The author, Andrew Amann, was born in the town of Sangre Grande, Trinidad, and Tobago, in 1936. He attended both private and government schools attaining a Senior Cambridge School Certificate, Grade one, in 1952. After working very briefly as a Civil Servant in the Warden's Office in Sangre Grande, he joined the teaching profession, becoming an assistant teacher (under training), at a Roman Catholic school in Arima.

Following in the footsteps of three of his "Windrush" cousins, he emigrated to England in 1957 and studied at Westminster College in London while working in restaurants to pay his way. He was called up for National Service but volunteered instead to join the Royal Air Force. He was stationed at RAF Waddington, a Bomber Command station in Lincolnshire. He courted a west country lass in the romantic city of Bath, married her and had six children. After serving as an electronic technician, in air radar, for 10 years, he again became a teacher after a two-year course at Bishop Grosseteste College. He was later to gain a MA (Ed.) degree from the University of Hull.

Having taught at both Secondary and Middle schools in Lincolnshire and Humberside for a number of years, he left to take up an appointment in the Youth and Community Service in Berkshire. He took early retirement from the post of County Youth and Community Education Officer and returned to Trinidad with his wife in 1992.

Andrew Amann

MILLIE'S QUEST

AUSTIN MACAULEY PUBLISHERS™

LONDON • CAMBRIDGE • NEW YORK • SHARJAH

Ordering Information
Quantity sales: Special discounts are available on quantity purchases by corporations, associations, and others. For details, contact the publisher at the address below.

Publisher's Cataloguing-in-Publication data
Amann, Andrew
Millie's Quest

ISBN 9781685629083 (Paperback)
ISBN 9781685629090 (ePub e-book)

Library of Congress Control Number: 2023902956

www.austinmacauley.com/us

First Published 2023
Austin Macauley Publishers LLC
40 Wall Street, 33rd Floor, Suite 3302
New York, NY 10005
USA

mail-usa@austinmacauley.com
+1 (646) 5125767

This book could not have been written without the knowledge gleaned from the following sources:

First in Trinidad; Michael Anthony. Syncreators Ltd.
Insight Guides, Trinidad & Tobago; APA Publications.
Chronicles of the 20th Century; Longman.
Through a Maze of Colour; Albert Gomes. Key Caribbean.
Forged from the Love of Liberty; Selected Speeches of Dr Eric Williams; Compiled by Dr Paul K. Sutton. Longman.

Inward Hunger, The Education of a Prime Minister; Dr Eric Williams. Andre Deutsch.

Angelo Bissessasarsingh's Virtual Museum of Trinidad and Tobago; the Internet.

I also wish to thank my patient wife, Rita Janet, who endured my obsession with writing, and the rest of my family who encouraged me to persevere and finish my first book.

Table of Contents

Author's Notes

This story, though based on someone's real life experience, is primarily a work of fiction. It portrays a period in time when Trinidad was still in the grip of the plantocracy. It was a British colony heavily flavoured with Spanish and French spices on a bed of African, Indian, Chinese, Portuguese, Syrian, and even Jewish cuisine. It traces marginally, without delving too deeply into politics, the development of a fledgling nation in the throes of seeking independence, from the end of the first world war to the struggle for self-government. It is the intention of the author to give an insight to today's young people, of the lives of their great grandparents, and to invoke memories of days gone by in people in their autumn years.

Seeking to lend authenticity to the tale, the names and location of real businesses are used and also, occasionally, names of real people. The surnames of most, however, are borrowed especially from what is referred to today as *gens d'Arime,* so as to impart genuine local. Historical events are true to the best of my knowledge, particularly the popular and enduring songs of the time. As a charming ditty extols:

All things shall perish from under the sky,
Music alone shall live, never shall die.

Trinidad

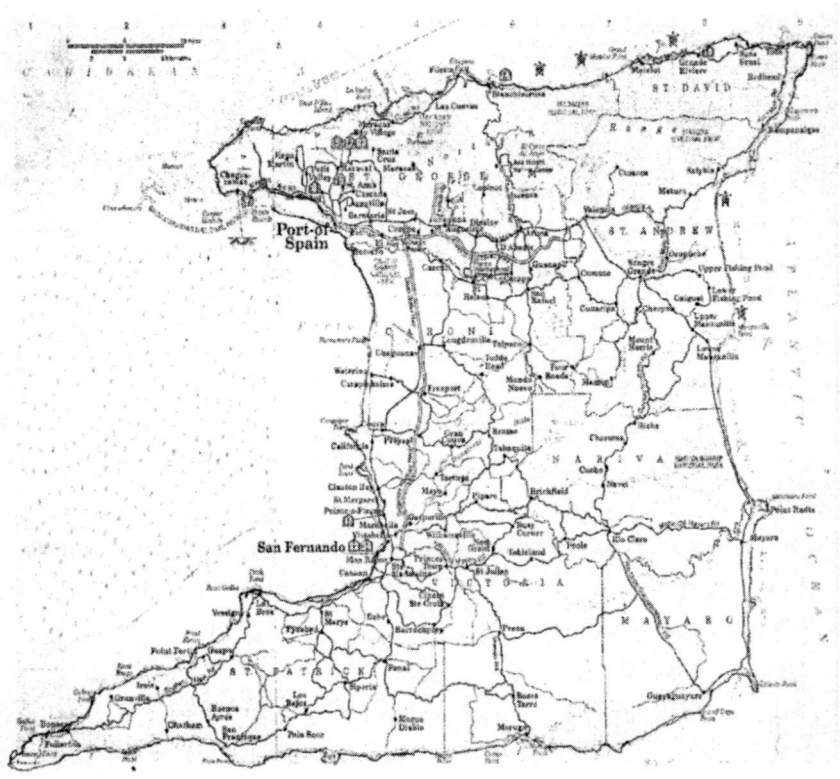

This map of Trinidad is relatively modern but shows the places mentioned in the story. A priority bus route has taken the place of the defunct railway network and highways have been built.

Prologue

Having found her reading glasses at last, Millie opened the letter which was whimsically addressed to:

My Nonagenarian Mum.

Dear Mum,

I've been making discoveries about our ancestry which may surprise even you. Having sent away to *My Heritage* for a DNA test, I received the following results:

I am 37.1% European, of which

23.0% North and West Europe,

13.1% South Europe,

1.0% East Europe.

I am 30.1% African,

21.8% Chinese and Vietnamese,

with the remaining 11% split between Mesoamerican and Andean, Filipino, Indonesian, Malay, and West Asian.

In all, there is a diverse ethnicity breakdown covering 42 regions!

What is of even greater interest is that *My Heritage* sends me DNA matches of nephews and nieces, second and third cousins, etc. who have taken their DNA test and have common ancestry. Some of their family trees trace back to your paternal great grandparents! This proves beyond doubt that your mother was right when she announced your father's name.

I intend to get in touch with some of these distant relatives (they are scattered all over the world), and when I do, I shall write and give you more details.

All members of my family over here are in the best of health and I trust that all of you in Trinidad and Tobago are the same. I heard from "little brother" John, recently.

Your loving Son,

Andrew xxx

Millie reread the letter and sighed: "It would truly have been like opening Pandora's Box if I had succeeded in my quest." She thought that her desire for "belonging" at that time could have had disastrous outcomes. She could vividly remember the yearning she felt to discover her biological father. Still, that was long ago and time is a great healer.

Memories of her childhood flooded her mind. There were happy, fulfilling moments that she could dwell upon. Strange that she could remember things from so far back when she couldn't remember where she had put her spectacles!

Part One
Millie's Early Childhood

Chapter 1
Awakening in Talparo

The blaring sound of a conch shell penetrated through to the dreaming Millie and she opened her eyes reluctantly. Her little sisters were still blissfully asleep lying crosswise on the double bed the three girls shared. Millie would be nine years old later that month and was going to join the Standard Two class at the Talparo R.C. School that day. The week before, her mother had taken her to Arima on the wagon driven by Alphonso, the proud owner of the two best looking black (well almost black) mules in the district.

In the town, they had gone into a Bata shoe shop where her mother had bought her a pair of "washeecongs," rubber-soled white canvas shoes (one size too big) that she would be wearing to school. They had also purchased a brand-new Royal Reader and two exercise books. She would no longer be doing all her writing on slates.

Miss Garcia, who taught the Infant Classes, had told her mother that Millie was "head and shoulders" above the other children in her class (which Millie thought was very funny as she was the smallest child in her class), and could comfortably skip a year and go straight to Standard Two.

The highlight of her trip to Arima was her hearing a honking horn and, on looking down Queen Street, seeing her first motorcar. It was a black Model-T Ford, driven by a liveried chauffeur wearing a peaked cap and a haughty expression. Behind him on the passenger seat, were Mr and Mrs Warner. Mr Warner was a high-ranking government official and, as she heard someone say, a very wealthy land-owner. In spite of the high esteem in which the couple was held, they smiled graciously at the onlookers and Millie felt sure that Mrs Warner, in an attractive wide-brimmed hat, had waved at her personally as they passed through the town on their way to Sangre Grande. In Millie's dream, she had been sitting in the Warners' car and waving at the bystanders as she drove by in their horseless carriage.

Millie was of a fair complexion with dark brown wavy hair and freckles. Her two sisters and her little brother, however, had inherited the colouring and most of the features of their African/Caribbean father. Millie didn't know who her own father was, just that he must have been white or nearly so. Her light complexioned mulatto mother, Meg, would always evade the question and told Millie that she would find out when she was old enough. This was a question that absorbed her mind at capricious moments. Millie was afflicted with a sense of unbelonging. She often felt as if she lived with the wrong family. She called James Browne, her stepfather, Papa, and he treated her like his own daughter, showing no favouritism. Although Millie was glad that her wavy brown hair was easier to comb than her sisters' tight curls, she had no pride in the colour of her skin as she was sometimes teased and called "red antz" by some of the children at school.

Only a few children at the Talparo R.C. School were not quite black in colour. There were four Chinese children, two boys and two girls, who belonged to the two Chinese shopkeepers in Talparo, and there were Millie's cousins, the Macleans, and an albino negro girl, Linda, who was nearly blind and had great difficulty in learning to read.

The Macleans, as the name suggests, were of Scottish descent. Ian Maclean had married Millie's aunt Marie and farmed twenty-five acres of land he had bought in Mahaica, the little village next to Talparo. Theirs also was a family with four children, three girls and a boy. People often remarked on the similarity between the Browne and Maclean families. Three of the Maclean children were of fair complexion, but one girl, Nora, who was a few months older than Millie, was dark-skinned with negroid hair. This of course led to much speculation in the village: was Nora really Ian's child?

It was the eldest Maclean cousin, Julia, who was most friendly with Millie. When Millie asked Julia why the Macleans were not teased as much as she was, Julia told her it was only the dull children, jealous and trying to get back at her because she was so bright. Millie always placed first, especially in English, General Knowledge and Mental Arithmetic and other children were envious of her.

The Maclean children, on the other hand, with the possible exception of Nora, were just average and did not stand out in class. Julia had advised Millie to pretend she did not know and not put her hand up when the teacher asked a question. Millie tried this but was occasionally put on the spot when the teacher, frustrated by the seeming apathy of the other children, singled Millie out to question her directly. Millie would usually know the answer but now found it expedient to appear unsure and reply in the form of another question: "Is it so and so?" This served to make it appear that she was lucky instead of a "Miss Know-it-all."

On this, the first school day of January 1924, Millie cut short her reminiscing and, tying up the mosquito net, knelt at the side of her bed to pray. She first pulled at her sisters' feet and reminded them: "Mama says to pray our morning prayers together!" Bleary eyed and reluctant, Olivia and Maria, six and five years old respectively, slid to their knees beside her as they recited the Our Father, Hail Mary, I Believe, I Confess and "Corbless," as Maria called the last prayer. Then Millie said her own prayer of hope for the new school year and included a prayer for Maria who was just starting school for the first time.

They carried out their ablutions using a jug of water Millie had brought in the night before from the rain barrel at the back of the house and the communal enamelled basin the girls used for washing. As they brushed their teeth with the tooth powder they had received as a Christmas present (normally they used salt or ashes) they were assailed by the aroma of fresh baked bread coming from the clay oven in the back yard. They could also hear the braying of the donkeys as Papa led them out to the estate to bring in the cocoa, coffee, or Tonka bean crops.

Having done her own hair with a few strokes of the brush, Millie then brushed and combed her sisters' hair amidst much "ouching" and "aahhing" from them. They then dressed in their brand new, home sewn school uniforms and marched down the corridor outside their bedroom to the dining room where their mother Meg was already slicing the fresh baked bread on the breadboard.

Mama quickly glanced at the girls, noting that the parting on Maria's cornrow hairstyle was not straight and Millie agreed to redo it after breakfast (muttering under her breath to Maria: "I told you not to fidget so!").

Mama then brought out little Pedro to sit at the table with them in his highchair and recited Grace Before Meals. They breakfasted on home-cured ham left over from Christmas and hot slices of bread with steamy mugs of sweet, thick cocoa and milk fresh from the goats. Papa had already gone out to the fields with the estate laborers having had just a cup of strong coffee and would return around ten for his breakfast. The girls would return home from school at lunch time as the school was only a quarter of a mile away. They would be accompanied by their cousins, the Maclean girls, who brought their own lunches to school but ate them at Aunt Meg's home.

"I hope you made the bed and left the bedroom tidy," Mama said, as she tied new red ribbons in the girls' hair. The ribbons, and some paper-wrapped sweets, were a present from Father Christmas.

"Yes Mama; we emptied the posie and we swept up too," replied Millie. "And we all said our prayers together as you told us to."

"Good," said Mama, "and keep yourselves clean and tidy and pay attention to your lessons. Off you go now and God be with you." As the three girls set off for school, each received a motherly kiss to send them on their way.

Chapter 2
A New School Day

The morning was bright and sunny and a slight drizzle during the night had wet the pit-run gravelled road just enough to prevent it being dusty. Maria clasped the hand of Millie, looking for reassurance on her first day at school. Maria had been taken to the school the week before by her mother and had met the headmaster and been shown her classroom, but was still somewhat apprehensive. Millie gave her hand a slight squeeze as she smiled at her and said: "You'll like Miss Garcia. She's very kind and claps her hands in a funny way when we get answers right."

"But you're not going to be in our class anymore," piped in Olivia.

"No, but I'll see you all at recess," said Millie, as she encouraged the girls to hop and skip their way to school.

The children were assembled on the forecourt of the school when Mr Farfan, the headmaster, came down the few short wooden steps from the building to the school yard. He was a son of the French plantocracy that held a privileged position in Trinidad at the time. He blew a single blast from a boy scout whistle he wore on a cord around his neck and the susurrating murmur of ten dozen children standing in serried ranks before him was hushed.

"Good morning, boys and girls," he said and an answering chorus returned: "Good morning Mr Farfan!"

"I hear some of you mispronounce my name. Although the last syllable is spelt f-a-n, it is not pronounced fan as in English. The French do not pronounce the n at the end so we say it as if we are talking about a place far far away. Do you understand now?"

"Yes, Mr Far far," chorused the children.

Mr Farfan continued: "We want you to be strong and healthy in mind and body and that is why we will start every day with five to ten minutes of P.E.

That stands for physical exercise. We'll begin by raising our arms high, making ourselves as tall as we can, then bending to touch our toes." Mr Farfan demonstrated and did it with the children ten times. He then said: "Your class teachers will now take their own classes, but as Mr Lee is absent today, I'll take standard two through their paces personally."

After a few minutes of calisthenics, the classes were then marched into the school and seated in their classrooms. Mr Farfan sat behind the teachers' table and proceeded to call the roll in alphabetical order of surnames but paused for a while when he came to Millicent Le Blanc. She answered: "Present Sir."

He looked at her keenly and asked: "You're the daughter of Marguerite Le Blanc?"

"Yes sir." She replied.

"Ah, I know your mother; she worked with my uncle in Arima years ago when your family first came to Trinidad." He then harrumphed and carried on with the roll call while Millie made a mental note to talk to her mother about that episode of her life.

Millie had known that her mother's family had come to Trinidad from Grenada but that they were originally from Martinique, which was why her mother could speak fluent French, as well as the creole patois, which was sometimes used at home among the grown-ups when they didn't want the children to know what they were talking about. She didn't, however, know much of the details of her mother's life and was interested to find out more, especially about the year before she, Millie, was born.

The first lesson of the day was Catechism which Millie knew to the letter as she had studied for her First Communion not too long ago. The morning passed uneventfully with the recitation of multiplication tables, spelling, and the story of what the children did over the Christmas holidays. Millie had a lot to write about, especially the coming of Parang groups to their home on three occasions. Millie remembered especially the group in which her uncle Ian played the violin and her stepfather's unusual reticence to entertain that group, telling them that they came at a bad time because it was after Christmas and all the grog was finished.

Millie thought that his reluctance was due to the fact that most of that parang band seemed already half drunk, especially Uncle Ian who had become unusually boisterous, but she did not put any of that in her composition. Her private thoughts remained private. She was an unusually reserved little girl in some ways and some people called her secretive which she thought unfair, as she was unaware of any secrets she held. As she wrote, she licked her lips in remembered pleasure as she recalled the taste of ginger beer, sorrel, sweetbread, paime, pastelle and other assorted delicacies they had enjoyed over the festive season.

As they walked back home for lunch that day, Millie asked her cousin Julia if many parang bands had visited their home in Mahaica. Julia replied that they didn't because their home was too far in the bush and her father's band went out playing most nights anyway. Then Julia giggled. "That means we still have lots of sorrel and ginger beer left over for us; so it doesn't matter so much."

Millie thought to herself: *That's just like Julia to see a good side to anything that happens.*

At lunchtime, it was Maria who had the most to say as they sat around the large rectangular table. They heard just about everything that Miss Garcia had said and done with her class that morning. Olivia, however, was very quiet and later confided to Millie that Miss Garcia seemed to expect her to know everything and be as bright as her older sister and that wasn't fair.

The Maclean girls giggled a lot and whispered quietly amongst themselves when Aunt Meg wasn't around. Aunt Meg considered it rude to whisper privately to each other when in company, and this seemed to make them want to do it more than ever. Millie didn't think much of their whispering for what she managed to overhear was usually harmless nonsense. Why bother to whisper that the Mendoza boy, Norman, gave Helen a lick of his lollipop? This time, however, the whispers were about the supernatural and Millie caught the words "douen" and "la-diablesse."

As soon as they were out of the house, Millie intended to find out why they were talking about these mysterious creatures of the dark woods and the night. They were supposed to be creatures that weren't seen in daylight but preferred to haunt the dark hours from dusk 'til dawn or lurk in the dark gloom of thick forests where mahoe, mahogany, cipre and silk-cotton trees reached up to the skies stretching out leafy branches to stop sunlight from reaching the earth beneath.

Having thanked Aunt Meg for the juice she provided to go with their meals, the Maclean girls quickly left. Millie gave her mother a quick hug and a kiss and shoving her sisters out, ran to catch up with her cousins.

"What happened with the la-diablesse?" she asked Julia.

Pulling her away from the smaller children, Julia confided: "I don't think it was a la-diablesse. I feel sure it was Belinda we saw. First, we saw a light moving in the bushes, not a flambeau, but an almost reddish-bluish kind of light. Then we saw a lady in a long dress come down the track and go into the bushes where we saw the light disappear. After a while, two little people, only about our height, came down the track and went into the bush too. Then we heard a howling noise and the two little figures came back out of the bushes and went up the track fast and then the lady in the long dress came out and followed them up the track and the light appeared again and then disappeared further into the bushes. Helen said the light must be a soucouyant."

"Did you tell tante Marie about it?" Asked Millie.

"Yes, but she told us to mind our own business and not to interfere in the devil's doings. That's what made us think of la-diablesse. She is a she-devil you know."

"Couldn't the two little people be Belinda's children?" Millie asked.

"Could be," Julia replied. By this time, they had reached the school and caught up with the younger children. The school bell was ringing and the children hurried to their respective classrooms.

That afternoon, Mr Farfan, still fretting about the absence of their class teacher, Mr Lee, gave paper and crayons to the monitors to distribute to standard two and told them that they had *carte blanche* (he loved to use French expressions) to draw whatever picture that came into their heads. He had a lot of administrative work to catch up on and although he had a few capable monitors who could keep order in the classroom he nevertheless thought it essential that a trained teacher be present to interact with each class each session. He therefore sat in Mr Lee's classroom that afternoon, leaving it only occasionally to see what was going on in the rest of the school.

Almost without thinking, Millie sat down and began to draw a tableau of a forest scene with a soucouyant, la-diablesse, douens, and in the background, a loup-garou with fiery eyes waiting to pounce on one of the unsuspecting douens to eat him up. As she drew, she reminisced that if a douen was the soul of a child who had died without being baptized, as Rebecca, one of her mother's helpers, had told her, how could it have a body that a loup-garou could eat? Can a soul get a new body? And why should the new body have its feet pointing backward? And why must the la-diablesse have hooves instead of feet? At least they were easier to draw.

Her thoughts were interrupted as Mr Farfan suddenly appeared at her left shoulder and said: "Very interesting, Millie, but I hope you do not believe all this superstitious rubbish about la-diablesse and douens. I know I gave you all carte blanche to draw whatever you wanted, but Le Blanc here, or should I say "La Blanche," the feminine form, has drawn things that only exist in the imagination. There are no such things in real life."

"But Sir," said Millie, "isn't it the same as drawing angels and cherubs?"

"No, my child, not the same at all, Angels have references from the Holy Bible to back up their existence. What you have drawn is the dark imagination of superstitious, uneducated people. We have been trying to stamp out these ridiculous beliefs for years." He paused, looking closely at her drawing. "Still, as long as you realize that what you have drawn is just a figment of your imagination, you have given us a good picture of a supernatural forest scene and displayed a precocious sense of the use of light and shade." Millie felt comforted by this compliment although she was not fully sure what he meant, and Mr Farfan went on to inspect other drawings.

During the short recessional period the children enjoyed, Susannah Henderson, the tallest girl in the class, teased Millie. "Mr Farfan said you were percushus about light and dark. That's because you is light in complexion and most ah we dark."

"No, it isn't," retorted Millie, rising to the bait, "it's because I like to see where shadows fall."

"Percushus Millie, percushus Millie," chanted Susannah, and Millie put her hands over her ears and ran back into the school. Susannah did not follow her.

That evening, after supper, as Mama was doing the washing up Millie asked her, "Mama what does precocious mean? Mr Farfan said my drawing was precocious."

"I think it means it was above your age. You do and say things they expect an older child to be doing," replied Mama.

"That's good, isn't it?" asked Millie.

"Well, good in some ways but it could make life difficult in others. People then expect more and more from you," said her mother. Millie pondered that remark for a while, then asked: "When did you work for the Farfans in Arima Mama? Was that before I was born?"

"Yes." Said her mother, drying her hands on an old rag, "come into the back room and I'll tell you about it." Millie was quite intrigued by then, thinking it was a story she didn't want the others to hear. She eagerly followed her mother into the back room where they sat side by side on a wooden bench Papa had made. Her mother then related how after fleeing from an erupting volcano in Martinique when she was eight, her parents took them first of all to Grenada where they lived for three years. Then her mother died and her father, Leon Le Blanc, was offered a job as a manager on a large cocoa estate in Trinidad. When they came to live in Trinidad she worked as a maid in the Farfans' home in Arima. There it was that she was taught to speak English properly and was treated like one of their family.

The Farfans, like most other white families, employed private tutors. Their children were not sent to the public elementary schools. She recalled that those were some of the happiest days of her life. She and the Farfan children played games and enjoyed themselves so much that she got over the grief of losing her mother.

Her older sister, Marie, had married Ian Maclean and settled on the small plantation he owned near Talparo, and her father occasionally took her to visit them on a horse and buggy he borrowed from time to time. When Marie was expecting her third child in three years and Meg was just sixteen, the Farfans were asked to release her for her to help her sister who was not very well and was having a hard time of pregnancy with Nora. This they somewhat reluctantly agreed to, though Meg overheard them saying that it would be a relief to get her away from the boys with whom they sometimes found her wrestling—something no girl of her age should be doing with boys. "It was never serious," Meg maintained, "but that is how I came to leave the Farfans. I never went back after that. Now you've heard the story it's time for you to get ready for bed."

Millie felt that there was more to the story than she was told. Why didn't Mama go back to the Farfans afterwards? Didn't she say that that was the happiest time of her life? Millie mused to herself as she scrubbed her teeth. Her sisters were already in bed but not asleep.

"Did you say your prayers?" Asked Millie.

"Not yet," said Olivia, "we were waiting for you, and we wanted to find out what you and Mama were talking about."

"Mama didn't want you to hear 'cause you're not old enough to understand," said Millie, preening herself.

"Ha, we still heard some of it through the wall. It was about something called a volcano and Grenada and the Farfans." Olivia smirked. "You shouldn't have been listening in to other people's business and you heard too much already; so now we'll say our prayers and go to sleep."

Chapter 3
Millie Delves into Folklore

The next day was bright and sunny as they tripped along to school, Millie wondered to herself if Mr Lee would be there to teach her class or she would have Mr Farfan again. Maria stopped every now and again along the way to pick up the orange and red immortelle flowers that fell onto the road. "Don't put them with your book," warned Millie, "it will get stained."

"What is stained?" asked Maria.

"Marks that spoil the book and won't come off," said Millie, as she removed the cockerel shaped flowers from Maria's satchel...

"Look, it's marked the inside of this new book-bag already." Retrieving her satchel, Maria peered into it and said: "It's the slate that mashed it on the side of the bag."

"Just one in your hand," suggested Millie, who guessed why Maria was taking it to school. "Then you'll have a good one to draw round when you get to school."

"All right," Maria conceded.

As they stood in their assembly lines in front of the school that morning, Millie noticed Mr Lee at the end of the line where class teachers normally stood during morning prayers. It was Mr Lee who took them through their paces for the P.E. session, but unlike Mr Farfan, he did not stretch and touch his toes with them.

After roll call, Mr Lee asked the class what they had done the day before, then called them out individually to read their own stories of what they had done during the school holidays. Millie had been expecting to read from her new Royal Reader and had practiced the first lesson at home, but read her own story instead, quite happily and fluently. She wondered if the Royal Readers were not used because not many of the newly promoted pupils had books. Mr

Lee praised her reading and acclaimed her a promising new entrant to standard two, which made Millie frown as she wondered what she had promised. She then thought of Julia's advice about not seeming to be too eager or bright and retreated into inconspicuous, but attentive silence for the rest of the morning. At least, now in standard two, she wouldn't stand out as the brightest in the class. There were many older children who had been in the class for longer, some who were repeating a whole year, having failed to pass the annual exam for promotion. She nevertheless decided to maintain a low profile.

That afternoon, after Mr Lee had examined the results of the previous day's art session, he decided to ask the children to write a story around the drawings they had done. His first day's lesson plans had been pre-empted by Mr Farfan's taking his class. He prided himself, however, on his ability to think on his feet and alter plans to suit any contingency. A few of the drawings he had seen, especially one of a cricket match in progress, had prompted him in his decision. The fact that he had a nagging headache and wanted as much peace and quiet as was possible in the thinly partitioned schoolhouse also contributed to his decision.

"How can I write a story about a bunch of coconuts?" asked Isaac Smith, in a whisper to Millie. "That's easy," whispered Millie, "Write about a monkey climbing a coconut tree and dropping nuts on people's heads."

"Ha, I like that," replied Isaac, who was the brother of Millie's albino friend, Linda. "I can make it a funny story." He then began to put pencil to paper, his grin spreading from ear to ear as he wrote.

Millie found herself thinking for a moment, her pencil tapping gently against her forehead as she recalled the tale of the douens she had heard from Rebecca. She then decided to make up her own story about becoming douens and their backward facing feet.

Millie's forest picture:

Chapter 4
Millie's Story: The Forest Dwellers

Once upon a time there were no people living in the dark forests, only a lonely spirit who called herself Materre. She longed for company other than the trees and the animals. She sat and thought very hard for many years. As she sat on the buttress roots of a silk-cotton tree, she stared at the trunk of a mahoe which had been struck by lightning. The tree trunk began to take the shape of a man. Materre got up went across to it and hugging it to her breast, kissed it. It came to life and embraced her in return. She then considered herself the happiest being in the world. She decided to call him Papa Bois. Together they would look after the woods and the animals.

They lived quite happily in the woods for many years. They were able to scare away greedy men who came into the forest to cut down too many trees and those who wanted to hunt and catch all the deer, agouti, and other wild animals they could.

They sometimes ventured to the edge of the forests and watched the villagers at work and the children at play. The joy-filled laughter of the playing children made Materre wish they had children of their own but she and Papa Bois never had any.

One day they saw a sorrowing young couple come to the edge of the forest to bury a dead baby. When the couple left, Materre quickly dug up the young child and kissed it. It came to life in her hands and she carried it into the forest.

Materre was happy looking after the young child. It was a boy and she named him Hoot. She fed him on deer's milk, fruit and mushrooms. Papa Bois went out every day to get things for the young boy to eat and drink and Hoot soon grew into a healthy toddler. He followed them everywhere and was especially interested when they went near the villages and he saw children playing. He wanted to join them but Materre and Papa Bois wouldn't let him.

When Hoot was about six years old, Papa Bois went out breaking traps which some hunters had set and Materre was busy looking after some wood pigeons who were suffering from a cough. He slipped away and went to play with some boys and girls.

At first, they laughed at him as he didn't have proper clothes but they soon accepted him because of his happy, joyful nature. He learned to catch a ball and could run very fast. They asked his name and he told them he was Hoot. He was having so much fun, talking and laughing with children instead of playing with dumb animals which he did in the forest.

Meanwhile, Materre and Papa Bois had returned to their home in the roots of the silk cotton tree and could not find their child. Materre went to the edge of the forest while Papa Bois went further inside. They both called out: "Hoot, Hoot," without hearing an answer.

As Hoot was playing with the village children, he finally heard his mother's voice calling out: "Hoot, Hoot!" He left the children and ran towards the forest. The children went home and told their parents what had happened. The villagers then decided to go in search of this strange child.

Having entered the forest, Hoot felt tired and sat down to rest against the trunk of a tree. He was worn out after playing so much for the first time in his life and soon drifted off to sleep.

The villagers followed his footprints into the forest and soon came upon the sleeping boy. They picked him up and carried him back to the village, wondering who he could be. He did have a close resemblance to one of the families in the village. They took him to Tante Marie, one of the oldest villagers who knew everyone in the village, Tante Marie looked at Hoot and said: "But he looks just like my grandson, Herbert, the one who left the village with his wife about seven years ago, just after their baby died. That's just how Herbert used to look like when I used to mind him."

Hoot, meanwhile, was twisting and squirming, trying to get away from the man and woman who held him fast between them, "I want to go back to Mama and Papa!" he cried.

"Who is your Mama?" they asked.

"Mama!" he replied, and they could get nothing more from him. The villagers decided they would feed him and keep him in a safe locked room that night and go searching for his parents the next day.

Meanwhile, Materre and Papa Bois had come upon the footprints and figured out what had happened. Papa Bois wanted to follow the footprints to where the villagers had taken Hoot. He wanted to go into the village to find their son but Materre said he shouldn't, as men were in the habit of setting their dogs on him and shooting at him whenever he went near them. She said they should go back to their home in the silk cotton tree and pray to the Great Spirit who would tell them what to do.

As soon as they got home, they prayed: "Great Spirit, we believe in your great power and wisdom. We want our son." A voice which seemed to come from high up in the trees replied: "He is mine. I lent him to you for a few years but he was promised to me at his baptism. You have shown that you can give care and love to little ones, so you can have any little ones you save from the grave if they have not been baptized and so promised to me."

So it was that Hoot was left to be taken care of by the people of the village. Materre and Papa Bois were very sad at this, but agreed to the wishes of the Great Spirit. They continued their caretaking of the forest and its animals as much as possible but nevertheless grieved for their lost son. Their grief grew less as years passed. They brought to life several babies who were buried without being baptized and raised them as their own in the forest. To make it difficult for people to track the douens, as the children came to be called, the feet of these little ones were trained to point backwards to confuse those who tried to follow them.

Chapter 5
Millie's Story Gets Published

Millie looked up from her work to find that all the other pupils had finished their stories and were reading quietly from their Royal Readers or other books as they had been told to do when finished writing. She took her exercise book up to Mr Lee's table for marking and returned to her desk to read.

"I expect your story to be twice as good as the others as you took twice as long to write it," Mr Lee remarked. Millie blushed deeply, unsure of Mr Lee's assessment of her. *Perhaps she should have written a shorter, simpler story,* she thought to herself. But then again, didn't all teachers say we must always do our best at all times?

Before Millie had finished reading a story about pirates from her new reading book, Mr Lee came to her desk and was holding her exercise book above his head. "This is the best story I've seen from anyone in this school. I shall enter it in the story competition in the Port of Spain Gazette—with your permission, of course, Millie," he added. Millie was astonished and blushed so deeply she could feel her face and neck grow hot with a suffusion of blood. She didn't expect her story to be good enough for entry in a newspaper competition and was flabbergasted that her permission had to be asked.

"Y-y-yes, Mr Lee," she stuttered, as the rest of the class grinned at her. Millie thought to herself: *Most of this story is what I heard from Rebecca; I'll have to tell Rebecca about this.* Mr Lee then proceeded to read Millie's story to the classroom.

Mr Lee explained to Mr Farfan, who happened by at that moment, what had taken place and Mr Farfan took the exercise book to read it for himself. He returned a short while later and said to Mr Lee; "This story has its merits and shows good imagination, but the subject matter will cause us some trouble."

"Why?" asked Mr Lee. "Everyone knows about these superstitions and this is a well written interesting story."

"But this is a Roman Catholic school and Archbishop Dowling is sure to object," replied Mr Farfan.

"I see your point," conceded Mr Lee. "Perhaps we should ask Fr. Macklin's opinion first."

"Yes, do that," Mr Farfan agreed.

That day many of the children pestered Millie with questions about douens and forest spirits. She had suddenly become the "expert" in that particular folklore. She answered what she could but told them to ask Rebecca, from whom she had heard the folklore.

That very evening, Mr Lee paid a visit to Fr. Macklin's presbytery. Fr. Macklin received him graciously and asked his housekeeper, Mrs Bonito, to make them a cup of tea. Mr Lee presented him with the story and asked if it would be all right to enter it in a newspaper competition. He told him also of Mr Farfan's reservations. After reading the story, Fr. Macklin scratched his head and thought for a moment. He recalled to himself the stories he had heard of "the wee folk" in the Ireland of his childhood. *Some people will always believe in superstition*, he thought. The thing to consider is how much harm or good could come from it. In this case, it might encourage many more people to have their babies baptized which will ultimately increase his congregation. If His Grace thought, it would harm the image of the Catholic School, perhaps it could be submitted with no mention as to which school the child belonged to. If not, he thought again, it would be a done deal once it was published and he might be able to convince His Grace that more good than harm would come from it. His Grace himself came from the land of leprechauns and the Catholic Church in Ireland had not suffered because of this myth. If the worse came to the worse, he could always write a letter of rebuttal to the newspaper saying that the story did not conform to the "official" teaching of the Catholic Church. *That would do it*, he thought. "Go ahead and submit it," he said. "The little child deserves a chance. It's only a story, after all." The good father made a note to talk to his fellow priests about it and gain their support, should it be necessary. After all, the more christenings they had, the better off the church would be. Don't they say, "the Good Lord works in mysterious ways His wonders to perform?"

Mr Lee submitted not just Millie's story, but also the one written by her friend, Isaac, not knowing that both stories were inspired by the same source.

To everyone's surprise and delight, Millie's story was awarded first prize in the competition and Isaac's came among the first six. It was the first time that the Talparo R.C. School had entered the story competition and Mr Lee felt sure that many people did not even know where Talparo was, this rural village in the geographical heart of the island. Not that its isolation was a bad thing; Talparo had escaped the ravages of the Spanish Flu' which killed many people in the towns. The neighbouring village of St. Raphael was much more popular. This achievement would put Talparo on the map in people's minds.

Chapter 6
Country Children's Stories Win Prizes

Millie was caught by surprise by an unexpected visit from Mr Lee to her home one Saturday morning. She had been helping her mother to make a cake and her arms were white up to her elbows from helping to sift the flour. It was with some trepidation that she opened the front door and found that it was Mr Lee calling. She invited Mr Lee into their drawing room. Mr Lee sensed her unease and immediately said: "I've come to bring good news. We have placed first in the Gazette's story competition!"

Millie almost collapsed into the Morris armchair behind her at the news but recovered in time and held on to an arm of the chair to steady herself. It had been nearly a month since she had written the story and the memory of it was beginning to fade from her mind. "P-please sit down, while I get Mama," she stuttered as she raced from the room to fetch her mother. Mama came in wiping her hands on her apron, Millie walking close behind, holding on to her skirt as if reverting to toddler-hood in her state of bemusement...

"Good morning, Mr Lee," she said. "I'm sorry I didn't come to the door myself as I was busy in the kitchen. I hope Millie was respectful."

"Of course, Mrs Browne, Millie is always full of respect. You have a remarkable daughter there. She won the story competition for elementary school children in the Port of Spain Gazette!"

"Millie told me something about writing a story about douens but I didn't take much notice. She's always making up stories about everything," her mother replied.

"She's a really good product of this fertile estate," Mr Lee re-joined. "Millie has an inventive imagination and an intelligence beyond her years. She must have inherited it from you or from her father," Mr Lee further ventured.

"I doubt that," her mother countered. "I taught her to read when she was only three and her head is always in a book. She even reads the old newspapers they wrap the goods in!" Meg laughed. She was nevertheless flattered and amused by the implied compliment and Mr Lee's ingenuous remark concerning Millie's paternity. That was a secret she had vowed to keep to herself.

The mention of Millie's father set Millie wondering. If her name was in the newspapers would her father see it? Would he want to get in touch with her? "Well," said Mr Lee, "the Sunday papers will have the results of the competition and will publish her story for everyone to read. We don't get that paper here until Monday but I'll make sure to have a copy for you. You'll enjoy reading your own story in print. Won't you Millie?" A blushing Millie replied a timid "Yes Sir."

"The letter I received from the Gazette says that all the winners will be invited to go to Port of Spain to receive their prizes next month. Travel expenses will be paid for the winners and their guardians. Isaac also won a prize and I've yet to tell the Smiths—"

"Great!" a surprised Millie exclaimed. "Isaac will be more than glad!"

Mr Lee, ignoring the interruption, smiled indulgently and added: "I have to tell the Smiths that Isaac will receive a book voucher to the value of a guinea as his prize."

In those days, a guinea was more than a month's wage for a field labourer. Millie was dancing around and clapping. Mr Lee remarked, "You seem more pleased for Isaac than for yourself." Millie blushed even deeper and said: "He didn't believe he could write a good story. He'll be more surprised than me."

"Than I," her mother corrected. Mr Lee smiled and thought to himself that he now knew why Millie's grammar was so good. He picked up his hat and said: "I must go now."

"I haven't even offered you a drink and you walked all this way," interrupted Meg. "Let me get you a glass of coconut water or orange juice. Oh! Sorry Mr Lee, the other children haven't come back with the oranges yet."

"Coconut water will be fine, Mrs Browne, then I really must be going."

By then, Millie had already run into the kitchen to get a glass and began pouring from the earthenware goblet which kept their drinks cool. Her mother took it from her, placed it on a carved wooden tray, and took it to Mr Lee.

"Delicious!" said Mr Lee after taking his first sip. "I wondered where the other children were."

"I sent them out to help their father who has taken this Saturday morning off. We're preparing a little birthday party for Millie who'll be nine tomorrow. They were getting too excited and getting in the way as Millie and I were making a cake," Meg explained.

"Of course," said Mr Lee and having finished his drink, thanked her again and left.

When the other children returned with their father, they were told the good news and became even more excited than Millie. "Can we go too?" they chorused.

Mr Browne replied: "Provided you all behave yourselves, I'll see what I can do."

"We will. We will." They chimed.

Chapter 7
The Birthday Party

The birthday party, which was held the next day, was supposed to be a quiet family affair, but turned out to be almost a village celebration. Her cousins from Mahaica, along with Aunt Marie dropped in to congratulate Millie. Many people brought food or drinks and those who didn't, gave Millie gifts of sixpenny pieces and even shillings! So great was their pride in her achievement. It seemed that only the De Verteuils were missing from the party. Mrs De Verteuil, however, sent one of her servants to tell the Brownes that they would lend their carriage to take Millie and her family to Arima to catch the train on the day of the prize-giving. That news was greeted with glee especially by the younger children who then assumed they would all be going.

It was truly astonishing the way the village grapevine had carried the tidings. It seemed that everyone had heard the news that not just one, but two Talparo children had won prizes in the national story competition. Of course, Fr. Macklin had been told and had announced it in the early Sunday morning masses as he thanked God for them and prayed for their continued success. The church-going congregation only represented about a third of the population of Talparo. It seems that the message had travelled from mouth to ear right along the main roads and up and down all the agricultural tracks that served as the arteries and veins of the cocoa, coffee, and citrus estates.

The Brownes and the Smiths were applauded by every Tom, Dick and Harry, not to mention Robinson, Maingot, and De La Bastide. Plantocracy as well as proletariat took vicarious pleasure in the accomplishment. So many people popped in to congratulate her that Millie began to hope that her real father would turn up among the well-wishers. Whether he would own up to being her father, however, was open to doubt. Millie resolved to try and observe the reactions of her mother to the visitors as she thought this would give her a clue as to who he might be. Her observations, however, yielded nothing of substance.

Her Aunt Marie had left early and in the late evening, her Uncle Ian came to fetch her cousins home. He kissed Millie on top of her head and said he wished Maclean children, Julia or Helen would do as well. Not wanting to have her cousins become jealous of her, Millie replied that she wished she could sing as well as they or run as fast. Her uncle grunted: "To each his own," as he led the children away. They had all had a wonderful time and been indulged by the grown-ups.

They had been allowed to play hide-and-seek around the house and to do skipping in the back yard. They had even marked out a hop scotch area under the cocoa house. The boxes and baskets of produce normally stored there had been moved aside to give them space for playing. Millie wondered if her father had visited while they were engrossed in play and she had missed him. She decided to find out from her mother in a roundabout way. "Did Mr De Verteuil or Mr Farfan come to the house, Mama?"

"Bon Dieu! No, child," her mother answered. "Rich estate owners don't come into poor people's houses! And Mr Farfan will see you tomorrow at school, anyway."

Millie had never thought of her family as being poor. They always had enough to eat and clothes to wear for church and school. Olivia did wear dresses handed down from Millie and Maria had Olivia's "grown out" clothes. Pedro, however, usually had new clothes sewn for him. They sometimes gave away clothes to the children of the estate laborers, some of whom were considered poor. Her stepfather, James Browne, was an overseer for the De Verteuils and that was considered a respectable job. In addition, they owned twenty acres of agricultural land. No, Millie decided to herself, they were not poor. It must be that white people prefer to mix with their own kind. Sometimes she wished that she wasn't so "light-complexioned" as her step father once said of her. It made her stand out in a crowd of mainly dark coloured children. She was also more easily burned by the sun. She was glad of her nearly straight, wavy hair, however, as the tight curls of her sisters were difficult to comb and plait. Once again, she found herself drifting into a reverie in which she fantasized that her father found her and she lived with a rich white family like the Warners and had servants who did all the menial work.

Chapter 8
Millie Gains the Recognition
of Her Fellow Pupils

The next day dawned bright and breezy. It was kite flying season and children at school would be flying chickichongs in the playground. These were small rectangular kites made of stiff paper with about an inch of their longer parallel sides folded upwards for rigidity and a thin paper ribbon tail for stability. When there was little or no breeze, the children would run with them to create the necessary air pressure for uplift but in windy weather the kites would stay fluttering in the breeze by themselves. Despite the breeze that morning, some boys ran along the road with their kites on the way to school. They stopped when they met Millie and her sisters and one of the boys, bolder than the rest, asked Millie if she would like to fly his kite. Flattered but embarrassed, Millie declined the offer but Maria anxiously begged: "Can I?" and the boy let her hold it for a while as they walked along the road to school. As they neared the school, the boy retrieved his kite and raced off to catch up with his friends. Millie wondered about the boy's unexpected offer and sensed that she might somehow be more popular from now on. She wasn't sure if that would be a good thing or not. As it turned out, her popularity was to be further enhanced, for after congratulating her achievement at the morning assembly, Mr Farfan announced that there would be an extended playtime that afternoon and that school would close early in honour of the occasion. Everyone, even Susannah Henderson, wanted to be Millie's friend. Millie smiled with tolerance at their efforts to ingratiate themselves. One girl who was genuinely pleased with her success was her friend Linda who came to her and asked: "You helped my big brother, Isaac, to write his story too, nah?"

"No," replied Millie, "all I did was to tell him that monkeys could do mischief with nuts. He imagined his story for himself."

"I wish you was still in our class," Linda sighed, wistfully. "I really wish I could be as good as you in English especially."

"That's because I read more than you."

"It's my eyes," said Linda. "They start to hurt and water when I read too long." Millie sympathized with her and thought to herself that glasses might help but knew that Linda's parents couldn't afford to buy them for her but said nothing and gave her albino friend a hug.

After lunch, Mr Lee produced two copies of the Port of Spain Gazette, one of which he presented to Millie as her own. Her story was on one of the centre pages. Everyone wanted to see it. Mr Lee asked everyone to be quiet as he beckoned Millie to the front of the class to read her own story from the newspaper. Her classmates had heard the story as read by Mr Lee but were anxious to hear it again. Millie felt her face flush and her knees turn to jelly as she stood before the class. As she got into the story, however, her embarrassment left her and she read fluently without stopping until she reached the end.

Isaac's story was also in the paper but he begged Mr Lee to let Millie read it to the class for him. This Mr Lee assented to as Isaac was known to stutter when faced with an embarrassing situation. Millie found it somewhat easier to read someone else's work and did not blush or have wobbly knees reading his work. She returned to her seat with the muted applause of the class ringing in her ears. That day, she actually enjoyed being a celebrity.

A covering article in the newspaper informed them that the presentation of prizes would take place at the end of the month. To Millie, the rest of the month passed in a blur. All members of the Browne family shared her excitement at the prospect of going to Port of Spain. Maria and Olivia had travelled in a buggy before and were excited to do it again but none of the children had ever travelled in a train. They could hardly repress their effervescence as they tried to be on their best behaviour to ensure that they would not miss out on the trip of a lifetime. Although Millie had seen the train as their coach waited at the level crossing in Arima, she had never been in a railway carriage and looked forward to being a passenger. She thought of the people traveling on the train as being specially privileged. Soon it would be her turn to wave at bystanders as they stand gawking at the side of the railway tracks.

Chapter 9
The Journey to Port of Spain

The long-awaited day arrived at last. They were woken at four o'clock that morning, their ablutions done, Millie was taking special care of Maria's hair. For once Maria did not protest, even when her hair was inadvertently pulled. So great was her excitement that she was prepared to endure any discomfort in order to ensure that she would be taken on the trip. After a hurried breakfast of hot chocolate and buttered coconut bake, they boarded the De Verteuil's buggy for the first part or their journey. An excited Pedro sat on his Mama's lap and stared wonder-eyed at everything. Maria also was beside herself with excitement. Her sister Olivia put a restraining arm around her to keep her from jumping to her feet and running to the window of the carriage at every new sight they encountered. The pit-run gravelled road to Arima passed through the villages of Brazil and San Raphael where there were many thatched cottages with their timite palm roofs and tapia walls. They trundled across several wooden bridges along the way, the wheels of their carriage making a roaring noise over them, distinct from the steady grinding sound that accompanied their journey across the pit run gravel. Livestock grazed contentedly at the side of the road and toucans, parrots and macaws flew overhead from time to time. They overtook many a pannier-laden donkey along the way and trundled over nine wooden bridges in all (Mama and Olivia were counting them aloud). Clear water gushed along in the streams beneath and sometimes fish could be glimpsed in limpid pools as the coach travelled on. A red-headed lineated woodpecker hammered away at the trunk of a dead boys canoe tree oblivious of the passing traffic. Estate laborers walking to work called out to the coach driver in three different languages: "Bon jour!" "Buenos Dias" or "Good morning," according to their ancestral heritage or the community they lived and worked in.

Mama chatted quietly to Pedro commenting on the scenery as they travelled on, while Mr Browne, who chose to sit up front with the driver, chatted animatedly as they compared the state of the various coffee, cocoa and citrus estates they passed through. Only Millie was quiet. She sat with a pensive look on her face as she looked out the window.

As interesting as her immediate surroundings were, her imagination took her miles away as she pondered at the effect the mention of her name in the Gazette might have on the rest of her life. Would her real father come to see her? Millie was jolted from her thoughts by the hoot of a horn from behind the buggy. The jitney belonging to the Chinaleongs, who owned a shop in Talparo, overtook them on its way to the Arima market. It was full of goods being taken to market by vendors who themselves sat in the back tray alongside their produce. Baskets full of ground provision such as yam, cassava, tannia, dasheen, eddoes, cush cush and topi tambu were stacked one on the other as every square foot of space was utilized. This jitney would return to Talparo later with bags of flour, rice, sugar, salt fish, etc. to be sold in the shop. It was one of only two motorized vehicles owned by Talparo people at that time.

Brief stops had been made along the way to rest the horses; at San Raphael, just before the Roman Catholic Church, they were allowed a drink of water. The passengers were also given the opportunity to stretch their legs, (or as Millie thought, *to rest their bottoms from the jolting of the buggy*.) At last, their coach rattled over the level-crossing which was left open as the train from Sangre Grande was not due for another half an hour. They drove more slowly now through the outskirts of Arima to the railway station at Malabar. Mr Browne would not be accompanying them to Port of Spain as he had transactions to complete for his employers in Arima.

They embarked from the carriage at the railway station and assembled on the west going platform to await the arrival of the train. The children could hardly contain their glee and had to be herded away from the edge of the platform by anxious adults. At last, the whistle of a train could be heard in the distance and the eagerly awaited locomotive came into view trailing a dense plume of smoke behind it. Pedro jerked spasmodically with excitement in his mother's arms and Maria jumped up and down on the spot, clapping her hands as she did so. Millie, however, kept darting anxious glances around her. "What's the matter, Millie?"

"Isaac's not here yet." Then, above the noise of the still chugging train, the sound of galloping hooves could be heard and a magnificent black horse came into view. On it were seated Mr Emmanuel Mendoza and Isaac, who was grinning from ear to ear.

Isaac's uncle, Mr Mendoza, had granted him the wish he had always wanted: to ride on Satan. Having dismounted, Isaac thanked his uncle and walking somewhat wobbly after his long ride and clutching a paper bag, he made his way to the group of passengers waiting to board the train. Turning once more, he waved to his uncle who was walking the beautiful stallion up and down in the road outside the station. Mr Lee, who had been looking out for him, reached out and took his hand saying: "Boy! I was beginning to think you wouldn't make it."

"Uncle Manny said Satan would make it," replied Isaac, "and it did!"

When they were all seated in one of the three second class carriages, Meg passed around a bag of rock cakes which the adults politely refused but the children eagerly accepted. The train seemed to spend an interminably long time at the station as bags of cocoa and coffee were loaded on to the goods wagons at the back, but finally the stationmaster blew his whistle, a guard standing at the front waved a flag, signalling that all was ready and the train started moving, slowly at first, then gathering speed with the accompaniment of clanking sounds as the carriage buffers and coupling springs jostled with each other. The carbon-tainted smell that permeated the atmosphere was more exciting to the children than the scent of incense at benediction in church. Their nostrils quivered as they gazed out the windows at the trees and occasional houses rushing by.

The train having accelerated to start with, was traveling at a faster pace than the children had ever travelled before. The sound of the train's whistle pierced the air and reverberated through the carriages and the train began slowing down. For the benefit of the children, Mr Lee remarked: "We're coming in to the Dabadie railway station; that's why we're slowing." The chucka-chucka, chucka-chucka sound seemed to decrease as the brakes were applied and there was a screeching sound that alarmed Pedro. However, instead of stopping, the train gathered speed again and the children saw a guard standing on the platform waving them on. "We have no passengers to pick up today," Mr Lee informed them.

From a few seats away, a child's voice was heard chanting: "Dabadie ain't have nobody, Dabadie ain't have nobody." This was in perfect time with the train's rattling chorus and the children all joined in the chant. The adults in the carriage seemed amused by this and smiled indulgently.

Before they had got to Arouca, however, the persistent chanting began to wear on the nerves of some of the grown-ups. Mrs Browne had an idea and said: "I know a fine game we can play while traveling. It's called "I see." Shall we play it?"

"Yes, let's!" chorused the children at once.

"I see with my little eye, something beginning with M," said Mrs Browne. "See if you can guess what it is."

Puzzled by this, the children peered out of the windows, hoping to see a man or a mango or a manicou as they sped by. "Monkey?" suggested Isaac.

"You're the only one here," jibed Olivia, who was immediately told off by her mother.

"That's very unkind!" rebuked Mrs Browne.

"I was only joking," said Olivia. "I didn't mean it serious."

"I don't mind," said Isaac. "I like to fool around a lot and that's why the children always say I'm up to me monkey tricks."

"Olivia should be looking for things beginning with M instead of being rude," Mrs Browne re-joined.

"Marigolds!" shouted Millie as they passed a small cottage with a garden full of marigolds.

"No," answered Mrs Browne, "we can only see the marigolds now but my M word was in view since we got on the train."

"Mountains!" Olivia exclaimed. "Yes, you're right. Now it's your turn to pick a subject and tell us the first letter."

"I see something beginning with I," said Olivia. Mr Lee interrupted: "You should say, "I spy with my little eye something beginning with I," Olivia. If Mrs Browne doesn't mind me butting in." He smiled at Mrs Browne.

"Of course not," answered Mrs Browne. "I had forgotten the correct form of the game myself."

"Engine," said Pedro, wanting to join in. This brought giggles of laughter from his sisters who chorused: "E for engine, not I."

"No, E is for egg," insisted Pedro.

49

"We should really say <u>E</u>ngine," stressed Mr Lee, "not <u>In</u>gine. Yet, Pedro was observant as we can see the engine as we go around slight bends in the tracks."

"It's Immortelle," shouted Millie as she saw the orange blossoms on the distant hills.

"Yes," said Ollie, "now it's your turn." They quickly grasped the format of the game.

"I spy with my little eye something beginning with T," said Millie.

"Train!" Isaac, Pedro and Olivia shouted in unison.

"Wrong," said Millie.

"Trees," suggested Isaac.

"No," said Millie.

"I think it's termites' nests," Mrs Browne ventured, wanting to get back in the game. Suggestion after suggestion came, each one greeted with a negative response 'til they all decided they'd had enough.

"It's telegraph poles," answered Millie.

Mr Lee then took the opportunity to explain that the telegraph poles and wires strung alongside the railway tracks were so that messages could be sent to signal boxes to alert the railway workers about the arrival of trains etc.

By then, the children had become absorbed in the commotion of passengers leaving the train and others coming on with their baggage. Some farmers from Lopinot with baskets of fruits and vegetables were being directed to the goods wagons at the back of the train so that other passengers would not be inconvenienced.

Wide eyed with excitement, the children took it all in. The train which was only a quarter full of passengers when it came in to Arima was now more than half full. Soon they were on their way again and the game of I Spy was resumed between stations.

At Tunapuna, they were told that pilgrims wishing to worship at Mt. St. Benedict got off there and walked up the mountain to the Abbey where the Benedictine monks lived and worked. The monks grew their own food and tended hives of honey bees which produced most of the honey in the island. Millie promised herself that one day she would go up there and see the Abbey.

After Tunapuna, they stopped at Curepe, and St. Joseph (which was the old capital of Trinidad), then came to the Croisee in San Juan. Mr Lee explained the Croisee was French for Crossing as important roads crossed each other there. There was a road that went up mountain passes to Santa Cruz and thence to Maracas on the north coast. Another road could take them south to Caroni. At the Croisee, vendors sold oysters, coconut water, phulourie, and other Indian delicacies. Indian women wore saris and their menfolk wore dhotis instead of trousers.

"These coolies* are going to be the biggest business people in Trinidad," said Mr Lee. "You mark my words. They can't read and write but they can count and make sacrifices and don't spend their money foolishly."

Most of the Indian women were adorned with gold and silver jewellery. They wore rings in their ears and noses and bracelets on their wrists and ankles so there was a musical tinkling of jewellery as they walked along the pavement. Mr Lee explained that many Indians preferred to barter with gold or silver. A man wishing to buy a goat might bring along his wife, and as the deal was struck, would remove one or two pieces of jewellery from his wife and exchange it for the goat. They knew the value of gold or silver better than shillings, florins and crowns and disliked the paper currency which was then coming into fashion.

The train eventually moved on again on the last leg of its journey into Port of Spain. It was now quite full of passengers and people were standing in the corridors.

*The term "coolie" at that time was applied to East Indians without the derogatory connotations later ascribed to it.

Chapter 10
The Reception at the Gazette Offices

A new, exciting treat awaited them as they left the massive Port of Spain Railway Terminal on the South Quay. They were to travel by tramcar on the short distance to the offices of the Port of Spain Gazette! The tramcars ran on rails set into the roads but were powered by electricity. An overhead wire trolley was connected to a grid of wire cables set over the streets of Port of Spain to deliver electricity from the generating plant set up by Edgar Tripp. The children were enchanted by the new sounds and scents. As the overhead wires sparked, Isaac exclaimed that he could smell the electricity. This caused the grown-ups to smile and Mr Lee thought to himself that he should investigate whether sparks could have a scent. Suddenly, they were at their destination.

A smiling lady and an old gentleman greeted them at the offices of the Port of Spain Gazette. "Are you the contingent from Talparo?" She enquired. Millie's ears pricked at the word contingent. She wondered if it had anything to do with the word continent with which she was familiar due to her Geography studies then dismissed that idea and decided that it must be another word for a group of people. Mr Lee answered that they were indeed from Talparo and added that they had had a pleasant and interesting trip to the capital. He introduced the party of country folk he had brought with him leaving Millie and Isaac for last. Mr Gomes and Miss Jones of the Gazette then introduced themselves and asked the party to follow them to a reception room where they were offered drinks of orange or grapefruit squash or mauby in glasses with ice. The children were all filled with awe and took the proffered drinks very hesitantly. Mrs Browne held Pedro's for him fearful lest he drop the glass. At home, Pedro drank from a tin mug.

Millie was savouring both her drink of grapefruit juice and the whole occasion as a wonderful adventure that only happened to other people she read about. She could hardly believe it was happening to her. She felt as though she were somehow suspended outside of her own body, floating above the crowd and observing what was going on around her.

Mr Gomes then asked the two children who had won prizes to accompany him to a special room to have their photograph taken. They were to stand absolutely still while the camera-man who ducked his head into a black bag attached to the camera took their picture. Millie asked if their pictures were going to be published in the newspaper. He replied that theirs and the pictures of four other children who had come in earlier, would be published. They were then escorted back to the reception room where they were presented with their prizes which were in white envelopes with their names printed on them. Upon opening her envelope, Millie discovered that her prize was a token worth two guineas!

They were asked if they would be willing to take part in a new venture which the Gazette was considering. It was to be a special page for children and would feature articles written by children. Millie felt quite excited by the idea and readily agreed. Mr Lee enquired how often the articles were to be submitted and was told that it was up to the contributors, as some pupils may want to send in an article every week while others may do so only occasionally. The Gazette would keep a store of articles and use them when it saw fit. Although a child may send in an article at the beginning of a month, it might be two months later that the story would appear in the Sunday Gazette. This seemed to satisfy everybody. They finally took their leave of the Press people and returned to the railway station for the homeward journey. The journey home was uneventful, the children having used up all their nervous energy, and the adults were also quite ready for a period of restful quiet.

Chapter 11
A Career in Journalism Beckons

The following day, as the children entered the school grounds, everyone was curious to know how the journey and the great occasion went. Olivia was bubbling over with excitement and was in her element, relating the strange sights and experiences of the journey there and back. Millie was happy to let her talk and tried to keep a low profile herself. When they got to their respective classrooms, however, Millie was asked by Mr Lee if she would like to give an account of her experience to the class. She said: "Please Sir, can I write it first?" To this Mr Lee assented and he gave her the task of writing it as her homework. She would be reading it to the class the next day. They then got on with their first lesson which was religious instruction.

Later that day, just as they came in from a "recess," Mr Farfan came to the classroom and enquired how the trip to the Port of Spain Gazette went. Mr Lee told him that it went very well and that Millie would be reading an account of the trip to the class the following morning.

"That's excellent!" exclaimed Mr Farfan, "It will be my pleasure to be part of her audience." Millie felt her knees grow weak at this and hoped that she would be able to do it well. Mr Lee then informed Mr Farfan of the commitment to submit further articles to a children's page the paper was planning to print in the Sunday Gazette. The headmaster was duly impressed and told Mr Lee that as long as it was under his supervision, he felt assured that it would be a beneficial venture. "The school might even produce some future journalists," he prophesied.

That evening when Millie got home, she told her mother what had transpired and how she felt nervous that Mr Farfan would be also there to hear her. Her mother assured her that everything would be all right and that she would help her with the account of the adventure. Millie was to write her version of events in her own way and Mama would suggest any improvements she thought necessary after reading Millie's work. To this Millie readily agreed.

In the classroom the following day, having prayed to The Holy Ghost, the third person of the Blessed Trinity, as her mother had instructed her to, Millie felt an exuberance of confidence and read her story with great aplomb. She was duly applauded as she returned to her seat and Mr Farfan commented that a career in journalism might very well be in store for her. He looked forward to reading further articles by her in the Sunday Gazette.

Millie wondered at this possibility. For her part, the thought of one day becoming a school teacher was as much as she had so far aspired. Newspapers were scarce in Talparo and the news was usually a day old by the time they became available there. She anxiously awaited the next issue of the Port of Spain Sunday Gazette in which her picture was to appear and privately hoped fervently that her natural father would see it and want to get in contact with her. Mr Lee had promised that he would make sure that she got a copy and would not accept any offers of payment in return. At this, Millie decided that she would make sure that he was well supplied with oranges, a fruit which he liked, and which, when anonymously presented on his table he could not refuse.

At recess time, she met with Isaac and asked him what he intended to do with his prize. He said that his father had heard that book tokens could be sold at slightly less than their marked value and would get them changed for cash. He shyly admitted that he wanted to get his sister Linda a pair of spectacles. Millie thought that a marvellously splendid idea and wondered if she too could help in that endeavour. She knew her mother would approve when she broached the matter to her that evening.

As expected, her mother approved of the idea wholeheartedly, but explained to Millie that buying a pair of glasses was not that simple. Linda would have to be taken to Port of Spain to see the eye specialist and because of her albinism she might have to undergo further tests and might need two pairs, one for indoors and another for outdoors. Millie nevertheless wanted to help her friend as much as she could and her mother agreed to help her. When she next spoke to Isaac, they conspired to keep it a secret project in so far as the rest of the school was concerned but acknowledged that they had to get the co-operation of both their parents. This was easy enough where Linda's mother was concerned, but it turned out that Mr Smith had other ideas as to how Isaac's prize was to be spent. He had already earmarked it to be used for buying galvanized sheeting for their roof which was leaking badly, especially over the children's bedroom. He considered their health a greater priority than Linda's reading. Mrs Smith tried to convince him by saying that it was because Millie and Isaac could read well that they were able to win prizes from the Port of Spain Gazette and they have a greater chance of getting a good job. These arguments did little to convince him, so the money would be used for the roof, and Linda's spectacles, trip to town, and eye examination would have to be forgotten for the foreseeable future.

Isaac related this tale of woe to Millie the following week and they both decided that they wouldn't give up on their project but would think about it seriously and come up with a plan to carry it through.

Meanwhile, Mr Lee had asked Millie to prepare another article for the Gazette and Millie decided to do a follow-up story on the douens in Materre's and Papa Bois' forest. Mr Lee had hinted that the Gazette might be willing to pay for any stories they accepted and printed. Millie welcomed the idea which she thought almost too good to be true. She decided to try her best.

When her picture appeared in the Sunday Gazette, Millie was thrilled. She knew that the paper was sold nearly all over the island and even made its way to some of the small islands such as Grenada and St. Vincent. Would her natural father see it and get in touch with them, she wondered. She thought that her mother must also wish to see him again, if only to say hello. The accompanying caption said that even children from rural Talparo were talented and that plans were afoot to produce a weekly children's page containing articles from children all over the island. While Millie agreed that this was a good idea, she felt it might reduce her chances of having her work selected again as the editors might want to use stories from other parts of the island, far-flung places such as Mayaro and Toco. She would nevertheless make the effort to write more stories. Much depended on it.

Chapter 12
Millie Seeks a Source of Inspiration in Vain

Millie thought of the source of her first story. Her cousins who had seen a mysterious light in the night had assumed that it could be la-diablesse and the little figures who followed were douens. From their imagination came the picture, she drew on paper and that had mushroomed into her published story. Chatting with her cousins could possibly provide her with more stories. Her mother, Meg, had run out of chadon bene, oregano and some of her other herbs, so Millie volunteered to go to her aunt's in Mahaica where there was always a plentiful supply of culinary herbs.

On reaching Aunt Marie's home, she could hear raised voices. Her aunt and uncle were quarrelling. "It takes two of us, you know. I didn't produce it on my own. You are as much or even more to blame," Aunt Marie was remonstrating.

"But every extra mouth to feed costs more money not to mention the clothes to buy and other things," Uncle Ian complained. "I'll have to butcher and sell my own meat rather than let Malcolm buy my pigs. It'll mean more work for us."

"Good afternoon," Millie called out. "Anybody home?"

"Yes, come in," Aunt Marie answered.

Millie entered the house and told her aunt that she wanted some herbs which her aunt was happy to provide. Her cousins were at the river washing clothes, so Millie didn't get to see them that day. Aunt Marie told her she would see them at school on Monday and Millie said, "That would be fine."

As Millie left, she pondered over the titbits her eavesdropping had gleaned. Aunt Marie must be having another baby. Uncle Ian is going to butcher and sell his own meat. This news she related to her mother when she got home. Her mother merely said, "It often happens on the change of life," which left Millie somewhat perplexed.

The news turned out to be true, however, and a week later, her uncle had taken up a stand in the junction. As Millie went to buy meat from her uncle who now sold pork on Saturday mornings, she found herself being congratulated on her journalism by nearly everyone she met in the village. Uncle Ian, however, was as taciturn as ever with her. Perhaps he hadn't seen the paper she thought, or he might have been thinking that one of his own daughters should have been in the limelight. He served a couple of young women who had come after her before he asked her what she wanted. He then weighed out her order to the exact ounce and handed it to her without a smile. Millie noticed that he had laughed and chatted merrily with the young women and gave them extra sausages, "as lagniappe" (a free extra piece) he had said. Millie mused, "To suffer the arrows of jealousy must be part of the price one paid for fame." She would not depend on her cousins for stories. She cast her net into the ocean of her imagination and dredged up a tale of her own.

Chapter 13
Millie's Second Story: the Forest Children

Materre and Papa Bois had wanted children even more after they lost Hoot, the first child whom they had rescued from an improvised grave. They therefore kept a lookout around the perimeter of the forest for people disposing of still-born or early-death infants. If these children were not baptized, they were permitted to raise them to life and rear them as their own in the forest. One day, they came upon a weeping young man digging a little grave. His pregnant wife, who was carrying twins, had miscarried and one of the twins was born too early and died. The couple hoped that at least one would survive. Materre and Papa Bois watched quietly from behind the forest bushes. As soon as there was no one else around they came out and dug out the baby, filling back the hole with earth.

Materre blew her warm breath on the child, placed her hand on its head and prayed. The baby stirred to life as though from a deep sleep and whimpered. It was a little boy! Papa Bois and Materre were overcome with joy and took him to their home in the forest to feed him on deer's milk and bring him up to be a healthy child. The other animals in their collection seemed happy to have the baby in their midst and adopted him as one of themselves.

A week later, tragedy struck the young couple again, and the second baby died. This time, the news was brought to Materre by a crow who happened to be on a tree nearby when the young man came to bury the other twin. Materre and Papa Bois hurriedly went to the grave site and retrieved the second baby. They brought to life a second boy who grew to be an identical copy of the first, only slightly smaller. If Papa Bois fretted or worried about the extra work, Materre was the opposite and welcomed the addition to their family.

The months went by and the babies grew at a faster rate than those in the villages outside of the forest. They copied the animals around them and even tried to climb like baby monkeys before they could walk properly. It was a full-time occupation looking after them and Materre could no longer accompany Papa Bois on long treks through the forest as she once did. She knew, however, that it would only be for a short while.

The twins were called Mack and Zack and normally answered when they were called once they were within hearing range, but Materre and Papa Bois preferred to summon them by whistling the notes of a Kiskadee, a type of flycatcher whose call sounded like the French words: "Qu'est-ce qu'il dit." Whilst for Mack they sounded the one "dit," to call Zack it was: "Qu'est ce qu'il dit dit." People who happened to overhear the calls were quite unaware of what was really happening. The twins played with each other and with the animals in the forest. Zack especially liked playing with the monkeys and often climbed up into the trees with them. Materre was fearful lest he should fall and hurt himself but Papa Bois felt confident that he could look after himself up in the branches. Zack soon became expert at swinging on lianas and could travel through the tree tops faster than Mack could run along the ground.

One day, when the twins were about 9 years old, they wandered some distance from the silk cotton tree which was their home and went in search of a pomerac tree which was laden with ripe, dark red fruit. Zack climbed and threw down fruit for his brother, who was content to sit on the ground and eat his fill. Having eaten more than he should, Mack lay back against the roots which protruded from the trunk of the tree and soon dropped off to sleep. Zack had remained at the top of the tree admiring the way some corn birds were weaving their nests on a nearby tree. So it was that they did not notice a group of six hunters who had stealthily crept through the forest and surrounded Mack at the bottom of the tree.

Mack woke with a start and scrambled to climb the tree out of their reach but the men were quick to grab hold of his legs and pull him down. Zack stayed quietly hidden at the top of the tree. "It's a wild child!" The men cried, not knowing whether it was a boy or a girl. The twins had long hair and looked more like girls than boys. They wore cotton shorts which were woven from the silk cotton by Materre. Mack tried to fight them off but was easily overpowered. His hands and feet were bound with rope which the men carried and he was tied to a long pole so the two men could carry him quite easily. Zack resisted the urge to help his brother fight the men off and decided to stay hidden among the tree tops and follow to see where they went.

The men travelled some distance through the forest until they came to a small clearing in which was set up a few make-shift wooden huts. This was obviously their camp from which they went out to hunt. They had caught some "wild meat"—manicou and agouti and relit their fire to cook a meal. Zack decided to fetch Papa Bois and Materre in order to rescue Mack.

Having returned to their silk-cotton tree home and related to his parents what had happened, Zack led them to the hunters' camp. There they saw that most of them had retired to their huts and they couldn't tell which hut they had put Mack in. They whistled to Mack: "Qu'est ce qu'il dit!" They heard a reply that sounded like "Ici ici," from one of the huts. They realized that Mack must have been locked in that hut but they couldn't get to him without the hunters seeing them. They had to think of a way of drawing the hunters off. Zack had an idea. "I can get them to chase after me and they can't catch me in the treetops." Materre was reluctant for him to try that idea but Papa Bois felt it would work.

Zack silently crept as near as he could to the hut where they thought Mack was being held then he showed himself and yelled at the men: "You can't catch me!" before running off into the forest. The men saw him and thought it was Mack who had escaped.

" Look!" They shouted, "don't let him get away!" They all started running after him as he scampered up a tree. "We'll catch him now." They said, but to their amazement Zack swung from that tree to another and then to another. Zack led them some distance from their camp, giving his parents time to free Mack. As he swung on a liana and landed on the branch of a sturdy tree Zack heard the call: "Qu'est-ce qu'il dit dit," and knew that Mack was now safe.

Zack had taken the opposite direction to their silk cotton tree home so it was safe for his parents to take Mack straight home. Having lost the hunters, Zack made his way carefully home to his forest family. Papa Bois was most unhappy about having hunters in his forest and made up a plan with Materre to scare them away. They made their way back to the hunters' campsite and hid themselves in the woods at opposite ends. By then, the hunters had returned to their huts exhausted from their fruitless chase after Zack. From the north end, Papa Bois made a frightful roar like an enraged lion. From the south of the campsite, Materre let out a bloodcurdling screech.

The hunters grabbed their weapons and came out of their huts but they could see nothing. Then Papa Bois and Materre carried out what they had planned. Both of them whilst moving clockwise around the clearing, intermittently called out their message. "**LEAVE *THIS* FOREST *AND* NEVER *COME* BACK!**" They repeated this message several times while circling the campsite. The hunters could hear this scary voice coming from all around them and became afraid. They huddled together in a circle in the middle of the campsite.

Papa Bois then crept silently nearer and from behind one of the huts, he threw a big Jack-Spaniard wasp nest into their midst. They cried out in alarm as the wasps stung them on their faces, ears, necks, hands, and every exposed part of their bodies. The hunters ran off in every direction and I'd like to think that to this day they are still running.

Chapter 14
Millie Puts Her Earnings to Good Use

It had taken Millie over two weeks to complete this story, for her mother had decided to edit it for her and made suggestions which Millie was content to use. After all, the idea of the story was completely Millie's and corrections of spelling and grammar were incidentals that she was only too happy to go along with. In fact, she welcomed them, and was particularly pleased when Mr Lee read her story and said the only addition he could suggest was the title: he thought, *"A Sequel" should be added to show that it was a follow-up to her last story*. Millie readily agreed to this, making a mental note to herself that the word sequel meant follow-up.

Millie was a little disappointed that her real father did not get in touch with her after her first story and later on when her picture, had appeared in the Port of Spain Gazette, but she lived in hope that one day he would perhaps read her story and decide to meet her. She loved her stepfather, Mr Browne, who always treated her as his own and was proud of her but her curiosity about her biological father remained.

As that year progressed, Millie was appointed class monitor for standard two and given responsibility for handing out chalks and paper for drawing and supervision over the filling of the inkwells, which was done by Isaac. Her stories to the Gazette were submitted every two months and she was paid a guinea each time one was printed in the paper. She was determined to use her new-found wealth in aid of her friend Linda's sight and with the connivance of her mother, they got Linda to see an eye specialist in Port of Spain and be prescribed spectacles which they paid for. All this was done with some secrecy as Mr Smith, Linda's father, was of the opinion that girls should not be educated and considered spending money on spectacles a waste. Mrs Smith, however, knew that her daughter would not be able to work outdoors because of her albinism, but with an education might be able to get employment in an office.

Somehow or other, Mr Lee got to find out that it was through Millie that Linda was now wearing spectacles which made a huge difference to her learning abilities and he wanted Millie to receive some recognition for her generosity. Millie's mother had to plead with him to keep it a secret lest they became a target for the many beggars and ne'er-do-wells in the village and also, for the sake of preserving the Smith family's self-esteem. Mr Lee agreed to this but privately vowed to himself to assist in furthering Millie's climb up the educational ladder as much as he could.

By the end of that year, Millie was set to enter standard four having spent only two terms in standard two before being promoted to standard three. Standards four and five were taught by Mr Farfan himself with the help of Prefects, young students who wished to be trained to become teachers.

As school attendance was only compulsory up to age ten, the number of children was greatly decreased in standards four and five. Boys over ten (and to a lesser extent, girls) were required to help "on the land." Thus, it was only children of favourable means who were kept on at school.

In Millie's case, although her family were not poverty stricken, she was not in the same league as the well-to-do children of the upper classes whose parents paid for them to be college educated. (The sisters of St. Joseph of Cluny had opened a branch of the St. Joseph's Convent for girls in Arima in 1895.) Millie was content to become a school teacher through the Pupil Teacher System operating at the time.

Chapter 15
Her Grandfather Passes On

Millie was aware that she had a grandfather somewhere in Trinidad but she had never met him and her mother avoided all mention of him. It was quite a surprise therefore when a distraught Aunt Marie appeared one day and announced: "Papa Leon est mort." Her sister Meg fell into her arms and the two ladies began weeping. The children were bewildered and asked Millie what had happened. She explained that Papa Leon, their grandfather, had just died. They wanted to question her further about this mysterious grandfather but Millie shushed them saying that she had to listen carefully to the adults who were talking in French. Not having learned French, Millie could only pick out a word or two in each sentence that she could understand. Her efforts were in vain as she was dispatched to the kitchen to make a pot of tea and missed most of the conversation between the bereaved sisters.

After three cups of fortifying tea, Aunt Marie departed and Millie was able to ask her mother about Papa Leon. She was told that he lived in the little village of Brazil, near San Raphael, where he managed a cocoa estate for the Francois family. Millie persisted in asking why they had never gone to see him or he come to visit them. Meg, still reeling emotionally from the shock of the news she had just received, sobbed out: "It was because of you." When I was discovered to be pregnant and wouldn't say who the father was, Papa said to me: "Unless an angel were to come and tell me that you are having an immaculate birth, I don't ever want to see you again. **Jamais!'** So, we have lived our separate lives ever since."

"Mama, I'm so sorry!" Millie cried, bursting into tears.

"Oh no, my little angel, it's not your fault. Don't ever think of blaming yourself. I'd rather have you than all the cocoa in Trinidad!"

This episode was to have a lasting effect on the mind of the impressionable Millie. She became determined, more than ever, never to give rise to any situation that might cause an illegitimate birth.

Chapter 16
The Wake

Papa Leon's wake was to be held at the Maclean's farmhouse in Mahaica. Meg made coconut sweet bread, cakes and ground a pound of finest Arabica coffee with a little Robusta (a blend for which Talparo was becoming famous) to take with them to the wake. The whole family set off on foot at half past five that evening. James Browne carried his own bag from which could be heard the occasional tinkling of bottles. When Maria asked what was in the bag, he replied that they had to take flambeaux as it would be dark on the return journey.

They arrived at the farmhouse to see a number of people lighting candles alongside the pathway to the house. A few benches and trestle tables were laid out at the side of the house and in the back yard. Meg and James exchanged greetings with acquaintances and then were met by Aunt Marie who expressed delight at receiving the basket from her sister Meg. Uncle Ian seemed equally pleased to take from his brother-in-law James the bag that he carried. Many more people seemed to be arriving every minute. In these villages, there were people who attended wakes whether or not they knew the deceased or their bereaved relatives. It was not unknown for the house of the bereaved to be left bereft of sustenance after a wake. In this case, however, so many people brought food and drink, that Millie suspected there would be a substantial surplus.

They were soon called to prayers and after the chaplet (as the rosary was called), was recited, a lay minister opened a bible at a random page. (This was in order to discern what message the departed one wished to impart to his family and friends.) The verse this day happened to be *The Lord is my Shepherd*. The congregation sang this so lustily that the cicadas ceased their evensong for the night. Half a dozen more hymns followed in quick succession so the lay preacher didn't get the chance he wanted to expound on the message of Psalm 23. A few hoarse voices called out for liquid refreshment, and coffee, juices and other drinks were served.

Discrete groups formed as playing cards and dominoes appeared on some tables, while women who hadn't seen each other for a while wanted to gather together to share their news. Millie and her mother and aunt found themselves in a group of women whose parents or grandparents came from the French islands of Martinique or Guadeloupe. These women wanted to know more about what they considered to be their mother country. One of them asked Meg whether wakes were held in a similar fashion in Martinique. She replied that this was so. Aunt Marie then added that one wake she remembered as a little girl was different from all the others. Her audience was intrigued by this and wanted to hear about it.

"It was my grandfather's, Boniface Le Blanc's;" she began. "He had taken ill and one morning couldn't be wakened. He had stopped breathing and had no pulse. Our neighbour and friend, monsieur le doctor, said that at eighty-four years of age, his time had come. That night at the wake, as drinks were being served, our father, Leon, *may his soul rest in peace,* opened a bottle of Napoleon brandy and began pouring it into glasses. The corpse in the coffin then sat up and asked: "Ou est ma verre?" The room was suddenly emptied! People who were near the doors rushed out. Those who were near a window jumped. Fortunately, we were on the ground floor and nobody was hurt."

"What happened then?" The ladies wanted to know.

"Well," said Aunt Marie, "his family didn't run away and the doctor stayed too. The doctor gave him a glass of water and brandy and said he'd be all right. He had fallen into a coma. Grandpere actually lived for a further three or four years."

Millie's curiosity about life in Martinique was now aroused and she determined to ask her mother more about it when they got home. Her mother then asked her to check on the little ones who had gravitated to a group of children of the same ages. Millie found them easily enough as "Ooos" and "Ahhs" from juvenile voices were coming from the side of the house. A bright carbide lamp was directed to a blank wall of the house and a man was making shadow images of animals on the wall using his fists and fingers. The children were trying to imitate him with varying degrees of success. Ducks and geese were the most common figures they managed to portray. Millie felt satisfied that they were well taken care of, as Julia and her other Maclean cousins were also in that group. She then returned to tell her mother that all was well.

She remembered that her friend Rebecca had told her about a story-teller who attended most wakes and had a head full of stories of the supernatural. She went in search of him and found him under a mango tree with a large gathering around him. This man, who went under the sobriquet of Tonton, was relating the story of a young man who was nearly seduced by la-diablesse. Millie was keen to hear this story and slipped into the group.

The story was situated at a wake, and Herbert, a young man, was the recipient of a fortune from the will of his favourite aunt who had just died. Somehow, the young ladies of the village had got wind of this and most of them attended the wake. Some baked bread and cakes which they brought. Others made ginger beer, sorrel, mauby, lemonade and wine. Two enterprising sisters were in the kitchen making a pelau with ingredients which they brought with them. They plied Herbert with all the treats they could and offered all the words of consolation they knew. At first, he bathed in the attention and flattery he received, but the cloying nature of his admirers began to wear on his nerves so he asked one of his older cousins to act as host while he slipped out for a walk in the cool night air.

On his way out, he noticed a strange young lady sitting and fanning herself on a log under a caimite tree. He thought to himself that she was probably escaping from the attentions of her many admirers, for she was strikingly good looking. He mused as he walked that he could now pick and choose among all the belles in the village. *He would take his time*, he thought, *and sample as many as he could.*

As he returned to the wake, the young lady was still sitting there. *(It was at this point in the story that Millie joined the story-teller's audience and her friend Rebecca spotted her and pulled her to sit on the bench next to her, whispering: "Shh, ah go tell yuh wha' he say later.")*

"Well," Herbert say to himself, "dis is my chance." He swagger over to the gyul and say in 'is bes' posh accent: "I say, young lady. I 'aven't 'ad the pleasure of seeing you 'round here before."

"Dat's because I ain't from 'round here," she answered.

"May I sit wit' you?" he arxed, plonkin' he bottom down on de log nex' to she. "Where you from an' what brung you to Talparo?" he enquired.

"I from town an' I staying by me tantie on Todd's road." Jes as Herbert feel 'e makin' 'eadway wid dis new craf', one o' the gyuls what was makin' de pelau come out de door an' say: "So is dere yuh is! We lookin' fuh yuh to say de chaplet fuh yuh dead tantie." Two ah de odder gyuls come out too, an' when dey see dis new fancy woman he talkin' to, dey turn as green as de moss alyu does slip on when yuh go to wash yuh clothes by de river. One o' dem hol' out she rosary beads wid a big silver cross on de end an' shout: "Is prayers for de dead we callin' yuh for! Well, de fancy woman leap up an' start runnin' down de track like a deer houn', an' everybody could see, instead of <u>foot,</u> is cow <u>hoof</u> she have!" Nervous laughter erupted from the listeners.

Just then, Aunt Marie came out and announced: "It's time for prayers again, please attend." They trooped into the house where the chaplet was recited again followed by a passage chosen at random from the bible. This time the message was from John the Baptist telling of the coming of the Messiah whose sandals he was not fit to unlace. The lay preacher immediately started on the theme of the need for repentance but Millie felt a tug on her arm as Rebecca motioned her to slip outside with her.

Once outside, Rebecca regaled her with the first part of the story which she had missed. Millie thanked her and stored every bit of the tale in her memory. She decided to write two versions of it, one in the creole dialect she had heard and the other in standard English. She would ask Mr Lee which version to submit. There was a certain comic appeal in the dialect version which she couldn't quite capture in standard English.

The two girls crept back into the house letting everyone assume that they had been on a call of nature. The lay preacher went on talking for another half an hour, and as he tended to repeat himself, Millie felt sure that she had missed nothing of consequence from his sermon.

Millie joined her cousins serving refreshments to the gathering and was pleased to hear some people praising the quality of the coffee which her mother had provided. She then thought of taking some to Mr Lee at school. She would tell him that it was an experimental blend and that she was seeking his opinion of it. Oranges were not in season and she wished to repay him for his kind attention.

James came from his All-Fours game in the wee hours of the morning and said it was time to leave; he had to work that day. As the younger children were already asleep, it was decided not to waken them but to have them collected in the daylight. Millie and her parents then made their way home by flambeau-light as several others were also doing.

Chapter 17
New Aunties and the Supremacy
of the King's English

The Browne family did not attend the funeral which was held in the San Raphael church. Millie asked her cousins, Julia and Helen, how it went. Julia reckoned that it was the biggest funeral she had ever seen. Helen added that she even met an aunt she never knew about who came from a place called St. Clair, in Port of Spain, and that she heard the story of their family's life before they came to Trinidad. Millie wished she could have been there. She realized then that they had relatives in other parts of Trinidad and even in Grenada and Martinique and hoped to meet and get to know them one day.

As she arrived home that afternoon her mother had just finished making their supper and was sitting in the bent-wood rocking chair on their front porch. "Mama," Millie began, "why have we never met our aunties from St. Clair?"

"How did you find out about them?" Her mother replied, "They didn't come to the wake."

"No," countered Millie, "but Aunt Camille attended the funeral and Julia and Helen met her."

"Ah, so that's who told you," Meg replied. "I have two sisters who came to Trinidad besides your aunt Marie. Papa Leon told them to keep away from me as I would be a bad influence on them and they believed it." Millie immediately wished she hadn't brought up the matter as a feeling of guilt washed over her. It must have been because of her that the sisters were apart. Her mother continued: "Now that Papa Leon has passed away, I think we'll all get to know each other again. Papa was a good man but he was too Old Testament in his ways." Millie pondered on this and transferred some of the guilt she felt on to the shoulders of her intransigent departed grandfather.

She suspected that it was Aunt Marie who had somehow got word to them about the death and must have known how to get in touch with her sisters. It would be through Aunt Marie, therefore that she would be able to find them.

At supper that evening, Millie noticed that her mother seemed even more depressed than usual and tried to cheer her up. "Mama, this saltfish accra tastes extra special. What did you add to it?"

"Only the usual onion and tomato—oh yes, there was something else. I almost forgot. There were some chopped chadon bene leaves left over from the pepper sauce I was making that I added to it."

"You must do it again," the children chorused. "We are really enjoying this." Millie was pleased to see Mama smiling with pleasure at the compliments and vowed to try to remember to cheer her up.

She related the "la-diabless" story she had heard at the wake to her mother who thought that it was one the Port of Spain Gazette would be happy to use. She was very amused by it herself. Millie then sat down to write it. She wrote it all down first of all in the original dialect it was delivered in by Tonton and Rebecca. Then she wrote her own version in standard English. Feeling that her English version lacked some of the nuances of the tale, she decided to take it to Mr Lee the next day for him to decide which version to submit to the Gazette.

Mr Lee, however, was quite intrigued by the original use of the common vernacular and couldn't choose. He decided to do an audience test. He asked Millie to read the standard English version to her class. The children responded favourably, saying it was a great story. Then he asked one of the older boys to read the dialect version to another class. This time, the uproarious laughter it produced caused Mr Farfan to come to investigate what was happening. Mr Lee told him of the experiment, and Mr Farfan, having read both copies, was in sympathy with their predicament and suggested that both copies be submitted so that the editor of the paper could decide. This was done, along with a request by Mr Lee to inform him of the reason for the choice of either version.

The standard English version was chosen and duly published. The reason given by the editor in a private letter to Mr Lee, was that "*both schools and the press are institutions for the promulgation of education to the masses, and to publish articles written in the native dialect would serve to legitimize its use, a practice we are trying to stamp out in favour of the King's English.*" This information was duly passed on to Millie who, with some misgivings, decided to restrict her efforts to writing in standard English. She had to exercise her skill as a translator as she continued to source her subject matter from the annals of "wake" stories as told by Tonton and recounted by Rebecca. These two people became the recipients of useful gifts while the publishing of her tales lasted.

Part 2
Millie as a Teenager

Chapter 18
Preparation for the School Concert

Millie was readily accepted as a pupil teacher from the age of thirteen under the patronage of Mr Farfan. Her academic brilliance had earned her the respect of her fellow pupils who were already in the habit of seeking her help with their studies. She, along with two of her classmates, were chosen to attend classes after school on two evenings a week and on some Saturday mornings.

One of her first experiences of responsibility came as the school was preparing for its annual Christmas concert. Millie was asked by Mr Farfan to be in charge of the music. Her job was to choose the carols and teach them to the children. She had previously taken part in the Nativity Play, either as Mary or one of the angels, this time she was one of the directors, a role she was happy to undertake. Mr Farfan also asked her to contact her uncle Ian to find out if his parang band would be able to play at the concert and she promised to do so.

She enlisted the help of her mother for the choosing of carols as she had in mind introducing a French carol Mama sometimes sang to them. Her mother and she readily decided upon *Oh Come all ye Faithful, Silent Night, The First Noel, Angels we Have Heard on High* and *Joy to the World.* She then got her mother to copy out the words of the French *Cantique Noel* which she intended to teach to her class. It was about calling neighbours to celebrate the birth of Jesus.

Promptement levez vous mon voisin
Le Sauveur de la terre est enfin
Parmi nous mon voisin
Envoye par son pere mon voisin
Allez mon voisin allez. Allez mon voisin allez

Allez mon voisin a la creche mon voisin
Allez mon voisin allez. Allez mon voisin allez
Allez mon voisin a la creche.

Veillant sur mon troupeau mon voisin
Autour de ce village mon voisi
J'entends un air nouveau mon voisi
Et de plus doux language mon voisin
Allez mon voisin allez. Allez mon voisin allez
Allez mon voisin a la creche mon voisin
Allez mon voisin allez. Allez mon voisin allez
Allez mon voisin a la creche.

Rempli d'etonnement mon voisin
Je laisse ma houlette mon voisin
Pour voir le Dieu naissant mon voisin
Qu'annoncait le Prophete mon voisin
Allez mon voisin allez. Allez mon voisin allez
Allez mon voisin a la creche mon voisin
Allez mon voisin allez. Allez mon voisin allez
Allez mon voisin a la creche.

Entrant dedans l'etable mon voisin
J'adore ce poupon mon voisin
Mais Jesus ineffable mon voisin
Allez mon voisin allez. Allez mon voisin allez
Allez mon voisin a la creche mon voisin
Allez mon voisin allez. Allez mon voisin allez
Allez mon voisin a la creche.

Mr Farfan's approval was sought for this carol and he readily agreed, saying that it was important that our rich and diverse cultural heritage be preserved. He even wished that someone would write the words in a book so that it would pass on to posterity. Encouraged by this response, Millie ventured to enhance the French cultural aspect of the Christmas concert by adding another song from her mother's collection. It had little to do with Christmas per se, other than the drinking of wine, but because of the rousing tune she decided to try it.

Chevalliers de la table ronde
Goutons voir si le vin est bon
Chevalliers de la table ronde
Goutons voir si le vin est bon
Goutons voir oui oui oui
Goutons vois non non non
Goutons voir si le vin est bon
Goutons voir oui oui oui
Goutons vois non non non
Goutons voir si le vin est bon

Si est bon c'est agreable
J'en bourais jusqua mon Plaisir
Si est bon c'est agreable
J'en bourais jusqua mon Plaisir
Goutons nous oui oui oui
Goutons nous non non non
Goutons nous si le vin est bon
Goutons nous oui oui oui
Goutons nous non non non
Goutons nous si le vin est bon

Et encore ce n'est pas beaucoup
J'en boirais cinq o six boutelles
Et encore ce n'est pas beaucoup
J'en boirais cinq o six boutelles
Et encore oui oui oui
Et encore non non non
Et encore ce n'est pas beaucoup

Si je meurs je veux qu'on m'enterre
Dans une cave ou y'a du bon vin
Si je meurs je veux qu'on m'enterre

Dans une cave ou y'a du bon vin
Dans une cave oui oui oui
Dans une cave non non non
Dans une cave ou y'a du bon vin
Dans une cave oui oui oui
Dans une cave non non non
Dans une cave ou y'a du bon vin.

Mr Farfan exclaimed when he saw the song: "But this is a song we sang in England! We learnt this along with *Frere Jacques*. You may use it as an encore, if needs be. It is not really a Christmas song as it mentions burying the dead; but it's a lively enough tune that people will appreciate." He then added that it reminded him of another English folk song that he learnt whilst studying in England. He promised to teach it to them at another time. It was called *On Ilkley Moor Baht'hat.*

Chapter 19
How to Get Parang Bands to Perform

In order to give the concert some Spanish flavour, Millie approached her uncle with the idea of his parang band performing at the school's Christmas concert. He claimed that the members of the band were very busy people who had to put work before pleasure and could ill afford the time. He would, nevertheless, talk to them about it. They would have very little time after getting home from work to wash, change into suitable clothes and go to a concert. He asked what refreshments would be available, and Millie replied that there was sure to be juices, sorrel, mauby and possibly ice-cream. He said: "I'll see what the others have to say."

Not being too happy with this response from her uncle and having told Mr Farfan that she would try to get the parang band to play at the concert, when Millie got home, she related the encounter with her uncle to her parents. James Browne smiled broadly when he heard her tale. "When you see your uncle again tell him that I will provide the rum but it will be off the school premises. The thing with parang bands is that they only play for a little bit of food and a lot of grog."

This promise of rum must have worked, for not only Ian Maclean's band turned up on the night of the concert but another band also appeared impromptu and took part. Christmas carols were sung by everybody and two of the French families who attended knew the *Cantique Noel* as well. It turned out to be the best Christmas concert the school had produced so far.

Millie's position as a pupil teacher was greatly enhanced by this and Mr Farfan was able to secure a teaching bursary on her behalf. This meant that her financial situation remained the same although Millie could no longer submit stories to the children's page of the Sunday Port of Spain Gazette because she was now too old. The Gazette offered Millie the chance of being a freelance journalist who could submit articles to the paper on an ad hoc basis but Millie declined, having committed herself to serious studying to become a teacher.

Chapter 20
A Possible Father Figure
Appears on the Scene

One of the other teachers, a Miss Lezama, was an expert at handicrafts and taught Millie to make artificial flowers with coloured crepe paper and also with wool and wire. Millie's creations were good enough to be sold at the church harvest. Meg, Millie's mother, was also good at handicrafts, and made trays and baskets from Seegin vines. They were allowed a stall at the Feast of San Raphael which was held on October 24th that year. It was well attended by patrons from the surrounding parishes and Meg and Millie displayed their wares to advantage.

After the mass, during which the church was absolutely full, the priest came by, blessing the stalls. Following the priest, was a contingent from the Santa Rosa Parish of Arima. A handsome man in his thirties suddenly reached across and put his hand on Meg's shoulder. "Marguerite!" he exclaimed. "It is you!"

"Jerome?" she enquired, "Did you not go to England to fight in the war?"

"Yes," he answered, "and I stayed on to study afterwards, but I'm back for good now." Meg reached out and hugged him with such a show of affection that Millie decided that her search for her father was at last at an end and was waiting for an introduction. The gentleman, however, releasing himself from her mother's embrace, sped off, saying, "I must tell father and mother at once." Millie asked her mother: "Who was that?"

"That was one of the Farfan boys from when I lived in Arima," her mother replied, still full of excitement.

Jerome reappeared then, herding before him an elderly man and woman who bore him a close resemblance. "Here she is," he said, introducing Meg to his mother.

"Marguerite!" His mother exclaimed, "Why have you kept away from us all these years?" They embraced each other and Meg, with tears in her eyes, said: "I must first introduce you to my fifteen-year-old daughter, Millie." They shook hands all around and Meg then took Mr and Mrs Farfan to the quiet side of the stall where they could converse more easily. Millie took Jerome to show him the flowers which he marvelled at, saying that he never saw wool being made into leaves and flowers before. Millie modestly declined to tell him that she had made them, but proclaimed her mother as the maker of the variety of trays and baskets on display. He bought a basket which he then proceeded to fill with flowers, taking his time to create an artistic bouquet. Millie meanwhile, strained to listen to the quiet conversation her mother and the elder Farfans were having and caught the words "viole" and "honte" which were among the growing vocabulary of French words she possessed. This unfortunately, dispelled her illusions of Jerome and fatherhood. Jerome paid double what she asked for the basket and the flowers, saying it was all for a good cause. He then invited them to visit when next they went to Arima and said that he had brought over a new gramophone which played excellent music he felt sure they would like to hear. She said she would try to persuade her mother to visit. Jerome also suggested that they should have a stall at the Santa Rosa harvest the following year.

Jerome's arrangement of his basket of flowers encouraged others to purchase baskets and flowers so that soon there were only trays left to be sold. The Farfans and most of the visitors departed and stalls were packed up. Their stall had made more money than ever before and it was with a feeling of accomplishment that they returned to Talparo that night.

Chapter 21
An Invitation Accepted

The following month, Millie accompanied her mother to Arima on a shopping expedition and having completed their purchases they paid a visit to the Farfan's home where Meg had once lived. Meg had also been pressed to visit by the elder Farfans. "How delightful to see you!" Mrs Farfan enthused.

"It was gracious of you to invite us, Mrs Farfan," Meg replied.

"Gertrude to you, Marguerite, please. You are not in my employ, and you are now a grown woman."

"Old habits die hard, but I'll try to remember, Gertrude," Meg answered.

"I'm sorry both Jerome and his father have gone to town today. They will be sorry to have missed you. Michel, however, our eldest, will be delighted to see you. He came over to listen to some music on our gramophone. When we told him that we met you at San Raphael, he was sorry that he didn't come with us," Mrs Farfan informed them.

Music could be heard coming from another room and they were led down a corridor and into the drawing room where Michel sat, tapping his feet to the beat of *Fascinating Rhythm* coming from a cone-shaped horn sitting next to a revolving black disc upon which an arm with a needle on its end was resting. Michel leapt to his feet and in two strides swept Meg into his arms in a welcoming hug. "Oh Michel!" Meg exclaimed, reaching up to put her hands on his shoulders and hold him at arm's length. "You have grown so tall!"

"And you are still *ma petite fleur*," he replied. "This is no doubt your lovely daughter," he added, holding out a hand to Millie. "I too have a daughter who is perhaps a little younger than you. She is just thirteen. She would have come with me but stayed at home to help her mother today."

"I would love to meet her one day," replied Millie.

Mrs Farfan then excused herself from their company to get some refreshments, leaving Meg and Millie to marvel at the gramophone which Michel was only too pleased to expound upon.

His Master's Voice was printed on a brass plaque and a picture of a little Terrier-cross dog looking into a speaker horn was on the inside of the raised cover. Michel explained that the needle on the end of the hovering arm picked up vibrations from the grooves in the revolving disc (which he called a record) and transmitted them along a wire to an amplifier which in turn sent vibrating signals to the horn shaped speaker, producing the music they could hear. Just then, the music came to an end but the record was still spinning with the hovering arm near to a paper disc in the middle.

Michel turned off the machine with a switch, stopping the record from spinning. He carefully lifted the arm (which was pivoted on one end so that it could move easily) from the record and placed it on a little stand at the side of the record. He then lifted the record off its turn-table and replaced it upside down. The writing on the paper disc on this side of the record said *It Had to be You*. There was a handle very like the one on Meg's Singer sewing machine which Michel carefully wound ten times. Switching the machine back on, he carefully placed the needle on the movable arm on to the outer rim of the record and the dulcet tones of a distant singer could be heard delivering one of the latest songs to the backing of a full orchestra.

Millie and her mother were enchanted. Mrs Farfan came in with a tray of drinks which she offered them. They accepted, thanked her and drank, but confessed to each other afterwards that they couldn't remember what they drank, so taken-up by the musical experience were they! Millie promised herself that she would own a gramophone one day. Unfortunately, their visit had to be terminated for them to catch the coach to take them back to Talparo, but they were invited to make another visit soon, to which they readily assented.

There were four other passengers on the coach to Talparo and these were regaled with the gramophone experience for most of the trip home. Millie needed little encouragement to sing what she remembered of the song *It Had to be You*. New songs were a rare treat for the residents of Talparo.

On reaching home, their experiences were related to the younger children who all wanted to see and hear for themselves the wonders they were told about. They begged to be taken to Arima on the next trip and Meg promised to take them, but not all at the same time. She promised to take them in order of age, Olivia, then Maria and finally Pedro.

"Not fair!" Maria exclaimed.

"Not fair!" Pedro echoed.

"Any more words of dissent from either of you and you will not go at all! Do you hear me?" Their mother admonished.

"Yes Mama," they both murmured.

"That's more than enough excitement for tonight now and you'll all get ready for bed."

"Yes Mama," was the meek response, as they hurried off to get washed and changed for bed. They knew they could not risk the wrath of a mother who generally meant what she said and would carry through any promised threat.

Chapter 22
Her Sisters' Talents Are Put to Use

The responsibility for the younger children's education had gradually shifted to Millie's capable shoulders and she supervised their homework and kept them up to mark reasonably well. However, they were not as academically minded as she was and their main interests lay in other directions. Olivia loved sewing and embroidery. Maria loved growing plants and rearing animals, while Pedro showed a keen interest in mechanical things and would take clocks and toys to bits to see how they worked and put them back together again.

As Christmas was approaching that year, Olivia was able to persuade her mother that they needed new curtains and table cloths which she was willing to sew for the festive season. This of course, entailed another shopping trip to Arima. While Meg was only too happy to agree, James needed convincing that the old curtains had become shabby. Maria, his youngest daughter, was the one who had the most influence on him. She was able to get him agree to things the others couldn't. Millie put it to Maria that although it was Olivia who would accompany them to Arima this time, it would bring her turn nearer the sooner Olivia went. Maria saw the sense of this and set about to convince her father to have their curtains changed.

As she was helping him prune some King Orange trees on the sunny side of the house one day, she looked up at the windows and said: "Papa, how come the curtains on this side of the house look almost white and on the other side of the house they're yellow?" James looked up as if seeing the curtains for the first time. He knew the answer and said: "That's because this side of the house gets more sunshine and bleaches them."

"Then why does my skin get darker when I stay out in the sun too long?" Her father couldn't explain that one and said that she should ask Millie, who was studying science. He had nevertheless come to realize that the curtains were old and faded at least on one side of the house. When Maria suggested that it would be nice to have new curtains for Christmas, he did not dismiss the idea, but said it would be possible if they got a good price for their coffee that year.

It so happened that coffee trees in other parts of the island that year suffered what he called a blight and his coffee commanded a fair price. The proposed shopping trip to Arima was therefore able to take place.

Chapter 23
The Launch of Olivia's Career

Cloths for curtains and for tablecloths and new Christmas dresses were chosen and packed away in the coach they had come on. They then had two hours to spare before the return trip and made their way to the Farfans' home for the promised visit.

"Good afternoon, Gertrude," Meg greeted, as Mrs Farfan came to the door in response to their knock. "Good afternoon, Marguerite," Mrs Farfan replied, "I'm so glad you remembered to call me Gertrude, "Mrs Farfan" makes me feel so terribly old," she laughed. "Come in. I see you have brought another of your lovely daughters to see us."

"Yes, this is Olivia, who has come with us to choose curtain material for Christmas and this is your Christmas present from us," Meg replied, handing her a basket of fruit which she gratefully accepted.

This time Jerome and his father John were also at home and were pleased to welcome them. Jerome was especially happy to see them and said how sorry he was that he had missed their last visit. He had gone to Port of Spain to acquire some new records which he insisted they must hear before they leave. They were ushered into the "drawing room" where they were served cool drinks. This was most welcome after their hot shopping spree.

Meg noticed that Mrs Farfan was appraising the fourteen-year-old Olivia, and explained that Olivia was the family member with an eye for colour and fashion who would be sewing the curtains this year. That was the reason for her appearance, along with Olivia's expressed desire to meet them. Mrs Farfan was particularly pleased to hear of Olivia's talent, especially when Meg acclaimed her as a much neater seamstress than herself. It turned out that a Mrs Diaz, who had been the Farfan's seamstress for years had recently passed away and the burgesses of Arima were looking for another.

"Would it be an imposition if I were to ask a favour?" Mrs Farfan enquired. "Please ask, Gertrude, anything we can do for you will not be enough to repay your kindness," Meg replied. "I too have some curtain material to be sewn up and I was wondering whether Olivia—"

"Of course, I'd be only too pleased to do it for you," Olivia interrupted.

"That's kind of you," continued Mrs Farfan. This time it was Jerome who interrupted, saying: "This record must have been meant for Olivia. It is one of the very latest releases." From the gramophone came the words of the song, *Ain't she Sweet?* "If Mother doesn't mind too much, we can have a musical interlude."

Olivia, blushing down to the tips of her toes, said, "I've never been so flattered in my life before. What an enchanting song!"

They listened 'til the song ended, then watched fascinated as Jerome replaced that record with *Sometimes I'm Happy*. He explained that he had been able to get the latest songs as soon as they were aired because of a friend in England who worked in the music industry. There were two other songs that they were treated to, *I Can't Give You Anything but Love Baby* and *Ole' Man River*, which they thoroughly enjoyed.

Millie was wearing a yellow dress that day and Mrs Farfan remarked: "What a lovely colour! I used to love wearing yellow when I was a girl."

Millie replied, "It's one of Olivia's creations; I saw a pattern in a catalogue, and Ollie made it up, better than the original." Mrs Farfan was impressed by the tailored look of her frock.

"When my dressmaker passed on," she explained, "I was tempted to buy her sewing machine, which is a new treadle type, but I'm not much good at sewing, myself, so I resisted."

"Really!" exclaimed Olivia, "I've been saving up to buy one of those as Mama's hand sewing machine is a bit slow when there's much sewing to do."

"I'll enquire for you if it's still for sale if you like. They've only recently come out so it must be nearly new."

"Oh yes please!" said Olivia, beaming with excitement.

Time seemed to fly as they enjoyed listening to the music and having a chatter and only too soon it was time to depart for Talparo with the sonorous tones of Al Jolson still ringing in their ears. They carried with them an extra package of material handed to them to be made into curtains for the Farfans.

Olivia especially, was full of hope, not only that she might be able to acquire a treadle machine, but that her career was launched.

Fellow passengers on the coach ride back to Talparo were regaled this time with snatches of verses from *Ain't she Sweet* and *Ol' Man River*.

Chapter 24
Another Parang Christmas Concert

Preparations for the school's Christmas concert were in full swing and Millie was again appointed one of its chief architects. Having had success with French songs sung by the children the previous year, Millie decided to try them with something Spanish. Her uncle's parang band was much appreciated by the children and they were keen to learn more of this exotic culture. She knew very little Spanish herself but thought she could rely on her uncle's help. She sat down and wrote:

Oh Virgin Maria, thou flower of innocence
God has seen thee and liked what he saw
So, He has sent me to tell you the score
That you're highly favoured above all maidens
That dwell on this earth who follow His teachings
And obey all his laws, you alone were chosen
To bear His Special Son
To him you will give birth tho' you know no man
Not even good Joseph who dotes upon you
And Joseph will be told that God is the father
Of your precious baby worth more than gold
An infant prodigious, told of from of old
He'll be the Saviour, Saviour of the world.

Millie took a copy of her song to her uncle and asked him to translate it into Spanish and compose a suitable tune for it. He was impressed with her effort and did the following translation:

O Virgen Maria, O flor de inocencia
El Senor ha te vista y mucho le gusta
El me despacha en consequencia
Contarte la Buena noticia.
Recontar que tu es bien parecida
Mas que todas las mujeres
Que viven en la tierra que copia doctrina
Y observa todas las leys.
Parir el Hijo, el Hijo subido del Senor
Tu va dar a luz aunque relaciona ningun hombre
Ni siquera el Bueno Jose
Cuyo admiracion tu posee.
Y Jose va ser contado que el Senor es el Padre
De suyo bambino precioso
Un infante portentoso que pronostica la Biblia
El sera el Salvador, Salvador del Mundo.

A lively tune was given to this and Millie was well pleased.

Mr Farfan had suggested that a few skits be included in the programme and Millie set her mind to write her own. She wanted the children to develop their confidence and have the audience in a happy mood also. Drama was seen as the perfect medium for this. Even the shyest boy, put into a soldier's uniform with a rifle placed in his hands, is transformed into a stalwart hero. Her sister Olivia, was happy to transform outgrown clothes into new costumes; Millie therefore had her own home-sewn costume designer.

Skit no. 1.

Scene: *A courtroom. A judge in white wig sits behind a table. A policeman in starched, ironed, uniform, and a farm labourer in ragged clothes stand before him.*

Judge: *Why is this man brought before the court?*

Policeman: *Gross disrespect, Your Honour. This man called me an ass.*

Judge: *It is indeed an offence to call an officer of His Majesty's constabulary an ass. Have you done so?*

Farm labourer: *Yes, Your Honour, but please may I ask one question?*

Judge: *Go ahead.*

Farm labourer: *Is it an offence to call an ass a constable?*

Judge: *An ass cannot understand, so he couldn't be offended; if anything, he should be flattered.*

Farm labourer: *(Turning towards the constable) You are a constable!*

Skit no. 2

Scene: *A playground. Two boys are facing up to each other in an aggressive manner. Children around them are egging them on to fight.*

1st boy: *You bumped into me on purpose!*

2nd boy: *No, I didn't! You bumped into me!*

1st boy: *You're a liar!*

2nd boy: *You're the liar and a bully to boot!*

1st boy: *I'm not! You've been provoking me for a fight since I came to this school.*

2nd boy: *You're a coward! (He bends down and draws a line on the ground) I dare you to step over this line! (The children are now chanting, 'Fight! Fight! Fight!')*

1st boy: *(Stepping over the line) Here I am now, I've stepped over.*

2nd boy: *You're on my side now, so we are friends. (Giving him a hug). (Disappointed, the children wail, "Ahhh").*

All the children were given strict instructions not to talk about what was in the concert outside of school so that it would be a surprise for their parents and other visitors in the audience.

A few "knock knock" jokes were also introduced to fill gaps between scene changes. Millie's friend Isaac had suggested these with his sister Linda as his "straight man."

(Examples)

Isaac: Knock knock.
Linda: Who's there?
Isaac: Voodoo.
Linda: Voodoo who?
Isaac: Voodoo you think it is other than me?
Isaac: Knock knock.

Linda: Who's there?
Isaac: Anita.
Linda: Anita who?
Isaac: Anita come in out of the rain.

These were especially loved by the other children who made up their own and sorely tried the patience of their teachers with them.

Chapter 25
Millie Passes Inspection

The inspector of schools, Mr Baillie, was due to visit the Talparo R.C. school the week before the concert and teachers were advised by Mr Farfan not to be awed by him but to give him truthful answers. On the day he arrived, Millie was teaching her class the Annunciation parang song she had composed. It was written on the blackboard and they had just finished copying it into their exercise books.

As he entered her class space the children stood and chorused: "Good morning, Mr Baillie," just as they had been instructed to do. He returned their greeting and turning to Millie, asked: "Are you the class teacher?" Millie replied: "Yes sir, I am Millicent Le Blanc, an appointed pupil teacher."

"Ah, yes. I remember reading something about your appointment. You must be among the youngest pupil teachers to secure a bursary."

"I have that honour sir," Millie responded.

"Carry on with your work, I do not wish to interrupt," the inspector said, taking a chair in the corner of the room.

"Please sit class," Millie instructed. "I will sing the first line, which will be repeated after every fourth line as a chorus." She then sang in a clear voice.

O Virgen Maria, O flor de inocencia.

The class repeated it after her. This process was repeated three times before they proceeded to the next line, which was treated in the same manner.

As they reached the line with the word *mujeres* Millie had to point out that the letter *j* in Spanish was pronounced as *h* in English. She then told the class that otherwise Spanish was very phonetic, unlike French, which they had had some difficulty with previously.

The entire song was sung just before the bell rang for the recessional break. The children were let out but Millie was asked by Mr Baillie to stay behind for a while.

"Is there a reason why you did not make the children learn the words first before you taught them the tune?" Asked the Inspector.

"Yes sir," answered Millie. "I've found that tunes help their memory. I also learned that in the days before newspapers messengers went from village to village, even in England, singing of the occurrences that had taken place because by that method they remembered it best."

The inspector then asked, "Why Spanish?"

Millie replied: "We try our best to preserve their cultural heritage, as you can see from the register, many of the children here have Spanish surnames. They have grandparents who speak Spanish. And as my "Notes of a Lesson" says, the aim of this lesson was: (i) To develop a sense of cultural heritage through music, (ii) To encourage the children's musical ability and giving of entertainment value."

He looked at the register then asked: "What about those with French, Scottish, and even English backgrounds?"

Millie answered: "We learnt the French *Cantique Noel*, the Scottish *Auld Lang Syne*, and Mr Farfan is even going to teach us the English folk song, *On Ilkley Moor Bar T'Hat*." (Millie then thought to herself: *Thank goodness he didn't ask about our African heritage. I couldn't very well tell him I intend to teach them the song Ole Man River, he might accuse me of condoning racism.*)

"Thank you," the inspector replied as he walked out the door. (He was heard to say to Mr Farfan before he left the school: "You have a promising pupil teacher in Miss Le Blanc even though she reminds me of a fighting Bantam.")

The school's Christmas concert that year was again a great success and Millie received praise from many quarters.

Chapter 26
The Girls Are Charmed by Stardust as Olivia Gets Her Singer

Olivia received word from Mrs Farfan that the treadle sewing machine was still for sale. Mrs Diaz' nephew would accept a deposit of two pounds and payment of ten shillings per month for the next eleven months. Olivia was excited at this and proposed to agree to the arrangement.

Having completed the sewing of Mrs Farfan's curtains, Olivia wanted to deliver them. It was the last week before Christmas and their mother couldn't spare the time to go to Arima again. However, cousin Julia was going to a job interview at a shop in Arima and Ollie asked if she could travel with Julia to Arima, to which Meg agreed. Maria, hearing of this proposal, claimed that she should be allowed to go to Arima too. "Please Mama," she begged: "You promised it would be my turn next."

"On one condition. You must promise to be on your best behaviour, and Millie will have to go too to see that you behave."

The four young ladies therefore embarked on the coach to Arima the following day, along with four other Christmas shoppers. Maria was amazed at the hustle and bustle of Christmas shopping. They went first with Julia to the Bata shoe shop where the manager agreed to give Julia a try out that very day to see whether she was suitable. Leaving her there, the three sisters went to the Farfan's home to deliver the curtains.

"How wonderful to see you again!" Mrs Farfan greeted them. "This must be Maria," she guessed, quite correctly.

"Pleased to meet you," replied Maria, attempting a curtsy, which elicited a giggle from her sisters. "Mama couldn't come, but we've brought your curtains."

Mrs Farfan opened the parcel immediately and exclaimed: "These are beautifully finished; thank you."

"We thought you'd want them before Christmas," Olivia explained, "so we made it a priority." Mrs Farfan informed them that Jerome and his father were out shopping but there was someone new to meet that day. Millie immediately thought: *Could it be my father at last?*

They were ushered into the drawing room where Michel, the eldest Farfan son, and his fourteen-year-old daughter, Florence, sat listening to the most haunting melody Maria had ever heard. It was a song called *Stardust*. Michel rose to his feet immediately and greeted them. After introductions were made all round, they sat to listen to the entrancing music coming from the gramophone. As the song came to an end, Michel graciously asked if they would like to hear it from the beginning to which they all agreed. He picked up the arm with the needle and carefully placed it on the outer rim of the spinning record, while explaining how it worked. They listened with rapt attention and when that tune came to its end, he turned the record over and the fascinating song, *Tiptoe Through the Tulips*, titillated their eardrums.

"Isn't it just smashing?" Florence asked.

"It is indeed!" Maria exclaimed. "Millie and Ollie told me all about it but until I experienced it for myself, I didn't appreciate how wonderful it is!" Michel then said that there were some who claimed that the invention of the gramophone would inhibit people from making music themselves and that it would even affect social conversation. Millie thought to herself, *If it would stop people gossiping about one another or babbling nonsense, then that would be a good thing*. But she didn't voice her opinion. If anything, it increased her determination to have one of her own one day. She entertained an idle thought: *I'll bet my father has one.*

Mrs Farfan brought them some drinks then asked if they would like to meet Mr Diaz, who lived one street away. Olivia readily agreed and Millie volunteered to go with them, leaving Maria to listen to music with Florence and her father.

Mrs Diaz, the departed seamstress, had a wooden house with three bedrooms. Her nephew had occupied the servants' quarters, a smaller wooden house behind his aunt's home. After her demise, he moved into his aunt's house.

Mr Diaz was pleased to see them and Olivia was so keen to make the purchase that she immediately told him: "I've brought the deposit."

He smiled and said, "You should see your wares first before paying out money."

Mrs Farfan agreed, "Of course, let's make sure the merchandise is in working order." He took them through the house to a room which was obviously his aunt's sewing room. It was still filled with bundles of cloth and various garments. The treadle machine stood in pride of place with a wooden slatted chair in front of it. It was already threaded, and placing a piece of cloth under the needle, he sat in the chair and began to pedal. His hands were both free to guide the cloth where he wanted. Olivia was filled with delight. It was just what she wanted. She tried the machine herself and handed him the two pounds deposit with pleasure. He went to write out a receipt.

Millie expressed her doubts about there being sufficient room on the buggy to transport the machine to Talparo as there were many parcels bought by the Christmas shoppers. Olivia agreed reluctantly and asked Mr Diaz if she could arrange collection at a later date. This he assented to, but told them that the machine would be moved to his old house at the back as he was getting married shortly and his bride wanted the sewing room cleared. They would have to collect it soon as the house was to be rented.

Millie's ears pricked at this, for her older cousin Julia had mentioned that she would be looking for a place to rent in Arima if she managed to secure employment, or to find temporary lodging with someone. She decided to inform Julia of this opportunity as soon as possible.

Thanking Mr Diaz, they returned to the Farfans' residence to find Maria and Florence listening to *Among my Souvenirs*, a song neither Millie nor Olivia had heard before. It was replayed for their benefit and they thoroughly enjoyed it. Millie wanted to copy the words for it and Florence said she would do it for her. Michel then informed her that a very enterprising young man could be found on Saturdays near the Arima Dial selling type-written copies of the lyrics of the most popular songs at a penny each. Millie was very interested to hear this as she dearly wanted a copy of the words of *Ole Man River*. She did not wish to impose further on the Farfan's kindness.

Having looked at her curtains which were now hung in her windows, Mrs Farfan again thanked Olivia and said that she wished she (Olivia) lived in Arima, as her friends, the Quesnels, the Cezairs, and the Da Silvas all were looking for a new seamstress. This gave Olivia considerable food for thought, as her clientele in Talparo was somewhat sparse to say the least. They took their leave then to continue Christmas gift shopping.

On returning to their coach, they met up with Julia, who said that she had had a very profitable day. Not only was she offered a job, but was given half a crown as her commission for that day's work although she had only been instrumental in selling eight pairs of shoes. Ollie then related her good news and Millie added that there might even be a place for Julia to rent in Arima if everything worked out right. She declined to elaborate on this as the other shoppers had just returned to the coach and she knew there was competition for rental property in Arima.

After departing from the coach in Talparo, the cousins chatted for a while. Julia wanted to know what kind of accommodation might be possible and

Millie told her about the Diaz property. It was small, but it was a whole house and the rent would be high for a single person. Olivia immediately volunteered: "I could share it with her."

"I don't think Mama and Papa would let you;" Millie countered, "you are not quite sixteen yet."

"But Julia is twenty, nearly twenty-one and we'd be together," Olivia argued.

"And I haven't agreed to it yet," Julia interposed.

"Well, will you?" Ollie asked.

"We'll have to wait and see what both our parents say," Julia concluded. The girls then went their separate ways, Julia to Mahaica and Millie and her sisters along the Talparo to Mundo Nuevo Road to their home.

The sisters debated among themselves along the way the best way to broach their parents with the idea of Olivia going to live in Arima. They finally concluded that they would need an influential ally and decided on involving Mrs Farfan in their scheme. They decided therefore to keep quiet until they had established firm foundations for their plans.

Chapter 27
Ian Lets the Cat Out of the Bag

Christmas that year was a joyful occasion in the Browne household. Instead of slaughtering one of their own animals as they had done in previous years, they bought a large ham from the Chinaleong's shop in the village. (This was done as a concession, for the Chinaleongs had bought not only their cocoa crop that year, but their entire coffee crop.)

The ham came completely covered in black tar. (Pedro took this to make a tar baby which he had read about in his school primer.) It was then encased in a network of string which was left on as it was put into five-gallon pitch-oil tin to boil on the clay oven at the back of the house. The aroma of boiling ham wafted into the street above and the occasional passer-by was wont to call out: "Madam Browne, like yuh havin' ham fuh Chris'mas! Ah comin' fuh meh share wen de parang ban' come roung." (Villagers had little compunction about invading each other's privacy.)

When the ham was cooked and its string bag removed, Maria decided to stick cloves into it to enhance the flavour. She had read somewhere that this was traditionally done with ham. Millie said that this practice applied to hams that were roasted and the cloves were put in before roasting. Their mother agreed but let Maria's experiment be tried. The result was nonetheless delicious.

The Brownes did not attend the Midnight Christmas Mass, which was held in San Raphael, but went instead to a Christmas morning mass held in the Talparo R.C. school. The Macleans also attended that service and the Brownes gave them an invitation to have Christmas lunch with them, which was readily accepted. The Brownes were in turn invited to lunch in Mahaica on Boxing Day. Everything went well with the Christmas lunch. Julia asked Ollie if her parents had agreed to her living in Arima and the plan to have Mrs Farfan suggest it to Mama was explained. It was after the Boxing Day lunch in Mahaica that the cat was let out of the bag.

Ian Maclean asked James: "What do you think of your daughter leaving home to live in Arima?"

"Millie didn't say she planned any such thing," James Browne replied.

"Not Millie," re-joined Ian. "I meant Olivia. Julia mentioned that they could rent a place together in Arima and only travel to Talparo on weekends."

"Well, this is the first time I'm hearing about this," James replied.

"Papa it was only an idea, we haven't decided anything yet," Olivia offered. "It's because I can get a lot of work sewing for people in Arima and it would be less lonely for Julia if she had a companion. She will have to live in Arima at least during the week as regular daily travel between Talparo and Arima is so difficult."

"I've heard that an Indian fellow by the name of Misir or something like that, is planning to run a daily bus service from Arima to Talparo. He already runs one to Port of Spain, but the railroad is giving him too much competition," Uncle Ian informed them.

"We'll wait and see how that turns out," James decided, "I don't like the idea of young girls living on their own."

Neither Aunt Marie nor Meg had added anything to the conversation and the girls thought that was a good sign. If they were not against the plan, they may be persuaded to be for it. The following week, after most of the celebrations were over, Millie took a trip to Arima on a Saturday needing to buy books for her studies and hoping to buy the lyrics of new songs. She was obliged to take her brother Pedro with her but didn't mind. She got him to pick a variety of fruits as a present to the Farfans and her mother gave her a beautiful basket for them.

Accordingly, they were welcomed to the Farfan home where Jerome entertained them with a new song called *On the Sunny Side of the Street*. Pedro was absolutely intrigued by the new machine and while Jerome took pleasure in explaining how it worked Millie chatted with Mrs Farfan about her sister Ollie's skill in dressmaking and her desire to expand her talents in Arima. Mrs Farfan had bought some dress material in the After-Christmas sale and had a catalogue with pictures of various dress designs. Millie was sure that her sister would be able to make the dress and proposed that she take Mrs Farfan's measurements, the picture of the required dress and the material to Ollie. Mrs Farfan agreed.

When they returned to the drawing room, Jerome was talking to Pedro about cricket, a sport he loved. He was telling him about a new batsman called Donald Bradman who the critics were hailing as better than W.G. Grace. Pedro had heard of Grace and wanted to be like him. Bradman, he wasn't so sure of. Millie related how she was pleased to be able to buy copies of the popular songs from the song vendor by the Dial and asked Jerome to thank his brother for telling her about him. That reminded Mrs Farfan that Florence had written out the words of *Among my Souvenirs* for her. She retrieved it from the bookcase where she had put it. Millie asked her to thank Florence for her as they left and promised that her sister would do a fine job.

Chapter 28
The Cinema Motivates Fashion Changes

The third decade of the twentieth century turned out to be a remarkable one. The Wall Street crash of over a year ago was sending ripples far and wide. Unemployment figures in the U.K. rose above 1.5 million. The pound sterling was devalued from $4.86 to $3.40 U.S. The Trinidad dollar, however, was tied to the pound and remained at $4.80 so the tables that the children recited at school, *One pound, four eighty. Two pounds, nine sixty. Three pounds, fourteen forty* etc. remained unchanged.

Changes in fashion, especially women's clothing, however, were taking place. Shorter skirts were being worn leading to the almost total eclipse of the petticoat. Brighter colours, once thought of as being somewhat vulgar, were becoming the norm. The cinema industry was reaching a new peak. The Swedish actress, Greta Garbo, talked on film for the first time as she was heard to utter the words: "Gimme a vhisky with ginger ale on the side—and don't be stingy, baby."

A new fibre, Nylon, was discovered by Wallace Carothers in America to have properties similar to silk, but was even stronger. This proved to be tailor-made for the stocking industry. Legs, therefore, were to be on display. Actresses were seen to be the leaders of fashion. Hemlines went up and down according to dictates of the latest films. Seamstresses who could copy the latest fashions were in great demand.

A traveling cinema tent owned by the politician Sarran Teelucksingh "brought the magic of the silver screen" to places like Arima from time to time so that the latest in fashionable taste was available to be savoured by the gentry.

Olivia's expertise was discovered by friends of the Farfans who wanted to know "who made Gertrude that beautiful dress?" In the fashion world Olivia became the teenage sensation. (Although the golden age of teenagers had not yet arrived.) It became imperative that she relocate to Arima if her success were to continue.

Julia, meanwhile, had rented the Diaz property on her own. She worked at the Bata shoe shop but found that the success she had enjoyed in sales during the Christmas season was no longer to be had. Commissions were meagre, barely sufficient to pay her rent and buy food. She also longed for company; she was at heart a country girl with the umbilical cords to her family severed. She had been introduced to the Farfans but did not have the same connection to them as her cousins and aunt. Her relations with them improved when she was seen as a "go-between" for getting messages to Olivia.

Michel's wife, Madeline, wanted dresses made for both herself and daughter Florence. Instructed by her mother-in-law Gertrude, she was able to find Julia's home one evening and introduce herself. Julia welcomed her to her humble dwelling and apologized for not being able to offer anything but water for her guest.

"That's quite all right," Madeline replied, "I've come to beg a favour. Would you be so kind as to take some material to your cousin Olivia to be made into dresses for me and my daughter Florence?"

"Of course," Julia answered, "I'd be delighted to help. Ollie prefers to take measurements herself, however, but her trips to Arima take up much of her sewing time. It's a pity she can't stay here with me."

"Why ever not?" Madeline exclaimed, "You have ample room here in fairly safe surroundings."

"Her parents think she should have better adult supervision than I would provide. In fact, they even think that I should have a parent figure watching over me, and I'll be twenty-one next month!" Julia explained. Madeline sympathized, "Well, something needs to be done to remedy that situation. Gertrude lives close by, and I'm not too far away. If I could tell them that we'd be *in loco parentis* that might help."

"Oh, yes indeed!" replied Julia.

"I'll talk to Gertrude about it," Madeline offered.

Chapter 29
A Conspiracy of White Ladies

A trial run to Talparo by Sookdeo Misir's bus service was advertised for the following Saturday and a trio of Farfan ladies, Gertrude Farfan, her daughter-in-law Madeline and her daughter Flo' booked seats on it. They had been given directions to the Browne's home which was less than half a mile from the crossroads where the bus made its terminus. The villagers were quite surprised to see three well-dressed white ladies walking along the Talparo/Mundo Nuevo Road, but even more surprised was Marguerite Browne.

"You walked all the way from the junction!" She exclaimed.

"Yes, and we loved the walk after sitting on the slatted wooden benches on the bus from Arima," Gertrude replied. "We've come to see Olivia for measurements. When Mahomet cannot go to the mountain, the mountain must come to Mahomet."

"I don't know that she deserves such praise," Meg replied. "Do come in and sit yourselves down while the girls pour you some cold drinks." Millie and Ollie had already fetched an earthenware goblet with coconut water from the kitchen and were pouring into glasses which they put on a wooden tray to serve their guests.

"I've still got your measurements from the last fitting, Mrs Farfan," Ollie ventured.

"It's for Madeline and my granddaughter that we've come," replied Mrs Farfan. "I'm just the chaperone."

"You shouldn't have had to come all this way; Olivia can travel to Arima," Meg suggested.

"Or wouldn't it be even better if Olivia lived in Arima?" Gertrude responded. "We would be honoured to have her amongst us, just as we were happy to have you live with us all those years ago."

Meg was a bit flustered by this and said: "But we can't impose on your family life like that!" Madeline then butted in, "It wouldn't be any imposition if she went to live with her cousin Julia, who needs the company, and we can keep a motherly eye on them."

"Well, if you put it that way, I might get James to agree," Meg conceded.

The ladies' measurements were taken and all three sisters from the Browne home walked back to the junction with the Farfans. The material was to be brought to them by Julia on the stage coach that night. The Farfans went home to Arima with a sense of accomplishment at their Talparo adventure (for that's what it was for them: "venturing into the bush") and Meg and Ollie felt elated that at last their plans were succeeding. Maria had mixed feelings about losing a dear sister.

Within a fortnight, plans were made to take Olivia's belongings and the treadle sewing machine back to Arima where industry awaited. The Farfans' dresses were completed to satisfaction and further orders were to keep flowing in despite the recession that was taking place elsewhere in the developed world. Unemployment had continued to rise in Britain. In Germany, Hitler's Nazi party came a challenging second in the elections. There seemed to be unrest all over the world, but Donald Bradman, the Australian batsman, cheered the hearts of sports lovers by scoring 452 not out in a single innings playing for New South Wales against Queensland in Sydney. This feat made Pedro change his sporting allegiance.

Chapter 30
Julia's Birthday

With her cousin, Olivia sharing the rent and being a companion to share her daily tribulations, Julia felt happy at last. Her misgivings about leaving home to seek her independence vanished. She could relate to Ollie the contretemps she had with that awkward customer who tried on a dozen pairs of shoes, insisting on trying on some that were obviously too narrow for her and thereby stretching some of them, then walking out without buying any! During that time the other salesgirl sold three pairs of shoes. They could laugh about it. Also, there were more frequent visits from Millie. One of the conditions laid down by the Brownes was that "big sister" Millie also keep an eye on Ollie.

Millie's trips to Arima (which were now more convenient due to the embryonic bus service) invariably included visits to the Farfans. On one visit, she brought a cake, which was intended as a surprise for Julia on her birthday the following day, and asked if it could be kept at the Farfans' until the next day as she wanted to surprise Julia. Mrs Farfan not only agreed, but insisted that they hold a party at her home where there could be music as well. Millie thanked her for her benevolence, agreeing but with the condition that the party fare be paid for solely by her and her sister Olivia. Florence was invited and she suggested bringing along some of her friends. This was a welcome suggestion, for her friends had brothers and so dancing partners were provided.

Julia was told that they were taking her to a cinema show for her birthday and was quite taken by surprise, when, as they stopped by to pay their respect to the Farfans, she found herself the centre of attraction. A banner proclaiming HAPPY BIRTHDAY JULIA was strung across the hallway and about a dozen people appeared shouting: "Surprise!"

She said to Millie later on that her knees suddenly felt so weak that she could have fallen if she didn't grab on to Olivia who was at her side. Everybody sang "Happy Birthday to you" and the laughter was contagious. The younger generation of the Cezairs, Da Silvas, Quesnels, and Sorzanos were all represented. Many of them were Olivia's clientele and introductions were made. It was the first "adult" party that the country girls were experiencing and they felt intoxicated without the use of alcohol. Glasses of mauby, sorrel, and fruit juices were passed around and Julia's "coming of age" toasted. The birthday cake, with 21 written on it, had pride of place on a centre table with plates of egg, cheese and fish-paste sandwiches spread around.

Jerome appointed himself "Master of Ceremonies" and played the records on the gramophone. Everyone listened to *Fascinating Rhythm* with many of them tapping their feet but no one was dancing. When the tune changed to *It Had to be You,* however, with its slow fox-trot tempo, the older Farfans, John and Gertrude, took to the floor and encouraged the young people to dance. A young man who introduced himself as Michael Quesnel, went to Julia and formally requested: "May I have the honour of this dance?"

"Only if you are prepared to teach me," Julia replied, "as I've never danced with anyone before."

"It will be my pleasure to do so," he responded, taking her hand.

"It's simple. I'll start with my weight on my right foot and move my left foot forward. You'll be doing the opposite so you start with your weight on your left foot and move your right foot backward. Then as I move my right foot forward to meet it, you move your left foot backward at the same time. I then move my left foot sideways and follow with my right foot, putting my weight on my right foot again. So, you move your right foot sideways together with mine and bring your left foot to meet it. The first two actions are slow, and the second two, fast. The rhythm is, slow slow, quick quick."

"Whoa!" Julia expostulated. "You said it's simple! I got tripped up just listening to you."

"It's easier to do than to say;" he replied, taking her on to the floor, "let's do it." Julia followed his steps tentatively at first then with more confidence. It was a little while before she felt confident enough to talk while dancing, but when Michael asked her what she really expected to be doing on her birthday, she replied that she had been promised a trip to the cinema. Her cousins had fooled her into thinking that they were going to the cinema tent which was visiting Arima for a fortnight. He immediately offered to take her himself the following night. She agreed with the stipulation that her cousins go along with them. This he consented to, saying: "The more the merrier."

Millie and Ollie, seeing their cousin's success decided to try it, Millie taking the leading role. Soon they were dancing with much aplomb; so much so that when the record was replayed and they were asked to dance by male partners they accepted eagerly. Following this they were taught some rudimentary jive steps to the music of *Ain't She Sweet* and *On the Sunny Side of the Street,* which they thoroughly enjoyed doing. When Julia told her cousins of the proposed cinema date, they were surprised but gladly accepted. They were going to see the Oberammergau passion play.

At the end of the party, Millie and Ollie insisted that they do the washing up and thanked their hosts profusely, claiming that it was the most fun they had ever had in their lives. They didn't realize at the time that they had been ushered into *the disco age*. That was the first of many house parties that the girls were to enjoy in Arima during the decade they were to look back on as their "swinging thirties."

Chapter 31
The Early Cinema

The traveling cinema tent was located at the north-eastern end of the Arima race course. It had been decided that they rendezvous at the Dial and walk from there. Michael was already there when the girls arrived. He informed them that they were to be joined by three other friends, Jean Cezair and his sister Amanda, and Daniel Sorzano from the birthday party, along the way. By the time they arrived at the cinema tent, however, their party had swelled to ten. Entrance fee was twelve cents each, so they paid five shillings for the group.

Seating was arranged with folding wooden chairs laid out in rows. They found an empty row and filled it. Julia at one end with Michael next to her, then Olivia and Millie, Jean and Amanda, Daniel, Barbara, Cecil and Denise. Daniel and Denise were Sorzanos and Cecil and Barbara, Pierres.

At six o'clock sharp, they were made to stand and sing *God Save the King* to a piano accompaniment and the lights were dimmed. A projector at the back of the tent started whirring and the screen in front lit up. Letters announced the name of the play they were about to see and its producers, directors and actors. A written narrative then described the story as it went along with moving black and white pictures (a little jerky at times) but no sound other than the whirr of the projector and some piano music. The audience sat entranced. (It didn't stop Jean Cezair's hand from reaching across the back of Millie's chair, however, resulting in her moving forward out of his reach.) As Millie glanced across to her right, she could see the other pairs at the end embracing each other. She said to herself, *that's probably what they come here for, but as I promised Mama, there'll be no hanky-panky for me.*

After the show Michel and Jean escorted the Talparo girls home, Jean walking beside Millie and trying to engage her in conversation. Getting tired of her monosyllabic replies, he asked her outright: "Have I offended you and am I just being a nuisance? Please tell me honestly."

Millie replied, "I made a promise to my mother not to become involved with any man until I'm twenty-one, and I'm keeping that promise."

"And how many more years shall I have to wait?" Jean enquired, smiling. "If that's not too rude to ask a lady."

"In three years, you'll probably be married with two children," Millie replied. She then walked quickly down the pathway to their door as they had reached their destination.

Chapter 32
Arima Carnival

On another visit to Arima that year, Millie and Ollie were to experience their first real Carnival. The Quesnels had invited them to a house party on the Sunday before Carnival at which everyone wore Domino masks and some dressed in period costumes. Olivia made Domino clown suits for herself and Millie and though they didn't look as elegant as Mrs Quesnel who was dressed as Marie Antoinette, they caught the eye of many who became interested in hiring the services of the dressmaker for future occasions.

That Monday morning, they were roused from their sleep by J'ouvert bands at about half past four. Revellers with painted faces and dressed in rags, some with tins which they banged with spoons, others blowing whistles or flutes, and some wielding brooms with which they made a pretence of sweeping front yards. They then demanded a penny for their services. Millie had heard of them from her mother but was experiencing the event for the first time. These bands went from house to house along the street and were given copper coins which they rattled in their tins.

In Talparo at that time, Carnival was comparatively a low-key affair. On Monday and Tuesday there might be: A Tamboo-Bamboo band in the junction beating their bamboo instruments while a small band of "*Wild Indians*" danced. (The government had banned drums the previous century.) A "*Midnight Robber*" dressed in black, wearing a large straw hat festooned with bones, brandishing a pistol and a dagger and reciting a litany of blood-curdling exploits to make the faint-hearted tremble, and a few Moko-Jumbies doing their balancing act. There was also a stick fighting competition which invariably turned out bloody. Many parents, the Brownes included, tried to keep their children away from Carnival.

That Monday, they were to witness a spectacular display of colour as bands portraying butterflies, exotic birds and even dragons paraded the streets to the accompaniment of musical orchestras with the full complement of brass and woodwind instruments. There was also a variety of individual portrayals of famous people such as Churchill, Hitler and Mussolini and a comic character called *Pierrot Grenade*. On the Tuesday, there was the judging of the bands, at which the Mayor presided.

Chapter 33
The Santa Rosa Fete

At the Santa Rosa festival that same year, Meg and Millie were invited to manage a flower stall. Millie created a variety of artificial orchids in both crepe paper and wool-and-wire. Her mother made an assortment of woven baskets and trays, some of which were reported by patrons to be similar to those made by the indigenous Caribs who lived in Arima. Meg said that her great grandmother in Martinique had passed the art down through the generations. Julia then added that her mother had tried to teach her the art of basketry but without much success. The flower stall also served to promote some flowered frock designs created by Olivia who came along to help.

The Farfans brought their friends to the stall and soon most of the goods on display were sold and orders were being taken for many items, especially Olivia's dresses. The friends who had attended Julia's birthday party also showed up. Jean Cezair introduced Millie to Albert Akong, a friend who had cycled from Sangre Grande. It was most embarrassing for Millie who had not told her mother about Jean. In her mother's presence, he said to Millie: "I would like you to meet Al, who'll be best man at our wedding."

Millie, blushing, countered by saying, "As you are not on your knees, I can't accept that as a serious proposal." The laughter that erupted at this riposte saved the situation for the time being. These two hung around to help after the others had gone. Albert was especially helpful, finding a broom and sweeping up before they left. As Julia did not have any personal responsibility for a harvest stall, she was free to wander with friends from stall to stall and learned more about Arima and its traditions. She indeed saw a stall full of indigenous Carib artefacts which had baskets similar in design to her aunt's. Millie joined her and they went together to see the children dance and sing around the May

Pole. The gaily dressed children sang as they weaved the May Pole ribbons around the pole: *I see, I know. La pita que tengo yo.*

They blew the tune on little flutes as well while two grown-ups played violins. When they had weaved themselves into a tight circle around the pole cymbals were clashed and they began un-weaving, dancing in and out until the ribbons were straight.

Another feature of the Santa Rosa festival was the Morris Dancers. These were men dressed in brown pants and wearing yellow shirts. There were two lines of them facing each other. They carried short staves which they clashed against their opponents in a rhythmic fashion from time to time. Millie thought these features very entertaining and wondered about introducing them to Talparo.

Before Meg and Millie caught the coach back to Talparo that evening, she asked Millie about the young man who so brashly announced the intended wedding. Millie had anticipated the question and was prepared to brush it off. "He just pretends to be Romeo to every girl he meets. He's not serious. I danced with him once at Julia's birthday party that I told you about and he was in the group of us who went to the cinema."

"I see," said her mother, whilst entertaining her own ideas about the young man. Nothing more was said and the matter dropped for the time being.

The takings of the day were all given to the church. The future proceeds, however, were considered private property. Meg and her daughters nevertheless decided to donate a percentage of the earnings from those orders to the church. This was to result in an avalanche effect, as Olivia's exposure to the Catholic congregation grew and she was forced to seek extra help. Julia being on the spot was an obvious choice, and she readily accepted the chance to earn more money. Millie also, was to find her skills being put to use, making corsages for bridesmaid dresses.

Chapter 34
Mr. Farfan's Farewell

At the Talparo school, changes were taking place. Mr Farfan was being replaced as head teacher by a Mr Belix. Mr Farfan had announced his retirement himself at morning assembly, regretting that he would be leaving at the end of that month. The school was stunned by the announcement and children asked their teachers how they could make him stay. It had to be explained to them that promotion to a more responsible job meant more pay and a higher retirement pension when one is too old to work. The children decided to collect money to buy him a farewell present. They asked Mr Lee to be in charge of this and planned to give it to him on the last Friday of the month. The teachers thought it fitting that a farewell party be held in his honour and planned it in secret.

Millie knew of his love for poetry and taught her class to recite Oliver Goldsmith's tribute to a headmaster from the poem *The Deserted Village,* in his honour. She chose the six best readers, giving them four lines each. The recitation took place before the presentation of a gold watch Mr Lee had purchased with help from the teachers. A little girl began:

Beside yon straggling fence that skirts the way,
With blossomed furze unprofitably gay.
There, in his noisy mansion, skilled to rule,
The village master taught his little school

A boy followed this with:

A man severe he was, and stern to view,
I knew him well, and every truant knew;
Well had the boding tremblers learned to trace
The day's disasters in his morning face.

Another girl continued:

Full well they laughed, with counterfeited glee
At all his jokes, for many a joke had he
Full well the busy whisper circling round
Conveyed the dismal tidings when he frowned;

A boy followed:

Yet he was kind, and if severe in aught,
The love he bore to learning was in fault;
The village all declared how much he knew;
T'was certain he could write, and cypher too;

A girl continued:

Lands he could measure, terms and tides presage,
And even, the story ran, that he could gauge.
In arguing too, the parson owned his skill,
For even tho' vanquished, he could argue still;

A boy finished:

While words of learned length and thundering sound,
Amazed the gazing rustics ranged around;
And still they gazed, and still the wonder grew,
That one small head, could carry all he knew.

The six reciters took a bow and received thunderous applause as Mr Farfan was noticed to wipe a tear from his eye.

His farewell speech cantered on the inevitability of change. The language used by Goldsmith in that poem was different from the language we use today and was also quite different from Chaucer's English. He prophesized that language in Trinidad in a hundred years' time would also be different. He had already noticed that what he called "the common vernacular" had crept into the language of politicians. The only thing constant in this world, paradoxically, is change. It was inevitable that his work had to change and the school also would undergo changes. He praised the teachers and told the children to thank their parents for their support and told them all to continue to put their best effort in all that they did.

The following month saw changes not all judged for the better. The "*new broom*" swept out some of the corn along with the husk. Mr Belix considered the Royal Readers too alien in its subject matter for West Indian children and preferred the West Indian Readers newly introduced by Cutteridge. While Mr Farfan hardly ever resorted to the use of corporal punishment, Mr Belix used the whip as the symbol of his authority. This did not go down well with the other teachers who held Mr Farfan in the highest regard. Mr Farfan, however, had accepted a promotion to the inspectorate and had moved on.

Millie had passed all the pupil-teacher exams over the last five years and took the first part of the Preliminary Teachers' Exam which she passed with flying colours. The two other pupil teachers from her school also passed the exam and it was assumed that at least two of them would be admitted to Teachers' Training College that year. The head-teacher's recommendation would determine who was selected. Mr Belix announced that due to the large number who had passed and the limited space at the college, only one from his school would go on to Teachers' Training College that year. He recommended Linda Smith.

Millie was crestfallen. Philosophically, she considered that Linda's needs were greater than her own and congratulated her friend on her success. Meg tried to console Millie by telling her that Mr Belix didn't want to lose his most efficient pupil teacher and that he was just settling in to the job. Millie, however, was becoming disenchanted with the changed atmosphere at the school. It was no longer the happy place it once was. Her only consolation was that her mentor, Mr Lee, was still there.

Mr Lee, for his part, was also disappointed, for (unknown to the rest of the staff) he had applied for the headship and failed. This dampened his enthusiasm for his work and it was beginning to show. He nevertheless considered it his duty to lift the morale of both teaching staff and pupils and made an effort to do so to the best of his ability.

Chapter 35
Disillusionment Creeps in as
Well as Disappointment

During her stays with her sister and cousin in Arima, they had attended parties at which she had met pupil teachers from Arima schools. Millie decided to find out more about conditions at schools in Arima and her chances of a transfer to Arima. Florence Farfan would not be of much help as she was a convent girl. But Jean Cezair's sister, Amanda, had said that she was a pupil teacher and Millie considered her a first port of call.

On her next visit to Arima to deliver six corsages she had made, this time experimenting with velvet cloth, she got Olivia to accompany her to see Amanda. By co-incidence, Amanda was one of the bridesmaids at a forthcoming wedding that Olivia was sewing for and it was under the pretext of finding out the suitability of the corsage that they called on Amanda. Amanda was delighted at the beauty of her corsage which was made of coloured velvet and copper wire but looked like a spray of natural orchids. She was told that it was never to get wet. That would not only spoil the crispness of the petals but would cause the dyes to run and ruin her dress. She thanked them for the information and invited them in.

Her brother Jean was there, involved in a game of chess with his friend Albert. They got up from their seats to welcome the girls but were politely told by Amanda to get on with their game as the visitors had come to discuss feminine business. The elder Cezairs were out for the evening and Amanda led them into the dining room which they had to themselves.

After discussing the colour scheme of the wedding and the foibles of fashion which required them to wear long gloves in a hot climate, Millie got around to asking Amanda about her school. Amanda taught at Arima Girls' R.C. and all the teachers were female. This was an alien arrangement to Millie who was used to having male colleagues and mixed classes of pupils. Amanda thought that it allowed the girls to become more assertive. It gave them confidence in their ability to compete with others on equal terms. Millie then asked about the attitude of the staff toward each other. Amanda claimed that it was generally good and helpful, adding with a laugh that it depended on the time of the month. Their headmistress, however, being an older woman, was generally equable, not being bothered by menstrual cycles. Millie then confessed that she was thinking of a change of schools and wondered about the possibility of moving to Arima. Amanda considered that this was only possible after becoming a fully qualified teacher. Pupil teachers were recruited from their own schools and as far as she knew, were not allowed to transfer. This put a damper on Millie's aspirations.

"Checkmate!" There was a shout from the other room. The girls looked in to see a crestfallen Jean and a jubilant Albert facing each other.

"This crafty Chink has beaten me again!" Jean moaned.

"Don't be so insulting to a guest in this house!" chided Amanda.

"He has called me worse than that. I don't mind. We're friends," Albert claimed.

"I should mind my manners," Jean apologized, "especially in the presence of beautiful young ladies. Do either of you play chess?"

"We play draughts," Olivia answered, "but I'm sure I can learn chess."

"I'll be happy to teach you," Jean offered.

"Some other time," Millie interposed. "We have some more errands to run and we are behind schedule. I'm afraid we must take our leave now." The sisters then departed with the trio escorting them to the door.

As they walked out of earshot, Ollie asked Millie: "Why did you cut him off so?"

"He has been making advances," Millie replied, "and I don't really fancy him."

"I think he's charming," Ollie ventured, "I wouldn't mind him teaching me to play chess."

"That's not all he'd be doing. I recognize his type. He'll lay on the charm like honey on toast waiting to catch an unwary fly," Millie advised. "You'd be better off learning from his friend Albert."

"I don't really have the time, anyway. It was just an idle thought," Ollie concluded.

They returned to Ollie's home just as it was getting dark and Ollie lit the gas lamp she had purchased for doing her work. It had to be pumped up and a fine gauze wick lit with a match. This gave out much more light than the pitch-oil lamp they were accustomed to in Talparo, but while the wick of the pitch-oil lamp was made of a sturdy canvas-like material, the wick of the gas lamp was very delicate and broke up if touched, as Ollie had learned to her cost. Still, the extra light it gave out was essential to her work.

Julia had gone to her parent's home for the week end and Millie would share the double bed so she didn't have to open the canvas cot she usually slept on when in Arima. After Ollie had finished her sewing, the girls chatted for hours in the dark; Millie, about the new head teacher in Talparo and Ollie, about the matronly dowagers who wanted dresses more suitable for younger, slimmer women, before they both drifted off to sleep.

Chapter 36
An Engagement Party Leads
to a Chinese Connection

The wedding in Arima for which Olivia had sewn the bridesmaids' dresses was between two of Arima's most notable families, a De Gannes spinster was marrying a De Verteuil bachelor. (*Spinster* and *Bachelor* were written on the banns which had to be published in the church weeks before the wedding.) Olivia was not one of the invited guests but was one of the throng who went to the Santa Rosa church to witness the ceremony. She persuaded Millie to accompany her for Millie's work was also on display. It was a splendid occasion and many people were admiring the bridesmaids' dresses. Amanda spotted Millie and Ollie in the crowd and pointed Ollie out as the dressmaker.

Olivia's already sizable clientele was to be made even larger and the popularity of both sisters increased. They were invited to an engagement party the following month at the home of the mayor of Arima, Timothy Aqui. One of the Aqui daughters was getting engaged to a Marchack from Sangre Grande.

Olivia sewed special dresses for herself and Millie for the occasion as they sensed that they were "moving up" in society and had to look the part. That they were invited mainly for the services they could render didn't even cross their minds, or if it did, they considered it worth their while. The Marchack's guests included Albert Akong, whom they already knew. It was quite natural that as the quartet of musicians began to play and guests took to the floor, Millie accepted Albert's invitation to dance.

Olivia, for the most part, was taken up with discussing suitable material and styles with the Aqui ladies, which she did not mind in the least. Their slim Chinese figures would show off the latest slit-skirt fashions she was itching to demonstrate. She made appointments with them to view prospective designs and take their measurements.

Millie and Albert were whirling around the dance floor to the music of a *Castellan* waltz, the one type of dance Mama and Papa had taught her, and she was enjoying it. Albert was only an inch or two taller than Millie (in her heels), so they were a handsome, well-suited couple. When she had danced the foxtrot with Jean, who was six foot two, Millie felt like a little child dancing with her father. "You dance very well," Albert complimented, "You've danced this waltz before with Jean, I suppose."

"No;" she replied, "we danced the foxtrot once, that's all."

"I got the impression you've been going out together for a long time," Albert re-joined. "Oh no. I've only met Jean on three occasions. If you must know. Not counting the time you were playing chess."

"Ah, I see," Albert summed up. "Then he can't object if I ask you to go to the races with me next Saturday."

"Jean can't but Papa might object." Millie laughed.

"Then I'll ask your Papa," Albert persisted.

"You'll have to go to Talparo for that," Millie replied, "and then you'll have to face a barrage of questions such as, "What are your intentions concerning my daughter, young man?" and "What is your financial position?" Are you ready for that?" Millie asked, laughing.

"You'll see," he replied with a smile as the music ended and he returned her to her seat.

Albert was very attentive and fetched the group of girls sitting together whatever refreshments they wanted. Olivia winked at Millie, "I see you've made a conquest."

"I don't think so. He probably flirts with all the girls the same way. He'll ask you to dance next, no doubt. Then you'll see what I mean."

Olivia did dance with Albert next and they seemed to be talking quite a lot. When Ollie was returned to her seat and Albert departed to fetch drinks, Millie said to her: "So now you see what I meant. You two were chatting away like old friends."

"It may have looked like that," Ollie replied, "but he was asking about you. He thought you were a florist and I told him you were a school teacher. Then he wanted to know where in Talparo you lived. He's more interested in you than you thought."

When the party was over Albert volunteered to walk the sisters home and they got him to talk about himself. He had his own barber shop in Cunapo, which he considered to be the shopping district of Sangre Grande and lived with his widowed mother in a house he had built himself with a little help from one of his three brothers. One of his four sisters was married to the owner of the Apollo cinema, the first cinema to be opened in Cunapo. He had been taught to cut hair by one of the Cezairs who worked in Cunapo. That explained his friendship with the Cezairs at whose home he was going to sleep that night. They bade him goodnight as they reached their door step and he departed into the dark. Olivia couldn't resist saying, "I told you so. He's smitten on you."

Millie merely replied: "Let's wait and see; only time will tell." Julia, who had had a hard day and didn't go to the party, was already asleep as they quietly prepared for bed.

Chapter 37

A Surprise Visit

No one was more surprised than Millie when at four o'clock the following Friday, Albert turned up at her doorstep in Talparo. He leaned his bicycle against a post and walked towards them smiling. "Good evening. I've come to see Mr Browne. Is he in?"

"No," a flustered Millie replied.

Her mother stated, "I'm Mrs Browne; what is it about?"

"Well, Millie here told me that if I wanted to take her out I'd have to ask his permission," Albert responded.

"No, it wasn't quite like that," Millie retorted, "and I don't remember agreeing to go out with you."

"I remember you now;" her mother recollected, "you were the young man from the Santa Rosa fete. Please come in and have a drink; you must be tired from all that cycling."

A bemused Maria was sent to the kitchen to fetch drinks as Albert entered their home for the first time, perspiring profusely. He sat on a bench in the front porch and drank a glass of coconut water. "Thank you. This is my favourite drink," he contended, "nothing revives a body more." Albert explained that he had ridden from Cunapo, through Cumuto and San Raphael and that it had taken him just over an hour. He would have to leave by five o'clock to get home before dark.

Maria ventured: "Papa doesn't often get home before six."

Albert replied: "Then perhaps Mother can plead my cause, I'd be grateful if you would." Millie's emotions were confused. She felt honoured that he had taken the trouble to ride all that way for her, yet annoyed that he had taken it for granted that once her parents approved, she would go out with him. Do most men behave like that? She mused. Albert had to return to Sangre Grande that day, his quest unresolved. Millie was left to explain to her mother exactly what had taken place between herself and Albert.

Later that evening James returned from work and was told of the visit by the young man. "You say he rode all the way from Sangre Grande on our rough roads?" He enquired incredulously.

"Yes Papa, but he had to leave early because he didn't have lights on his bike," Maria explained.

"Well, he's showing determination if not much common sense," Papa declared.

"He at least had the sense to leave early," Meg defended.

"I'll grant him that, but, what I'll say is—if he's serious enough to come to ask my permission to see my daughter then I'll leave it to the daughter to decide. Millie has the respect of every one in Talparo and I don't think she'll disrespect herself in Arima. Will you, girl?" He asked, turning to Millie.

"No Papa, I won't," she answered meekly.

"I'd like to know a bit more about him;" Papa pursued, "like, what he does for a living and what is his family like. Does he have his own house or is he renting?" Millie took a deep breath then answered: "Albert told us he had his own barbershop and that he and his brother built a house for his widowed mother in Sangre Grande. His brother-in-law is the owner of the Apollo cinema in Cunapo. He is also a good friend of the Cezairs in Arima and he was invited to the mayor's house for an engagement party where I met him."

"Is that the only time you met him?" Her step-father asked.

At this point, her mother cut in and said, "We met him at the Santa Rosa festival and he seemed a decent, helpful young man; he even swept up for us without being asked."

"So, he was chasing after Millie from then," James concluded.

"No Papa, at that time he thought I was Jean Cezair's girlfriend."

"What would have given him that idea? And who is this Jean Cezair anyway?"

Her mother came to her defense then. "The Cezairs are friends of the Farfans, and Jean Cezair is a friend of Albert. Jean pretended to be Millie's fiancé at the festival. He is just a joker. I was there with Millie at the time."

Millie sighed with relief at her mother's intervention and Papa went off muttering: "It makes me wonder what Olivia is getting up to in our absence."

"Thanks Mama," Millie whispered. "It would have been difficult for me to explain that I was fending off Jean's flirtations at the time."

"So, you'll be happy to go out with Albert? He seems much older than you," her mother enquired.

"I don't really know, Mama, I think I might accept his first date as he went to all the trouble to come to Talparo and then we'll see what happens from there."

"Take Ollie with you," Meg advised.

"I intend to," Millie answered.

"Where are you going?" Pedro asked, coming through the door.

"We are not going anywhere," answered Millie.

"Mama or Maria will explain it to you. I'm tired and going to bed." Pedro had been out hunting squirrels and had a bag with him containing squirrel tails. He would be paid a shilling for each tail as the government wished to help cocoa farmers eradicate these pests which threatened the agricultural industry.

"What have you done with the dead squirrels?" Maria asked.

"I gave them to Alphonso, who would keep the skins and cook the meat for his dogs," Pedro replied. "Now will you tell me Millie's mystery?" Maria then narrated the events of the day.

Chapter 38
An Invitation to the Cinema

It was two weeks later that Millie had the chance to spend a weekend in Arima. When she started to tell Ollie about Albert's visit, Ollie said she knew because Albert had visited her one evening to ask when her sister was coming to Arima again. She nevertheless wanted to hear Millie's side of the story.

Millie explained about their father's reservations and her mother's support, the latter a surprise to Ollie. Ollie had expected their mother to be more distrustful of men and therefore protective of her daughter and her father less strict with a step-daughter. Millie said that Mama was impressed by Albert when he voluntarily swept out the stall at the Santa Rosa festival, something the men in their experience wouldn't do. "Can you imagine Pedro doing that?" Millie asked her sister.

Ollie replied: "Not Pedro, but I suppose if Albert runs a barbershop, he must be in the habit of sweeping up regularly. I could do with him here, all the bits of thread and snippets of cloth that keep piling up!"

"Yes," laughed Millie. "I sometimes wonder if you expect a Rumpelstiltskin-like dwarf to come in the night and weave a carpet for you out of the debris on the floor. When did you tell Albert I'll be here?"

"I guessed it might be this weekend but I told him I wasn't sure," Ollie replied.

Just then, there was a knock at the door and a male voice calling out "Good evening."

On opening it, Ollie said: "Speak of the devil."

"Who are you calling the devil?" Albert asked, smiling as he caught sight of Millie. "Can I come in? It'll only be for a moment."

"Enter my humble abode, but sit down at your peril. I seem to have pins and needles on every surface here," Ollie apologized Millie felt her heart quicken at the sound of his voice and sought to control her emotions and appear calm.

Wiping his feet on the mat, Albert entered and stretching out a hand to Millie said: "Good evening, Millie, I've come to apologize for any trouble my visit to Talparo may have caused you."

"Apology accepted if you include the act of taking it for granted that I'd be willing to go out with you. If you remember what you asked, it was "whether Jean would object" **if** you asked me out."

"My! My!" Albert replied, "You'll make a good chess player. Such attention to detail! Such irrefutable logic! My heart in that instance over-rode my brain. I apologize for the lapse. Will you please go out with me?"

Millie paused for a moment then replied: "I might, if you agree not to patronise me as well as take me for granted."

"Sorry I didn't mean to sound patronising, it just took me by surprise that you were so **absolutely** right. It was like I was caught in a checkmate in two position! I surrender," Albert answered, sounding quite flustered.

"If you two are going to have an argument, I'd better step outside for a minute," Olivia interposed.

"No need for that," Millie responded, "I believe Albert has seen the error of his ways." They all laughed at that, breaking the tension.

"There's a great film showing at the newly opened Princess cinema near the racecourse. Will you two ladies come with me to see it tomorrow night?" Albert asked.

"What's it called?" Millie enquired.

"*Innocents of Paris*," Albert replied, "with Maurice Chevalier and Silvia Beecher; I've heard mention of them as two upcoming stars."

"Sounds innocent enough," quipped Millie. "What do you say, Ollie?"

"I'd be happy to," Olivia replied.

"That's settled then; I'll meet you here at six," said Albert as he took his leave of them.

The cinema still smelled of paint, they noticed, as they took their seats in the area called *House*. Seating was provided in three sections, the *Pits*, nearest the screen, *House*, the middle section, and *Balcony*, the highest, raised section, at the back. After the National Anthem, they were treated to Pathe News, which dealt with problems in Germany with the Nazis. This was followed by news of the Japanese army taking over Shanghai and President Hoover of the United

States sending the 31st Infantry Regiment to join British, Italian and French reinforcements to protect the large foreign population of Shanghai. The news ended with sports, as India competed in its first ever test match at Lords. India was beaten, thanks to the bowling of two Bills, Bill Voce and Bill Bowes. The Olympic Games were mentioned as a forthcoming event to be held in Los Angeles later that year.

Paramount Pictures took over from Pathe and the list of names of actors, producers, camera men etc. filled the screen to accompanying music. When the story began, however, our audience was surprised to hear for the first time, the actors' voices as they spoke. There was a slight lack of synchronization at times as "dubbing" was in its infancy, but it detracted little from the thrill of hearing the actors speak and sing.

Maurice Chevalier in the persona of Maurice Marny sang *Louise* to an enthralled audience both on and off the screen. Millie decided that if the film was ever shown again, she would take her mother to see it. She herself was captivated by the young French actor and would enjoy a repetition. This was to be the start of a love affair in two senses.

"Wasn't that wonderful?" Olivia was ecstatic about it.

"Wonderful!" Millie echoed.

Albert began singing: *"Every little breeze, seems to whisper Millie—"*

"That doesn't rhyme, and you don't sound French," Millie interrupted, laughing.

"I may not be French, but I'm trying to be chivalrous." Albert punned. "I pictured myself singing that song to you while Maurice was singing."

"Then I'll accept that as a compliment," Millie replied, "but not while we're out here on the street."

"Sorry to embarrass you, but my heart takes charge of my brain when I'm near you."

"Then we better stay apart," Millie teased.

"Only until the end of the month; that Charlie Chaplin film, "The Great Dictator," is on then and I'd like you to see it with me," Albert requested.

"We'll certainly consider it," said Millie, as they reached their home, "and thank you very much for a wonderful evening out."

As the sisters prepared for bed that night, Millie was noticeably quiet while Olivia enthused about the film. "Do you think he's really in love with me?" Millie finally asked her sister. "He did ask both of us out."

"That was just for decorum," replied Ollie. "He must be aware that young ladies do not go out with men without a chaperone. Didn't he say he has sisters?"

"Yes, I suppose you're right," Millie conceded. "But Julia might be here with us at the end of the month instead of going to her parents. We can't expect him to pay for her as well."

"Julia can offer to pay for herself," Ollie reasoned, "then we'll see what kind of man he is." Millie's thoughts went back to Maurice Chevalier's voice. *I wonder if my father spoke English with a French accent like that? It's so romantic. Mama would have been charmed by him. Perhaps he was already married. Men are such deceivers*, she thought as she drifted off to sleep.

At the end of the month, Julia did offer to pay for herself but Albert wouldn't hear of it and escorted all three ladies to the cinema where they laughed so much that their hankies were thoroughly soaked with their tears.

Part 3
Millie's Adult Years

Chapter 39
Mama Loves Maurice

Millie's earnings from making corsages and button-hole florets, along with her teaching stipend, enabled her to take her mother to the cinema. It was a first-time experience for Meg who was looking forward to it ever since she had heard Millie describe her own experience. Millie thought her mother deserved a treat for having worked tirelessly for her family for all those years without once even having her birthday celebrated. The film being shown that weekend was *The Love Parade,* starring Maurice Chevalier and Jeanette MacDonald. Olivia thought it was a great idea, and decided to share the cost for the whole family to attend. Papa, however, had to be excused at the last minute as one of their donkeys was about to give birth.

It was a musical comedy which, without the brash slapstick funniness of Charlie Chaplin films, yet possessed a subtlety of humour which pasted a smile of happiness on the faces of the audience throughout the film. The songs were integral to the story, knitting all the threads together seamlessly. They gave the Browne family months of fuel for their arguments of which was best song, *Dream Lover, My Love Parade*, or *March of the Grenadiers.*

To say that Meg was enthralled would be an understatement. Maurice Chevalier became the archetype to which all other actors were later compared. Jeanette MacDonald, however, was only criticized for her smoking, something Meg thought no women should do. Millie was pleased with her mother's reaction to the film and promised to take her again whenever the opportunity arose. She wondered whether her mother's reaction to the voice of Maurice Chevalier was a response to the voice of the man who was her natural father. English spoken with a French accent was so romantic. Surely other people must know who that man was. Perhaps her other aunts might know. She would have to find out where they lived and pay them a visit.

Chapter 40
A Sisterly Reunion

In order to find out where her other aunts lived, Millie decided to visit her aunt Marie in Mahaica one day. She went under the pretext of seeking a remedy for pimples which were appearing on her face no matter how clean she kept her skin. Aunt Marie was regarded as "the medicine woman" by many villagers due to her knowledge of medicinal uses of many different herbs.

Millie was greeted by her aunt with great pleasure. She was complimented on how well both she and Olivia were doing, as Julia kept her informed of their progress. Millie thanked her and told her of her problem with pimples. Aunt Marie examined the skin on Millie's face and told her that the leaves of the Dartier, or Christmas Candles plant, might help. If she crushed the leaves and rub the juice into her face at night that could improve her skin. She also thought that Millie's skin tended to be dry and could benefit by the application of juices from Herbe a Femme, or Petit Pain Doux.

Millie thanked her and asked how she came to know these remedies. Marie answered that her grandmother was a renowned herbalist in Martinique and taught those who wanted to know about plants. Millie's mother was a little too young at the time. Millie then enquired about the sisters who lived in Port of Spain and was told that her Aunt Camille was also a herbalist. She then confessed that she was very interested in meeting her estranged aunts and was given Aunt Camille's address in St. Clair. Thanking her aunt for her help, Millie bade her goodbye.

So it was that as the Easter vacation started, Millie persuaded her mother to accompany her on a trip to visit her Aunt Camille. From Talparo, they travelled by bus and train to Port of Spain, then took a tramcar to St. Clair. They got off on St. Clair Avenue and walked up Alexandria Street to the number Millie was given. A blonde blue-eyed little girl of about seven or eight answered their call and replied that Camille Le Blanc lived in the smaller house at the back.

Camille was surprised to see them but recognized her sister Meg at first glance. The two sisters hugged each other and both cried, their tears streaming down their faces. "It's been so long!" Aunt Camille sobbed. "I wanted to come and see you when I went to Papa's funeral, but Mr Du Bois had to return immediately and he was already so kind as to take me himself to the funeral I couldn't impose on him further."

Meg said: "Never mind, we are together again, after twenty-one years."

Millie was introduced to her aunt who hugged and smothered her with kisses, making her face wet as well. Aunt Camille was glad that they had come that week for the Du Bois family were moving to Coblenz Avenue in St. Ann's the following week and they might not have met. She was their head house-keeper and they wanted her to continue in their service wherever they went. Mr Du Bois' work with the embassy had taken him to Grenada a few years ago and she went back to Grenada with them. There, she was reunited with her brother Gabriel and met his family.

Millie was amazed that anyone could talk so much, as her aunt carried on non-stop for over fifteen minutes, even as she poured them cold drinks and sliced sweet-bread for them. She would never get the chance to ask about her father. It was a mistake to have brought her mother with her, and yet, how could she not when her mother hadn't seen her sister for so long? All because of her; no, not because of me. She corrected herself. Because of Papa Leon's false pride, inflexibility and self-righteousness. For a moment she felt, she hated her grandfather, then she pitied him instead. He didn't even know what he was missing.

Listening to their conversation, Millie discovered that she had three more aunts that she didn't know about and another uncle who lived in Trinidad. There were Aunt Pauline and Aunt Florence who lived in St. Ann's, Aunt Cecile, in Grenada, and Uncle Jerome who had come to Trinidad. Even her mother was unaware that Jerome had come to Trinidad and lived in Maracas. Getting in the odd word proved difficult, but Millie managed to ask for the addresses of her relatives and Aunt Camille's intended address.

Too soon it was time for their return journey to Talparo. They had a tearful farewell and made their way back to catch a tramcar to take them to the train station in Port of Spain. Millie felt glad that they had come but sad that her mission failed.

Chapter 41
Albert Bares All

Millie was in the habit of visiting her sister in Arima once a month and invariably saw Albert on those occasions. After six months of this slow courtship, Albert declared that he must see her more often and asked if she would mind him visiting at weekends in Talparo. Millie was impressed that he asked, instead of taking it for granted, and agreed. She also, was beginning to look forward to meeting him. Her feelings were somewhat ambivalent as she had heard rumours about him being a ladies' man. Amanda had hinted that Albert was involved with someone in Sangre Grande. His behaviour to her so far was above board. He would take her hand as they crossed the street and on the last two occasions that he escorted them home had kissed her on the cheek. She decided to ask him.

On the next occasion that Albert turned up at her home in Talparo (after his initial visit), he had acquired a carbide lamp which he affixed to the handlebar of his bicycle. This was made by his youngest brother, Verne, who was also a cyclist. Pedro was there that day and showed Albert his own carbide hunting torch. Millie asked them to put the smelly torches away as she brought some drinks and cake to their front veranda. Maria then called Pedro aside, whispering to him that he should give the couple some privacy. Even their parents, after greeting Albert, had retreated indoors.

Alone at last, Albert carefully said: "I've come to ask you if I may ask your father for your hand in marriage."

"What an odd way of putting it!" Millie teased. "You haven't asked me if I would marry you."

"That's what I'm doing!" Albert insisted. "Will you?"

"I'll have to think about it," Millie replied. "You may already have a wife in Sangre Grande for all I know."

"I haven't," Albert protested. "I confess I was going out with someone once but she was having an affair with another man at the same time and I gave her up. I was going to tell you all about it but we haven't had the chance until now."

Millie's heart was beating rapidly. Did she want to hear about Albert's love affairs? Was he going to tell the whole truth? Yes, she told herself. If I'm going to get any more involved with him or cut off our relationship, I need to know more. "All right, you have the chance now. Tell me everything," Millie offered.

"Shall I start at the beginning then?" Albert asked.

"Please do," Millie answered. "It was about ten years ago, at one of my sisters'. We were celebrating my twenty-first birthday. I'd been drinking. We all were, about twenty of us, when one of the girls decided, "Let's give Al a kiss on his birthday," and they did. One of the older ones (she must have been about twenty-eight) went further. She gave me a lingering kiss, pressed her body against me and whispered, "I have a birthday present for you in the work shed." I was aroused. Somehow, we ended up in the shed at the back of the house alone that night and you can guess what happened."

"Yes," answered Millie, "but I'd like to know what happened after that."

"To be honest, I thought I was in love with her. She was older and already had one child and no husband. She said the father of the child was a member of the West Indian Regiment who had gone to war and not returned. She worked in a shop in Cunapo and her mother looked after the little boy. I tried my best to help out and even started thinking of marrying her. Then one night I—I found them together and—broke it off." Albert paused, looking distressed. He got up and walked to the banister railing.

Millie felt a mixture of emotions overwhelm her, sadness, betrayal, disillusionment, and finally, sympathy. How much was Albert to blame? Not a lot. She decided. Even the strongest of men have their Achilles heel. "Here, finish your drink," she said, handing him his glass. "There's more to tell, isn't there?" She asked.

After taking a long draught, Albert resumed his seat and continued: "Two months later, she came to me and said she was having my baby! I refused to believe it! I wanted nothing more to do with her!" He paused again and held his head in his hands. "It was after the baby was born, a girl, a little paler in complexion than her brown-skin mother, and with Chinese eyes, that I could see it was mine."

"So, what did you do?" enquired Millie. "I told her I would help support it but I wanted nothing more to do with her."

"And do you still? Support it, I mean," Millie asked.

"Yes, as a matter of fact, my mother looks after her during the day while Agatha is working and she collects her after work." It was the first time that Albert had mentioned the name of the lady in question and Millie wondered about it.

"And what is the baby's name?" She asked.

"Amoy," Albert answered. "We named her after a dear old Chinese lady I knew."

"She must be about ten years old now, the baby I mean," enquired Millie.

"Yes," admitted Albert. "In a few more years, she'll be off my hands."

"But she'll still be your daughter," Millie persisted.

"Of course," he replied: "I'll always keep an eye on her as she grows up. I don't want her to grow up like her mother." Millie found herself admiring his sentiment and then thought: *What on earth am I letting myself in for? I can back out now. Or can I? No*, she answered herself. "He is trying to do the right thing, and I can help him. I must not be self-righteous and have false pride."

"All right, now that you've made a clean breast of things, you can speak to my father. But I hope you know that only puts you on probation," she laughed. "You'll have to prove yourself in the coming months."

"Oh, thank you," he replied, going down on one knee and kissing her hand.

Millie went inside to speak to her father and came out with him after a short while. "It is better to talk out here while Mama is keeping the others busy in the kitchen," James declared.

"Thank you," Albert answered. "I merely want to ask your permission to marry your daughter."

"Merely sounds as though it's a little thing!" James replied. "It is the biggest, most serious thing a man can do with his life, and with the life of the woman."

"I do realize that. The word "merely" slipped out. I apologize," Albert said.

"Then come on in and have dinner with us. It's not every day we celebrate an engagement." James shook his hand and led him into the house.

Chapter 42
The Engagement Ring

The following Friday, Millie travelled to Arima to spend the week-end with her cousin Julia. It was Olivia's turn to spend a week-end in Talparo. Julia greeted her cousin warmly and looking at her fingers enquired: "Girl, where's the ring?"

"What ring?" Millie replied, feigning innocence. "So, you think I don't know. Belinda came in to Bata shoe shop, so say, to try on a pair of shoes, only it was really to tell me that Albert ask Uncle James for your hand. She didn't even buy a tin of Nugget shoe polish."

Millie wondered how Belinda knew, then remembered that Maria and Belinda were now as thick as two thieves. Maria would have told her. So now the whole village must be in the know. "All right," Millie conceded. "If you must know, Albert did ask, and he's meeting me here tomorrow morning to go to Khan's to choose a ring."

"Congratulations, girl!" Julia exclaimed. "Only I thought it would have been Jean Cezair you'd be marrying."

"You're free to have Jean, I never really fancied him," quipped Millie. The two young women carried on with their bantering as they carried out their ablutions and even after going to bed. Millie debated whether to tell her cousin about Albert's disclosure and decided to let her know the truth instead of malicious rumours.

They were up and dressed and having a second cup of coffee when Albert came to the door the next morning. "Good morning, ladies," he greeted.

"Good morning to you too," they chorused. He declined the offer of coffee or anything else and they left the house together.

They bade Julia goodbye at the door of the shoe shop and proceeded to the jeweller's shop down the street. There they paused for a moment outside the window looking at the display of sparkling gems before entering.

"Have you a particular stone in mind, Millie?" Albert enquired.

"I think I'd like a single diamond, a solitaire," Millie answered.

Mr Khan, the proprietor, beamed at them. "Can I show you a tray from which you can choose?" He asked.

"Please do," Millie replied. He took out a tray of rings from below the counter and placed it before her. Millie held up a medium sized solitaire and showed it to Albert. "How about this one?" She asked.

"Try it on," Albert replied. It was too large.

Mr Khan said: "Size doesn't matter; I can alter it. Let me measure your ring finger."

"Try some of the others," Albert urged, "some of these look smaller." Millie tried two others but said that she preferred the first. "Then that's the one you shall have," Albert declared. Mr Khan said it would be ready in a week's time and asked for a deposit of thirty dollars which Albert promptly paid.

As they left the shop Albert produced a jade ring which he gave Millie. "My mother wants you to have this. She said my father gave it to her. It's supposed to bring luck."

"Thank you," said Millie, slipping it on to the middle finger of her right hand. "Tell your mother thanks for me. Do you know Albert, that this is the first time that you have mentioned your father to me? You led me to assume that he was dead, but that's all."

"Yes, he died when I was ten years old," Albert replied. "I do not remember much about him; he was just a middle-aged Chinaman who smoked a pipe. We had a cocoa estate near Sangre Chiquito in those days, and a little shop too. Ma said he lost it all, gambling." Albert's face seemed clouded over and Millie began to regret asking about his father. He then asked: "What about your father? I've been told that James Browne is your stepfather."

"That's true, but he's been a real father to me, no favouritism. He is the only father I know. I've been trying to find my birth father but with no luck so far. Perhaps this ring will bring me luck." Millie rubbed the green stone on her hand and smiled up at Albert.

Albert bent and gave her a quick kiss on the cheek. "That's for luck," he said.

The couple had decided to have a celebratory lunch at a newly opened parlour/restaurant called Apang's. Millie had never been there before but it seemed that Albert had. As they entered the establishment the owner himself, a middle-aged Chinese gentleman greeted Albert. "Boy, is about time yuh come to try meh han'. Is two weeks since I open, an' is only now yuh come?"

"Man, I busy fuh so, wen ah ent trimmin' hair ah buildin' ah extension to meh house. I getting' married yuh see; meet meh wife-to-be. Apang, dis is Millie," Albert offered.

"Pleased to meet you," Apang replied, bowing and offering his hand. "Dis crafty half Chinee go settle down at las'. Lemme gi' yuh de bes' table in de place."

When they were seated and Apang had gone to fetch them a menu himself, Millie said to Albert: "I've never heard you talking like a *peong* before."

"When I'm with my *peong* friends I talk like them. When I'm with posh friends I talk proper English."

"My family isn't posh," Millie contended.

"You mightn't be rich, but you're educated and that puts you in the posh bracket," Albert replied. Apang returned with a hand-written menu and apologized that the copies he'd ordered were still at the printers.

"What's your favourite Chinese food?" Albert asked Millie.

"I've never eaten Chinese food," Millie confessed. "So, this is going to be a new experience for me, I'll trust you to choose for us."

Albert opened his eyes incredulously. "In that case, I'll order my favourite. We'll start with Wonton soup, followed by Sweet and Sour Pork with fried rice." He handed the menu back to the waitress Apang had delegated to look after them, but Millie asked to see what else was on offer and was given the menu to peruse. After reading through it, she laid it on the table to be collected by the waitress on her return.

"Did you see anything you might have fancied?" Albert enquired.

"No," Millie replied. "I was just curious." The phrase "curiosity killed the cat" came to her mind then and a laugh escaped her throat.

"What's so funny?" Albert asked.

"I'll tell you later," was the reply.

Millie enjoyed the Wonton soup and watched Albert devour his with relish. She wondered if after they were married he would want her to cook Chinese food. *She could learn*, she thought. The bowls were taken away and the main course served. They had to help themselves from the dishes which were placed on the table. The food came in delicate China dishes which made Millie reflect on the fact that the tableware they called China did in fact originate in China and China had one of the oldest civilizations in the world. She asked Albert if his mother served meals like this. He told her that on occasions when they had guests she might. His father had liked to cook and had taught her to cook Chinese food, in fact, had taught him as well. Millie pondered on this as they thanked Apang and the waitress and departed. It was a thoroughly satisfying meal and Millie said so to Albert.

As they left the restaurant, Albert asked: "Are you going to tell me now what made you laugh?"

"Yes," answered Millie. "My cousin and my sister said that Chinese people eat cats and dogs and the words 'curiosity killed the cat' came to my head as I told you that I was just curious about the menu."

"I've never known any Chinese people who would eat cats or dogs," Albert defended. "There are too many racialist people in Trinidad. Do you know that when I was a boy at school they teased me with the rhyme, *Chinee never die, flat nose and chinky eye*?"

"That's as bad as calling people of my colour *red antz*," Millie replied.

Albert smiled at that. "We can only dream that sometime in the future, people of all races, creeds and colours will be regarded the same and respect and dignity given to everyone."

"Make that a prayer and I'll say amen to that," added Millie. "And another group in that list should be illegitimates."

They strolled in the direction of the race course and found a bench to sit on in the savannah. As they sat, Millie sought to appease the situation. "Do you know that in the old days when English or other European sailors were adrift at sea, they ended up killing and eating the ship's pets?"

"Yes, those were special circumstances," admitted Albert. "And I can imagine in times of famine in China, or anywhere else in the world, if people were desperate enough, they would eat just about any animal to survive."

"I don't believe that Chinese people would eat cats and dogs, I'm sorry if you thought I meant that," Millie apologized.

"I didn't think that," Albert replied, putting his arm around her shoulders. Looking around, he whispered in her ear, "I love you. There's no one around."

They kissed, their first real kiss, flavoured with Sweet and Sour sauce, that they would remember for the rest of their lives.

Chapter 43
An Engagement Party

The Cezairs, on learning of Albert's engagement, decided to hold an impromptu party for the couple that Saturday evening. All their friends were invited and it seemed that they could all attend. It was as if everyone were simply waiting for an excuse to have a Saturday night party. Even the quartet of musicians, the Fermin brothers, who had been hired to play at the Aqui's engagement party, volunteered to provide their services free of charge.

When Albert informed Millie of the intended party she immediately panicked: "But I've nothing to wear!"

"Don't worry," he assured her. "This isn't the sort of socialite affair like we had at the Aqui's; it will be a 'come-as-you-are' type of party." He left Millie at her door and went to help with the preparations for the party.

As soon as Julia got home from work that evening Millie told her of the intended party and they began to get ready. Julia admired the jade keepsake Albert's mother had given her and said that her father had a jade figurine of Buddha that he rubbed for luck. Millie smiled, rubbed her ring and made a silent wish for her father to make himself known.

Albert arrived to escort them to the party at a quarter to six. "You both look ravishing," he complimented.

"Thank you," they chorused. He added: "I hope you haven't spoilt your appetite by having dinner already for Amanda has prepared something special for you." They were intrigued by this but Albert wouldn't tell them what it was, saying it would spoil the surprise.

On arrival, they were greeted with shouts of "Congratulations!" by a motley group of young and old acquaintances. They were casually dressed, the women in blouses and skirts and the men in khaki trousers and shirts. An elderly Cezair, whom Albert called "uncle" Tony, took Millie's hand and

151

kissed it, saying: "Welcome to the biggest family in Arima. Al is like a son to me, so you will be a daughter."

Drinks were served and the guests toasted the couple, wishing them a long, happy and fruitful union. Amanda and Claire Chin, one of Amanda's friends from the convent, then invited everyone to help themselves to Dim Sum, a variety of Chinese puddings they had made especially for the occasion. This treat was spread out on a long trestle table and guests simply helped themselves using paper napkins. Millie thought this a most convenient way to serve snacks and considered doing something like that for parang sessions at Christmas time; it would save washing up of wares. She and Julia particularly enjoyed the fried shrimp Wantons, and Millie told her of the Wanton soup she'd had at lunch time.

The Fermin brothers, with guitarist Cecil Chance, then struck up one of the latest tunes to hit the music world: *The Peanut Vendor*. The band consisted of drums, saxophone, clarinet and guitar. The Cezairs owned a piano and Jean was happy to join them, making a quintet. For the "*Vendor*," no one seemed quite sure what dance steps should be taken but simply followed the beat of the music as they danced.

Millie danced most of the time with Albert but when a waltz or foxtrot was played "uncle" Tony or one of the older men would say "Excuse," and take her to the floor. As she danced with him, Millie inquired how "uncle" Tony got to know Albert. She then learned that Tony Cezair was the first owner of the barbershop in Sangre Grande which Albert now owned.

When Albert was only ten, Albert went to work for Marlay and Company in Cunapo. Tony saw him washing glasses behind the bar in Marlay's rum shop and told his mother (who catered his daily lunch), that Albert could be apprenticed to him and become a barber. She agreed willingly and so did Albert, who learned the art quickly and prospered. When some fifteen years later, Tony decided to move to Port of Spain, opening a new shop there, Albert inherited the Sangre Grande establishment.

During a break from dancing, Julia and Millie swapped stories. Julia had danced with Amon Chin, the brother of Claire, who had helped with the buffet, and discovered that the Chins owned a "Take-out parlour" on Prince Street in Arima and Dim Sum could be bought there. Millie told Julia about "uncle" Tony's role in establishing Albert as a hairdresser.

As the girls chatted, Tony came across to them bearing three drinks on a tray.

"You didn't introduce me to your sister," he complained. "I've brought you some lubrication for your throats."

"Thank you," they chorused.

"Julia is my cousin; our mothers are sisters," Millie informed him.

"But you are like two peas in a pod," Tony replied.

"Thanks for the compliment, but Millie is the pretty one," Julia responded.

"Don't put yourself down Julia. I wish I had your natural charm," Millie chided. Tony intervened: "I'm sorry if my words are the source of a quarrel between such charming members of the fair sex. Let's drink a toast to a growing extended family."

"Oh no, we're not quarrelling," they laughed. "Cheers. May this pumpkin-vine family spread over the islands."

Among Amanda's friends from school was Florence Farfan, who then came over to congratulate Millie. "My dad sends his best wishes," she said, looking at Millie's left hand and not seeing a ring. Millie noticed her glance and explained that they had bought the ring that day but had to have it altered to fit and would receive it next Saturday. She also told Florence that she had intended visiting the Farfan family the next day before returning to Talparo. Millie was aware that in a close community as existed in Arima it was very easy to slight someone without meaning to.

Albert claimed her for the next dance and as they danced, she informed Albert that she and Julia would be going to the nine o'clock Mass in Santa Rosa in the morning and tentatively suggested that he join them. To her pleasant surprise, he readily agreed and shortly after, they thanked their hosts as the party ended and he escorted the cousins home. Millie was quick to claim that they had imbibed too many drinks, implying the need to relieve their bladders, and thus avoided an attempt of a goodnight kiss.

Safely behind doors, Julia chided her cousin. "You could at least have given your fiancé a goodnight kiss."

"I know what that could lead to," Millie replied.

"Not with me around," Julia remonstrated. "You would have been quite safe."

"Anyway, it's too late now," Millie concluded.

Chapter 44
Albert Goes to Church

The following morning as the cousins set off for church Albert came hurrying to meet them. "Good morning, ladies," he enthused. "Did you think I wouldn't make it?"

"You gave your word," Millie answered. "And so far, you have been true to your word." The girls both wore long-sleeved, high-necked dresses and mantillas whilst Albert wore a grey suit which was obviously borrowed as the sleeves were too long for him. Millie silently praised him for making the effort.

Albert took her arm as they mounted the short steps to the vestibule of the church. He dipped his fingers in the font and knelt on one knee facing the altar as he made the sign on the cross. Millie and Julia blessed themselves and followed him down the aisle to an empty pew. Kneeling next to him, Millie whispered in his ear: "So you have done this before."

"Of course," he whispered back, "Ma used to take us every Sunday at six o'clock and sometimes during the week too." His actions were to prove his words as he not only sang the hymns and knew the Latin responses, but recited the Credo and the Pater Noster perfectly. *It augured well for their marriage*, Millie thought. He at least was, or had been, a practicing Catholic.

After Mass, they paid a visit to John and Gertrude Farfan. The Farfans had attended an earlier Mass and had just finished having breakfast. Millie introduced Albert to them as her intended husband and they welcomed the trio to their home. They were offered coffee and toast which they accepted but asked for some water first, a custom that had been ingrained in them from childhood. When the Farfans heard that Millie would be getting the ring the following Saturday they said: "We look forward to another visit from you then."

Chapter 45
A Dim Sum Soiree

On her return to Talparo, her sisters greeted her with the words: "Let's see the ring." Millie had to explain that the jewellers had kept it to make it smaller to fit her ring finger. Her mother was impressed that Albert's mother had given her the jade ring. If it had been given to her by Albert's father, it must have been precious to her. That action spoke of a desire to please and welcome a daughter-in-law-to-be she had never met and she must therefore have been greatly affected by what she had heard of her, possibly from sources other than Albert. It boded well for the marriage.

Olivia and Maria could hardly contain their excitement and stayed in Millie's room chatting into the slumber most portion of the night. They wanted to know what the Chinese food was like, how the party went, who she danced with, what music was played and everything that went on. They only stopped when Papa put his head round the door and said: "That's enough girls. Ollie remember you've got to catch the first bus in the morning."

The following morning when Millie turned up at school the other teachers stole surreptitious glances at her left hand, for the jungle vines had been humming with gossip over the weekend. They all knew that Millie was getting engaged. When they didn't see a ring they felt disappointed but knew from the inner glow that emanated from Millie that all was well with her. At the first break time, Miss Lezama broached the subject, asking Millie: "Did you have a good weekend?"

"Oh yes indeed!" answered Millie. "One of the very best. I believe you must have heard that I was getting engaged; well, I am."

"Congratulations!" A chorus of voices sang out. This caused Mr Belix, who must have been the only one not in the know, to put his head round the blind and enquire: "What's this about?" When informed of Millie's engagement he said what was uppermost in his mind: "So I'll soon be a staff member short." Then added: "Well, I must add my congratulations. When is the wedding to be?"

"We haven't set the date yet," answered Millie. "Albert is building an extension to his house and we will wait 'til it's completed." The bell was rung, signalling the end of recess and they retreated to their respective classrooms.

To Millie, the rest of the week seemed snail-paced. Friday couldn't come soon enough. That Friday morning, she packed her grip and took it to school with her as she was going to catch the bus directly after school. Her youngest sister, Maria, was also going to spend to weekend in Arima and was waiting at the bus stop for Millie as she left the school. They travelled in companiable silence, aware that other passengers on rural buses were only too keen to listen to other peoples' conversation and spread gossip. On a seat next to her, Millie found a discarded copy of the Port of Spain Gazette and began to read. There was a story of a Trinidad born African-American who had flown from coast to coast across the U.S.A. His name was Hubert Fauntleroy Julian, alias *The Black Eagle* and he was the first man of African descent to do so. Millie thought she would use that article to show her pupils that people of colour could achieve whatever they wanted.

Olivia was happy to welcome them to her home as Julia had just left to spend a weekend with her parents. She was also relieved that her landlord would be put off dropping in "just to see that she was all right" as he had lately begun to do. His wife was expecting their second child and according to him, "was behaving very broody."

Maria had brought some freshly made cocoa sticks and they made themselves a pot of rich drinking chocolate which they sweetened with condensed milk. The sisters opened up a tin of Sunrise biscuits and they ate these with cheese for their supper.

As expected, Albert turned up bright and early the following morning to escort Millie to the jewellers' shop. Maria's eyes had made such an eloquent plea to Albert that he said to Millie: "It would be fine if your sister came along as well, wouldn't it?"

"Let's ask her," Millie replied.

"If I wouldn't be in the way, I'd love to," Maria quickly responded. Olivia had much sewing to finish and said she would join them at Chin's parlour at lunch time. She had visited it after being told about it by Millie and found it highly satisfactory.

The trio traipsed into Khan's e as its doors were opening and Mr Khan came to greet them. "Welcome, I see you have brought another lady for a ring," he teased.

"Oh no," Millie replied. "My sister is only along as a bodyguard." They laughed at that and Mr Khan produced the ring which fitted Millie's finger perfectly. Millie and Maria then ostensibly busied themselves examining a display of earrings while Albert completed the financial transaction.

As it was too early to head for Chin's, they decided pop in to see the Farfans as promised. Mrs Farfan admired the diamond which sparkled on Millie's finger and thought it similar to her own, which it was. They were therefore complimented on their taste. Jerome was in and persuaded them to listen to his latest records, which were: *Love is the Sweetest Thing, Smoke Gets in Your Eyes* and *Stormy Weather*. They enjoyed the songs very much and Albert promised Millie that they would have a gramophone of their own when they were married. When she had tactfully discovered that they hadn't made any plans for that evening, Mrs Farfan invited them to come for Supper at seven and bring Olivia with them.

They went along to Prince Street and found Olivia already at Chin's parlour, waiting in a queue. Chin's was a popular place for people who wanted a quick but tasty lunch and many shop clerks and office workers frequented it. Albert took over from Olivia, who had brought a picnic basket with her and paid for a variety of Dim Sum which they then took to the savannah near the race course.

They were happy to sit in the shade of a Tamarind tree to enjoy their repast. Albert was asked about his childhood and he regaled them with stories of fishing and swimming in the Cunapo river, hunting for manicou and agouti in the forest and the occasional trips to Manzanilla to bathe in the sea and dig in the sand for chip chip. The girls were most intrigued by his description of the Manzanilla beach as they had never been to the seaside. Their only glimpse of the sea was from their trip to Port of Spain and there was no sandy beach there. Albert suggested that they should organize a family outing to Manzanilla sometime before the wedding and get to know each other's relatives there. They thought it a great idea and decided to discuss it with the rest of the family.

Millie remembered Mrs Farfan's invitation and told Olivia about it. Olivia could only spare the time if she returned to her work immediately so they had to leave the savannah and wend their way back. Maria had some shopping to do and asked Millie to help her choose a pair of shoes. Albert sensed that he would be in the way and begged to be excused saying he would escort Olivia home on his way to the Cezair's. Maria and Millie were thus left alone to try the patience of the shop clerks. With Millie's help, Maria chose a pair of sensible shoes which yet had style.

At a quarter to seven, Albert turned up to walk the young ladies to the Farfans. Ollie was just finishing the dress she would be wearing to the supper so they didn't set off until ten minutes later. They arrived on time and were welcomed by Michel Farfan, his wife, Madeline, and daughter Florence. "Congratulations, we had to join in the celebration," they enthused.

"It's a pity your mother couldn't be here too," Michel added. Millie introduced Albert to the two Farfans he hadn't met and they went through to the dining room. Gertrude Farfan had just finished laying the table with a buffet of **Dim Sum**.

Maria started to exclaim: "We've just—"

"Had a lovely surprise!" Millie butted in. "Madeline's solitaire diamond is just like ours."

"And so it is!" Michel noticed for the first time. Maria looked at Millie and blushed. Millie's prevarication had saved the day. Albert smiled knowingly and remained silent.

"Florence told us that you liked Dim Sum, so that's what we're having," Mrs Farfan stated.

"Oh yes we do," Millie agreed. "It's so exotic and tasty." Jerome and John Farfan entered the room then and added their congratulations to the couple and the buffet.

After everyone had helped themselves to the fare and had a drink, Jerome invited Millie and Albert to look through the record collection and compile a list for their listening and dancing pleasure. Little did they realize that the selection they settled upon that night was to become their all-time favourite songs for the rest of their lives. Among the songs chosen were: *It Had to be You, I Can't Give You Anything but Love, Among my Souvenirs, Moonlight and Roses, Ramona, Stardust, Tiptoe through the Tulips,* and *On the Sunny*

Side of the Street. This soiree lasted until the bewitching hour, when they went home.

Chapter 46
Le Mot Juste

On their return to Talparo on Sunday evening, Maria was the more excited of the two sisters. One would have thought that Maria had just become engaged. She related everything that had happened, including her almost faux pas at the Farfans. Millie played down her part in her sister's rescue from the awkward situation, claiming that she did indeed notice the similarity in the rings. Both her parents and her brother then admired the ring and Meg said how *exquisite* it was. Pedro assumed *exquisite* was a French word and asked what it meant in English. They all had a laugh at that and Millie explained that it meant *elegant*, which was yet another French word commonly used in English and that many words had their roots in the Romance languages. This left Pedro as bewildered as ever and he left the room thinking: "Why can't we just use one word like *pretty*, which everybody could understand?"

On the following day at school, most of her fellow teachers stole surreptitious glances at Millie's ring but said nothing. The children, however, were openly curious. One little girl naively enquired, "Miss, is true you gettin' married?"

"Yes," Millie replied. "It will be in a year's time from now, so you won't lose me yet."

"So why you haveta wear a ring so early?"

"It's to stop other men from pestering me," Millie said with a laugh. This brought out a burst of giggles from her class.

Mr Belix then appeared from behind the partition. "Did I hear you were being pestered, Miss Le Blanc?"

"No Mr Belix," Millie replied, "I was merely explaining why brides-to-be wear engagement rings."

"I see," he replied, going off muttering under his breath, "and to show off that they've caught a man."

Millie quickly brought her class under control and continued with her lesson on synonyms and antonyms. Her brother's reaction to unusual words had made her question the use of different words and remember Mr Farfan's phrase, *le mot juste,* that he was wont to use from time to time. She began writing a list of words on the board: *Enormous, immense, exorbitant, large.* The children were then asked to give examples of words that meant the same as those on the board. They offered: *Huge, big, monstrous, grand, gigantic, extreme.* One boy improvised: *Gynormous.* Millie then commended him on his effort but had to explain that that particular word was not in the dictionary and was not accepted as a proper English word. She added that it might one day become accepted if enough people of influence began using it. Prominent authors using it in books would be a start. He could become an author, anything he wanted was possible. The Gazette article about Julian's flight across America was then read to the class. It was an inspiration for them that a black man could achieve anything he aspired to.

She then asked the class to use the ten words on the board in sentences and elicited from them the subtle differences in meaning between words we regard as synonyms. The enthusiasm of the class in this exercise again attracted the attention of Mr Belix who this time praised their efforts but exhorted them to "*exult quietly in their exuberance*" as they were disturbing other classes.

Millie felt some sympathy for the classes which were being disturbed but thought that lessons learned with exuberance were remembered better than those learned in quiet decorum. It was for this reason that she often took her classes outside when the weather permitted; unfortunately, it didn't that day.

She felt that the coming of a new head teacher had put a damper on her enjoyment of teaching and toyed with the idea of writing to the Gazette to find out if there was still an opportunity of employment with them for her. The school term dragged on slowly and Millie was glad when the August vacation began.

Chapter 47
The Visit to St. Ann's

Her cousins had heard of her visit to St. Clair to see her aunt and wanted to pay a visit also. Millie wrote to the new address in Coblenz Avenue, St. Ann's and received a reply. Her Aunt Camille would be very happy to see them, all of them, if possible. As it turned out, Olivia was too busy to go and so was Frank who was helping his father plant a new crop of pink grapefruit.

So it was that six young people, Julia, Helen, Nora, Millie, Maria and Pedro travelled from Talparo by bus, train, and tramcar to visit relatives in St. Ann's. They got off the tram near the Botanical Gardens at the northern end of Queens Park Savannah and walked about half a mile to the address Millie had obtained from her aunt. They were to stay overnight and carried grips with their change of clothing and toiletries. They also brought with them a few bags of fruit and vegetables as presents.

As before, Aunt Camille was elated to see Millie and be introduced to the nieces and nephew she had not met. Aunt Camille had told her daughter Pauline, who lived nearby in Cascade of the impending visit and "Aunt" Pauline (Adult cousins were customarily given the honorary title of aunt) was also present to greet them. The aunts were happy to receive the gifts of fruit and vegetables but protested that it was too much weight for the youngsters to carry. Pedro laughed at that and said that they were accustomed to walking a mile with a fifty-to-sixty-pound bag of tonka beans or cashew nuts on their backs.

Aunt Camille again had her own quarters at the back of her employers' residence and Maria remarked that it was bigger than St. Clair or the one Olivia and Julia shared in Arima. The aunts ushered them in to a dining room with a trestle table on which was spread a variety of delicious food and drinks. They were invited to wash their hands at a basin with indoor plumbing; something they were using for the first time. They then sat down to drink ice-cold glasses of soda and eat the specially prepared dishes of food their aunts had provided.

Aunt Camille noticed Millie's engagement ring and declared: "So you intend to keep quiet about the wedding, Millie."

Millie blushed and replied, "Oh no Auntie, it's just that we haven't set a date as Albert is building an extension to his house which his mother is living in, and we can't make definite plans until it's finished."

"Tell me about this Albert then. I hope you know it's not a good thing to be living under the same roof as your mother-in-law." Millie agreed with this and said that her mother-in-law-to-be might be a nice person after all, for without meeting her, she had given her the jade ring, which must have been of great sentimental value to her. She then went on to tell Aunt Camille of Albert's cycling to Talparo to ask her father for her hand in marriage and his devotion to her.

The conversation was non-stop, as the young people were asked about life in the country, which the aunts compared to their experiences in Grenada. Julia and Helen were able to relate the little they knew about Papa Leon as they were sometimes given errands to perform by their mother, Marie, who seemed to be the only one he kept in contact with. They were given parcels to take to him from time to time and were always bemused by the messages he gave them to relate to their mother as it was always in patois. It appeared that Papa Leon had never learned to talk in English. Millie was quite intrigued by this revelation but wanted to find out what her aunts knew about her mother.

Getting Aunt Camille aside in the kitchen as she helped to wash the wares, Millie asked her what Papa Leon had told her about her mother, Meg. Papa Leon had merely told them that Meg was *tres obstine* and had brought *gros deshonneur pour la famille,* she was to be *ostracisee.* Aunts Camille and Pauline had no idea what Meg had done or with whom. This trip did not help her quest.

Julia was asked about her job as a sales clerk for Bata in Arima and confessed to her aunts that it was only just more bearable than staying under her father's roof all the time. Her income depended on commission and when sales were slow this barely covered her expenses. Aunt Pauline told her that there was a job available at the moment as a house-keeper for a doctor with two young children. He had recently lost his wife and was looking for someone trustworthy to look after his children, cook and keep his house clean and tidy.

Both Julia and Helen claimed interest in this position and Aunt Pauline promised to look into it on their behalf.

Three of them were to sleep at Aunt Pauline's home in Cascade and the other three at Aunt Camille's. Julia, Helen, and Nora volunteered to go with Aunt Pauline, leaving Millie, Maria and Pedro at Aunt Camille's. Millie and Maria shared the double bed in Aunt Camille's guest room while Pedro slept on a sofa in the living room. There were no mosquito nets but Aunt Camille lit anti-mosquito coils which she called *Mokoto*, to keep them safe.

The next morning, they were up bright and early. There were no blasts of conch shells or donkeys braying to awaken them, just the sound of early morning traffic on its way to Port of Spain. They were to pay a visit to Aunt Pauline's house about a half mile away. Aunt Camille was busy and couldn't take them, but a little girl of about ten and her brother of thirteen or fourteen from "the big house" where Aunt Camille worked, volunteered to show them the way. These children were going to play with some friends who lived near Aunt Pauline's.

Millie noted as they walked along that most of the people they saw were white. The few coloured people she saw wore aprons or overalls for work. The houses were quite grand and built mostly of brick and concrete with smaller servants' quarters at the back. Gardens were well tended and proliferated with flowers. The roads were well paved with asphalt. It was a far cry from rural Talparo. As they ascended a hill, however, a few wooden houses could be seen. It was in one of these that Aunt Pauline lived.

At the side of Aunt Pauline's house, a little stream came gushing down the hillside. A small group of children were having fun by putting twigs in the water upstream and watching them race down to the bridge. Nora and Helen were on the bridge with them whilst Julia stood watching from Aunt Pauline's porch. Some of these children were friends of Millie's escorts.

Nora looked a bit downcast as she and Helen joined their cousins and went into the house. Julia noticed her demeanour and asked what was the matter. "Nothing," Nora replied. "It's just that one of the children asked me if I was your maid."

"Oh, never mind that, most of the whites in this district have coloured maids. They didn't mean anything disrespectful," Julia explained. Nevertheless, this episode put a dampener on Nora's spirits for the rest of the day.

Aunt Pauline was glad to see them again and offered them cups of chocolate made from the cocoa sticks they themselves had given her. Aunt Pauline's husband, Jose, was a Master Mariner and worked on one of the steamships that ferried people and goods to and from Tobago; she explained that he spent very little time at home and when he was home, he spent most of his time asleep. She was very glad therefore to have their company. Her only companion was the rediffusion speaker box in the living room. This was an experiment being carried out in the area at the time. Her two children were grown up and lived in Tobago so it was nice to have people around to talk to. It was a shame that they intended to return to Talparo that day. Julia said that it was on account of her mean boss who allowed her very little vacation time. This reminded Aunt Pauline of her promise to find employment for one of the girls with the widowed doctor.

"We might catch the doctor at home now if we pay him a quick visit. Would the two of you like to come with me to see him?" She asked Julia and Helen.

"Yes please," Julia said happily. Helen seemed a little uncertain but decided to go along nonetheless, leaving Millie with the other three.

Millie was happy to stay and listen to the rediffusion programs which alternated between music and news. Pedro and Nora wished they could have a speaker box like that in Talparo, but Millie explained that they would have to have wires brought to it all the way from Port of Spain. They listened to *Temptation* sung by Bing Crosby. Then there was news about Mahatma Gandhi leaving the Sassoon hospital in Poona, India. He weighed only 90 lbs. after fasting in prison to protest against a refusal to allow him to continue his work with the Untouchables. This was followed by two songs which were to become favourites over the years, *Stormy Weather* and *It's Only a Paper Moon*.

Aunt Pauline returned with Julia and Helen then, as they had enjoyed a very short but productive visit with Dr Chalfont who was happy to employ Julia on Aunt Pauline's recommendation. He needed someone immediately, however, and Julia needed to give her employer two weeks' notice. He preferred the older of the two girls but Aunt Pauline suggested that Helen start in Julia's place for the first two weeks and gain some experience which would help her towards future employment. Helen acquiesced to that suggestion. Her only problem would be her clothes. She had only brought two changes with her. Dr Chalfont then asked if it would it bother her to have some of his late wife's garments. He noted that Helen was about the same size. He had not got around to getting rid of his wife's clothes yet. Aunt Pauline urged her to accept and she did.

They had an early lunch at Aunt Pauline's that day and a quick "drop in" to say goodbye at Aunt Camille's before leaving to catch a tramcar to take them to the railway station in Port of Spain. The five of them found it difficult to leave Helen behind but thought it was best for her. Helen accompanied them as far as the Queen's Park Savannah where they said goodbye with much hugging and kissing before they boarded the tram.

Passing through the city on the tram, they marvelled at the big shops they saw, Stevens and Todd's, Glendennings, Muir Marshalls, Forgarty's, Salvatori's and the extensive Marine Square. There was no time for shopping (or money for that either), as the train ran on schedule and they couldn't afford to miss it. They got on the waiting train, which would get into Arima at four o'clock, in time to catch the Talparo bus.

On the train, Millie said that they would miss having Julia and Helen around to talk to and have fun together. Julia said that Helen would be back with them in a week's time and she herself would continue to visit Talparo regularly. Millie voiced the opinion that this was unlikely as she was sure that Helen would find other employment when the fortnight was up and visits to Talparo by both sisters would soon taper off. Nora, Maria and Pedro were upset at this and begged Julia not to forget them.

"Of course not," Julia protested. "I didn't forget you when I lived in Arima, why should I forget you if I live in Port of Spain? My visits would depend on the time off I can get from work, so it might not be very frequent, but there's nothing to stop you from visiting me." This appeased the younger ones somewhat as the idea of "going to town," as visits to Port of Spain were called, appealed to them very much.

Millie anticipated that their parents might not be too pleased to have their eldest daughters both live so far away. She therefore counselled Julia to tactfully remind them that they themselves had left the parental home at an even younger age. The train got to the Arima station just in time for them to catch the bus to Talparo and they were lucky to get the last five seats left.

Millie, Maria and Pedro said goodbye to their cousins at the junction and trudged their way home, weary but elated. On arriving home, Maria could hardly contain her excitement. She told her parents of the big houses they had seen. There was indoor plumbing (which she called "pipe water inside") and electricity in most homes! Pedro enthused about the rediffusion. Only Millie was quiet. Her mother Meg sensed that something was disturbing her peace of mind and asked if any of their relatives were ill. "Oh no," Millie replied, "They are all very well and send their regards; it's just that Julia is going to take up a job as housekeeper for a widowed doctor and Helen will follow her, I'm sure, as Helen is already filling in for Julia from tomorrow. Julia has to give her Bata employer two weeks' notice."

Meg thought that Millie should be pleased for them as it would give them freedom from the constrictions of their Mahaica home. Millie interpreted this to mean "getting away from under Uncle Ian's thumb." She had often heard Helen and Julia complain that their father didn't want them to have friends in the village and restricted their activities to church and school. They even accused him of being colour prejudiced! "They are both over twenty-one now and have level heads on their shoulders," she said to her mother. "Anyway, they'll have Aunt Pauline and Aunt Camille looking after them. It's just that I'll miss having them to talk to."

The initial reunion excitement over, they washed off the travel dust and went to bed having lit a *Mokoto*, a parting present from Aunt Camille.

Chapter 48
Olivia's Undoing

As it turned out, Helen was offered employment with another family in Cascade and did not return to Talparo when Julia took up her appointment. Olivia was therefore left on her own most of the time. Millie thereby felt obliged to increase the frequency of her week-end visits to Arima. Albert was happy with this as Arima was easier to get to from Sangre Grande, whether by bus, train or bicycle. He was happy to take the two sisters out to dinner at Apang's or Chin's from time to time. Albert found it embarrassing to take them to his friend Apang's restaurant as Apang would often refuse to accept his payment, saying: "This one is on the house, old friend." He thought it made him "look cheap," so they more often than not, dined at Chin's.

It was at Apang's, however, that as they were dining one evening, Olivia was violently and most embarrassingly sick. She had tried to get away from the table, but before she could reach the washroom door, what she had eaten was all over the floor. Apang was most considerate about it, refusing help from Millie who wanted to mop the floor and then not accepting any payment from Albert. It was perhaps fortunate that only two other customers were in the restaurant at the time and both of them were regulars who would not be put off by the incident.

After escorting the sisters home, Albert took his leave as he sensed that they would prefer to be on their own. Olivia was pale and trembling and Millie immediately helped her to bed. "Ollie, is it something you've eaten?" Millie asked solicitously, as they had been halfway through their meal when Olivia became sick.

"I wish it was," Olivia replied, bursting into tears. "I think I'm pregnant." Millie was shocked. "How could that happen?" She naively asked.

"It was Desmond, Mr Diaz," Ollie explained. "I asked him if he could reduce the rent as Julia was no longer sharing with me. He said: 'Call me Desmond, Mr Diaz is too formal. Of course, we could come to a friendly arrangement.' He put his arm around my shoulder as if to comfort me, and I didn't pull away as I thought it would offend him. 'You could pay half until you get someone else in to share.' He whispered into my ear. 'Thank you.' I said, turning to face him. The next thing I knew his mouth was on mine and he was kissing me. He pushed me on to the bed and I tried to scream. He said, 'Shush. My wife is in a very delicate condition and doctor says she'd lose the baby if she got upset.' You can guess what happened next."

Millie too burst into tears. "He raped you, the swine! I'll report him to the police!"

"No, that wouldn't do any good," Olivia sobbed. "I should have done that at least the next day, but I was too ashamed. Then, when I told him I was going to report him, he said it would be my word against his. He would say I offered to go to bed with him instead of paying rent. I haven't any receipts for the last two months."

The two weeping sisters hugged each other as Millie tried to think of a solution to the problem. "You'll have to leave this place and come home to Talparo. I'll explain to Mama what happened. I'm sure she'll understand only too well," Millie advised.

The next day, a Saturday, they made arrangements with Alphonso, who had brought goods to the Arima market by coach, to transport Olivia's sewing machine and other belongings to Talparo the following week.

Millie had to tell Albert the truth of what happened with Olivia for he would eventually find out. He found Desmond Diaz's behaviour outrageous and was so incensed that he wanted to go with some friends and administer what he called "a good licking" on Diaz. Millie dissuaded him from such a rash action, claiming it would only make matters worse and that Olivia did not want it to be known what had happened. She swore him to secrecy. Albert accompanied them to the Talparo bus that afternoon and promised to visit Talparo at least fortnightly.

Chapter 49
Return to Talparo

Olivia's arrival was a surprise to her family in Talparo and she quickly went to her room while Millie took their mother aside and explained what had happened. Meg was dismayed but not too surprised. She always knew that a young woman on her own was very vulnerable. Her past experience was an example. She felt comforted by the knowledge that her husband James was not like Papa Leon, and would welcome his daughter home. Meg thanked Millie for bringing Ollie back and went to the girls' bedroom to see Ollie. A tearful Ollie was telling Maria what had happened and her mother took her into her arms, exclaiming: "My poor child! Why should this happen to you as well?" They sat on the bed and sobbed together. Maria and Millie joined them.

When James got home that evening, Meg met him downstairs at the water butt as he was washing himself before entering the house. "James," she said, "we have a surprise waiting for you."

"I hope it's a nice one, as I've had a tiring day," he answered.

"Ollie has come home," Meg informed him. "She will not be working in Arima anymore."

"I'll be glad for that, but why is she here?" He asked, suspiciously. Meg explained the situation and he trudged wearily upstairs to console his daughter.

Olivia cried in his arms as he steeled himself to console her with a hug and suppress the angry words of recrimination which would not be of any consolation to her. True love was all she needed now and he would do his best to give her that.

Millie's thoughts went from her sister's experience to her mother's. Could both have happened in a similar way? Did they both trust the man who had done that to them? Why wouldn't her mother name the perpetrator? Is she scared of his threats or does she want to protect him? He could be a married man of some importance to the community; but who could it be? These questions swirled in her head, the answers to them elusive.

Her second line of thinking was that of self-searching. Did she really want to meet her father if he was a cold, calculating rapist as Desmond Diaz was? If, as it seemed possible, her mother and father did care for each other and somehow their love-making got out of hand, as she had read of in romance novels, she would still like to meet him. But then, what kind of a man would simply abandon a girl he loved and his own child? Could it be that he doesn't know that he fathered a child? That could be the answer, she concluded. Although aware that she was grasping at straws, she would continue her quest.

Chapter 50
Albert Offers His Assistance

The following Friday, Albert arrived on his bicycle. He had acquired a bottle-shaped dynamo which was attached to the back wheel and produced electricity which passed through wires to a lamp in the middle of his handlebars. Pedro was excited by this contraption and asked numerous questions about its performance.

The drawbacks were that there was no light when the bicycle was stationary, and there was too much electricity produced when going too fast. The bulb in the lamp blew and left you in darkness. Albert explained that this had happened to him last night with nearly disastrous consequences. He was going downhill and approaching a corner when the bulb blew. Fortunately, he knew the road and managed to turn in the dark before he was able to stop and change the bulb.

During this visit, Millie was happy to have her sisters and brother around, because for some reason not quite clear in her mind, she felt uncomfortable when alone in Albert's company although she knew that he was not the sort to try to take advantage of her.

Albert, for his part, felt the need to offer some sort of consolation to Olivia about her predicament. He related that his youngest sister, Emma, had been seduced by an employer and had given birth to a lovely baby girl whom they now all adored. Olivia said she would prefer a son, as girls were too vulnerable, but she would teach him to treat girls with kindness and respect.

James Browne came out to join them on the front verandah then and Albert greeted him respectfully: "Good to see you Mr Browne, I dropped by to offer my services with the moving of Olivia's furniture tomorrow. I'll be spending the night in Arima and can help load the coach in the morning."

"Thanks for the offer, but we'll manage all right with the few belongings she has and Alphonso isn't getting to Arima before ten o'clock, so you don't have to be up early."

Mr Browne replied, "I have some business to attend to in Arima anyway so I'll be there. You are welcome to join us as I feel I might need someone to restrain me if I set eyes on that demon of a landlord."

Albert smiled. "I know what you mean, but I'm sure you can handle yourself with dignity, Mr Browne." Albert then prepared to depart for Arima.

Chapter 51
The Retreat of the Dastardly Diaz

The next day, Pedro also wanted to join them, so Millie, Olivia and Pedro travelled with their father on the coach to Arima. They only had to stop on the way once when Olivia felt sick. Albert met them at the house and they began removing Olivia's belongings. As Pedro and Albert were carrying the sewing machine out of the door, Mr Diaz appeared. "I'm having that in lieu of rent," he ventured.

"I'm only owing half a month's rent," Olivia replied, "and I've already got it for you in this envelope." She threw it at him. James Browne then descended from the coach and advancing on Diaz, asked: "Is this the landlord?" Before the "yes" came out of Olivia's mouth, Desmond Diaz ran. He bolted up the two steps to his front door and shut it behind him. He must have recognized the look of paternal affront in her father's eyes and was taking no chances. Albert and Pedro wanted to follow him but Mr Browne restrained them, saying, "We don't want to make a fuss. Some people are watching out their windows already." A few curtains actually twitched.

They continued loading Olivia's belongings and material given her for making dresses, into and on top of, the coach. When they were satisfied that everything was accounted for Olivia locked the little house and pushed the key under the door of the Diaz' home. Olivia said she would prefer to travel back to Talparo by bus rather than the jolting coach and Millie was happy to go with her, leaving Pedro and father to go home with Alphonso, after father's business was concluded.

Albert said to Millie, "We owe Apang an apology and I promised him we'd come by soon to try and make amends for the embarrassment caused, that is, if Olivia is up to it."

"Yes, I agree and I'm willing to see him now, especially as I can now put dastardly Diaz behind me. I only hope Apang hasn't guessed the real reason why I was sick." Albert kept silent on this matter but lead them into Apang's where he paid for lunch enjoyed by the three of them. They then walked to the bus terminal where they said their goodbyes and the girls departed for Talparo.

Chapter 52
An Easter Monday Excursion Is Planned

Millie volunteered to take the finished dresses to Arima for Olivia the following weekend and to deliver them to their respective owners. She also had to make excuses for the slightly late delivery in a couple of instances. She claimed that Olivia was suffering from severe migraine and could not be expected to work for the next month or so, and that her place in Arima was given up due to a "falling out" with the landlord.

At one home, that of the Cardinez family, she encountered much concern on Olivia's behalf; especially from a young man who solicitously asked if he could pay Olivia a visit at her parent's home. He wanted to thank her personally for altering his shirts so that they had the tailored fit he desired. Millie said she would convey his thanks and appreciation but he insisted on getting the address of the Browne family in Talparo. Millie gave it to him and thought no more of the matter.

Her last port of call was at the Cezairs, where she hoped somewhat fancifully, that she might meet Albert. They had not made arrangements to meet on this week-end and she thought they would not see each other until the following Friday evening. There was no way of communicating with each other in the interim. She was pleasantly surprised therefore when he appeared from their dining room where he was having a snack. She explained why she was in Arima for the day and he claimed that it was "her vibes" that had caused him to take a bus trip to Arima that evening. (Actually, he had come to order some galvanized iron sheeting for the extension of his house.)

Millie accepted some refreshments offered her and she sat chatting with Amanda, Jean and Albert, about the problems of communicating in Trinidad, whether by post or telephone. A few shops acted as Postal Agencies in rural districts and mail was sent by bus in most instances. Two full days seemed to be the minimum time taken to get a letter from A to B, providing that such letters were addressed adequately and the sorting done efficiently. Only a few government buildings, such as police stations and warden's offices, had telephones. Albert claimed that jungle tribes with their drums were better equipped to send messages from one end of an island to the other. Jean he that the next generation would have "walkie-talkies" and be able to talk to each other everywhere.

As they had their respective buses to catch and took their leave of the Cezairs to walk to the bus station, Albert had an idea. "Do you remember we agreed it would be nice to get our families to know each other before our wedding? I can find out if the bus company would run a day trip to Manzanilla beach."

"That sounds great," Millie agreed. "I've heard of people chartering buses for special occasions. It could work out to be quite economical if a large enough number can be persuaded to go. I'll try to get my family interested. Perhaps Easter Monday might be a good time."

"Good," Albert replied. "I'll find out the cost and let you know. See you next Friday; please God," he said, as he got on to the Sangre Grande bus and she on the Talparo bus.

Millie thought she would be able to encourage all her Talparo family to go, with the possible exception of Uncle Ian. She would even send Aunt Camille and Aunt Pauline letters inviting them. They could travel by train to Arima and join the bus there.

Maria and Pedro were overly thrilled at the prospect of an outing to the sea-side and Mama recounted stories of days spent at the beaches in Grenada. James had been to Manzanilla beach with some friends in his youth and one of them had drowned. He therefore warned them that there was to be no swimming in the sea. They reluctantly agreed, Millie emphasizing the fact that the object of the outing was to meet prospective family and picnic together.

Albert duly arrived on his bicycle the following Friday evening. Millie asked about the chartering of the bus and he said the company was willing to have the bus pick them up from Talparo but could only drop them off at Arima on the return journey. The Talparo travellers would have to make other arrangements to get home. The cost was one guinea for the day but the driver would expect tips from passengers alighting. This, he believed was an

American custom they were adopting. There was expected to be a full complement of twenty-four persons.

The Browne family were happy with that and thanked Albert for arranging it. He was invited to have supper with them that evening and they enjoyed a meal of cray fish, caught by Pedro in the river that day, and ground provisions from their garden. Albert declined second helpings claiming that riding on too full a stomach did not agree with him and thanked his hosts profusely on his departure. He would be working on the roof of his house that week-end. Millie said she was hoping to see the house soon and he promised she would on the day of the outing.

She visited the Maclean farmstead the following day and told her aunt and uncle of the proposed beach picnic and the intention of getting acquainted with Albert's family. Aunt Marie was thrilled with the idea and recounted the same stories Meg had told her of beaches in Grenada. Uncle Ian, however, claimed to have made arrangements to visit a farmer in the south of Trinidad who was growing a new type of hybrid oranges.

Nora and Frank were delighted at the prospect of a beach outing, and the chance of seeing Julia and Helen whom they were missing already. Millie had told them of inviting family from St. Ann's and Cascade as well. Uncle Ian informed them that they would have to pay for themselves but that he would provide an agouti and a manicou for their picnic lunch. Millie thought that her uncle's response was just as she had expected. She was becoming an expert on foretelling people's reactions, especially where her own relatives were concerned.

Millie's next visit was to the coach owner, Alphonso. To take passengers from Arima back to Talparo meant that he would have to go to Arima to pick them up. He had no plans to go to Arima on Easter Monday. He therefore suggested that instead of having the bus come to Talparo to pick them up, he could take them to Arima that morning, spend the day himself at the Arima Easter Monday races, and take them home that evening. It would cost them a little more, but Millie felt it was worth paying extra for the ease of mind, knowing that they would get transport home. She therefore booked his coach for the trip. There would be nine people traveling to Arima that morning, but there might be eleven on the return journey if Julia and Helen decided to go home with them.

On her return home that evening, there was a vaguely familiar young man on their front gallery taking to Ollie. Millie did not recognize him at first, but when he thanked her for giving him the address, she remembered the Cardinez fellow from Arima. He then introduced himself as Carlton, and said he had come to thank Olivia in person and to bring her some more work from his mother, which he stressed was not of an urgent nature.

Olivia seemed pleased, but whether it was for the work or the visitor, Millie was not sure. Her mother Meg was pleased for her and brought out some lemonade for their guest. Millie was grateful for a drink also, as she had had a long walk. She informed them that plans for their Manzanilla outing were now in hand as she had booked their trip to and from Arima. Carlton's ears pricked at this and he mentioned that he had been to Manzanilla once before and thoroughly loved it. Millie explained that it was a way of meeting with her future in-laws and he wished them all a pleasant time. He then had to leave to catch the last bus back to Arima

Having been informed of the Maclean's decision to cook "wild meat," Meg said they would take a chicken pelau. It would make a welcome change from the vegetarian and fish dishes they were having all through the Lenten season. It was expected at picnics to exchange plates of food, and Pedro especially, was looking forward to tasting his auntie's manicou. They also wondered what fare Albert's family from Sangre Grande would provide. James said he would take a bottle of rum but it would only be offered to adult non-bathers. It was the consumption of alcohol which had caused a drowning he had experienced as a youth. This had caused him to have a phobia of the sea, drunk or sober.

Chapter 53
A Letter to Albert

Millie was concerned that her family would number at least thirteen or fourteen; more than half of seating capacity of the bus. As it was two weeks before Easter, she wrote a letter to Albert informing him of the arrangements she had made and asking him to change the pick-up point from Talparo to Arima. She felt sure he would get it on time. She sent it to the only address he had given her, *Albert Akong, Eastern Main Road, Sangre Grande,* and hoped it would get to him on time. She had read that in England, houses were being numbered to facilitate postal delivery.

Albert's youngest sister, Emma, went to the Sangre Grande Post Office at the corner of the Eastern Main Road and River Road (built next to the railway station in 1898, a year after the railway came to Cunapo) hoping there might be a chance of employment for her in the Sorting Department. There wasn't, but she was given her brother Albert's letter to deliver to him. Albert was not in his barbershop in Marlay's building as she went past, so she took the letter home.

Her mother Isabella looked at the handwriting and said: "This looks like a French person's writing. My parents from Guadeloupe used to write in this cursive script. I'll bet it's from his intended. He said her mother was Martiniquan." Emma was intrigued by this and was tempted to open the letter but her mother reproved her. "You wouldn't like it if Albert opened a letter addressed to you. If it has news we should know, Albert will tell us." They placed the letter on the grandfather clock, out of reach of little children like Amoy.

Albert came home from a house call later that afternoon. He had been trimming the Warden's hair at his home in what was beginning to be called "Upper Sangre Grande." As he opened the letter, he said: "Great! Remember the Easter Monday outing I mentioned to you the other day? Well, it's on. Millie's family will be coming, that includes her aunts and cousins. The bus from Arima will bring them here to meet you and we'll go on to Manzanilla for a sea-side picnic."

"Can I go too?" cried Amoy.

"Sure, you can," Albert replied, "I'll tell your mother to bring you here that day."

Emma then said she would have to bring Marla, her little toddler, along as well, and her aunts would want to bring their children. They therefore got pencil and paper and wrote out a list of family members who would like to join them. This list numbered fifteen and did not include Isabella's siblings and their children (These would no doubt be invited to the wedding and would be introduced in due course). To carry this many, the bus would have to allow at least five standing passengers between Sangre Grande and Manzanilla.

Albert promptly replied by letter to Millie that the numbers did not present a problem and that everyone was looking forward to having a great time.

His mother and sister, however, began to fret over the state of their house. They thought the curtains looked shabby and the cushions on the Morris chairs grubby. Albert tried to assure them that it was no worse than the Browne's house in Talparo and that the house would not be under scrutiny, but to no avail. They insisted on new curtains and clean cushion covers before Easter. Then they deliberated on what foods they would take.

Chapter 54
Preparations for the Excursion and Some Easter Customs

In Talparo, preparations began to take place from Good Friday. The Macleans marinated their agouti and manicou separately. Aunt Marie had claimed that in Trinidad all "wild-meat" tended to taste the same because of the treatment meted out by amateur cooks. She thought that while manicou needed stronger seasoning with garlic and chadon bene, agouti, flavour with rosemary and thyme, had its own exquisite palate. The meat was cut into small pieces and left in marinade sauce for two days.

It being Good Friday, Aunt Marie decided to make egg-shell rattles. This, apparently, was a custom from her childhood. She sent Frank to the black-smith's to get some long hairs from a horse's tail and Nora to the woods to get some pine resin. She then took three large eggs and made small holes at the sharper end of each of them through which she extracted the fluid (which she later used to make a cake). She heated the resin in a tin can and dipped the ends of three pencil sized sticks in it and allowed it to dry. One end of a horse hair was knotted to a piece of matchstick which was then inserted into the hole made in an eggshell so that it anchored itself firmly. The other end of the horse hair was tied into a loop and passed over the resin coated pencil sized stick. The egg-shell was then twirled around the stick and made unusual musical sounds unlike any rattle the children had ever heard. They were delighted with them; so much that Nora and Frank made half a dozen more which they decided to take with them on the outing and offer as gifts to anyone who liked them.

The Browne family made their own traditional pelau which included pumpkin and pigeon peas with the *arroz con pollo*. This would enhance the taste of the chicken as well as enable the dish to go further. Meg also prepared some boiled eggs which she dyed with different colours and made some little baskets to put them in, six at a time. These she intended to give as presents. Baskets of fruits were also prepared. Pedro was sent to collect as many different fruits as could be found on the estate. These included citrus, mangoes, pomme-cytere, caimite, soursop, sugar apple, and different varieties of bananas. He dropped off two bags of fruit and dashed off to the "junction" as he wanted to take part in the beating of the "Bobolee," an effigy of Judas Iscariot which villagers made every year. It was customary in villages throughout Trinidad to have a "Bobolee" bashing session, usually after church services, on Good Friday.

Pedro met his cousin Frank, who had also come armed with a stout stick, to join a group of boys who belaboured the hapless dummy with blows until head and limbs were severed from the body, its clothes torn to shreds and the coconut fibre stuffing disintegrated. Girls were not usually part of this vigilante mob but some stood around to cheer the boys as they completed the gruesome task. Vengeance for the betrayal Jesus having been achieved, Pedro saw Rebecca who was an occasional helper on the estate. He told her of the intended Easter Monday outing and asked her help with the care of the animals in their absence.

Rebecca was willing to oblige and said that she had seen a favourable omen that morning. It was a Good Friday custom to break an egg into a glass of water and observe the shape that resulted. It transpired that Rebecca saw a figure in a bridal dress.

This signified a forthcoming marriage and Rebecca thought of Millie instantly. She was happy to tell Pedro of this and asked him to convey the good news to Millie. Pedro assented, but the plight of his other sister, Olivia, came to mind. He said nothing of this, however, and returned home to tell his parents that the feeding of the animals on Easter Monday was taken care of.

Feeling over-heated after his exertions at "Bobolee" bashing, Pedro announced that he felt like going to the river for a swim and asked if any of his sisters cared to join him. His mother overheard this and said: "Don't any of you dare go swimming today! Good Friday is the day Our Lord died. Anyone who goes swimming on a Good Friday will turn into a fish!"

"I've still got to wash the sweat off me," Pablo replied.

"And our tank is low on water after this dry-season," Millie intervened. "I'll go with him to see that he doesn't swim."

"I'll go too," Olivia added.

"And me!" Maria chimed in.

So it was that the four youngsters traipsed down to the river that Good Friday; Pedro, with the conviction that here was his chance to debunk another "old wives" tale; Millie, with the feeling that she was needed to protect the younger ones from doing foolish things; Olivia, with the expectation that Pedro would do something exciting; and Maria, with the hope of joining in Pedro's daring-do.

The river passed through cultivated estates, the owners of which used its water for their crops especially in the dry-season. Cocoa, coffee, citrus and bananas were the main crops but other fruits were planted from time to time. A field of pawpaw came right down to the river's edge and one tree had fallen into the water. This is where the Browne family usually washed and bathed.

The basin, as they called the large pool used for swimming, was deserted that day. Pedro stripped to his underpants and sat on a rock with his feet dangling in the water. Maria, too, took off her dress and sat in her underwear on a boulder nearby. Millie had brought a book of poetry with her and sat under a tree where she soon became absorbed in her reading.

Olivia whispered to Pedro, "This is your chance. She's not looking." Pedro silently slipped into the water and dived under. He was a good, strong swimmer and could hold his breath for well over a minute. Ollie and Maria winked at each other as Millie read on.

Two minutes passed and Pedro didn't surface. Wrinkles of worry crossed Olivia's forehead.

"Millie!" Olivia called out. "Pedro dived under and he hasn't come up!" Roused from her reverie, Millie ran to the water's edge and peered into the coffee-coloured confection in which their brother was submerged.

"I counted a hundred and fifty!" Maria shouted, "and he's never stayed under this long."

The girls walked to the far end of the basin where the river flowed out behind a large rock, but he was not there. They walked back to see if he was playing a joke on them by hiding behind the fallen pawpaw tree. There was no sign of him. In desperation, Maria dived in to see if he was stuck somehow in tangled roots on the bottom. Lurking in the murky depths, there were shoals of coscorob, river mullet and the occasional morrocoy, but no Pedro. Had he turned into a fish?

Diving again this time nearer the pawpaw tree, she discerned what looked like a head about two feet under the surface of the water. The body it belonged to was obscured by the large leaves of the pawpaw tree. She surfaced and swam to the tree. Reaching across, she pulled out the stem of a pawpaw leaf which was sticking out of the water. A spluttering Pedro then emerged from the water.

"How dare you frighten us so?" Millie screamed at him. "Don't you know that Ollie is in a delicate condition? You could have caused her to lose the baby!"

"I didn't think of that," Pedro replied lamely. "I only wanted you to wonder if I had turned into a fish."

"You can only be a tadpole," Maria jibed. This broke the tension and a round of nervous laughter ensued. Relieved that nothing more untoward had occurred, they conspired to tell their parents nothing of the escapade.

Gloria Saturday saw the entire family at church. They first sought the grace of the Sacrament of Confession, then with the blessing of the holy water and partaking of the Eucharist, they resolved to reflect by their lives, the Resurrection of Jesus Christ. Millie prayed that the forthcoming union of herself and Albert would not be the cause of friction with his family and that both families would like and respect each other. The communal picnic on Easter Monday could set the scene for an amicable relationship. She prayed therefore that all would go well with their outing and it be a sign of happy days to come.

Easter Sunday was spent restfully and both Browne and Maclean families retired to bed before the chickens went to roost that day as they were to be up at three o'clock on the Monday morning to cook the food they were taking to the beach that day.

Chapter 55
The Excursion to Manzanilla

By six o'clock on Monday morning, everything was ready to be loaded on to Alphonso's large coach which was drawn by four splendid animals. The Maclean family had already been picked up and their baggage tied on top of the coach. The feeling of excitement was palpable. Olivia, however, felt miserably sick. It was the third month of her pregnancy and she thought she had gotten over her morning sickness. The feeling of nausea overcame her and she said she would stay home that day. Aunt Marie, who knew of her condition, had anticipated the situation and gave her a warm herbal drink from a thermos-flask (which she called an *icyhot*.) This seemed to work wonders as Olivia felt better almost immediately and was able to go on the trip.

In Arima, they were joined by Aunt Camille and Aunt Pauline, along with Julia, Helen and Aunt Pauline's husband, Jose. They had come on the early morning train and would travel back to Port of Spain on the last train that evening. They transferred their luggage to the waiting bus which had a CHARTERED sign emblazoned across the top of its windscreen and proceeded to Sangre Grande. The chatter on the bus was non-stop and excitable, as the relatives all had much to say to each other. At one point, the bus driver called out: "Ah feel ah should replace de fus R in the sign on the windscreen and put a T." This was met with blank astonishment by his passengers. It took a while for the penny to drop, but when it did there was so much laughter and explanations that the noise was even greater for a full ten minutes.

They passed through agricultural lands and came to Valencia, a small village named after the famed Spanish city. Journeying along the Eastern Main Road, they entered a forest reserve where tall trees stretched their branches over the road forming a canopy through which flickering sunlight could be seen. Mahogany vied with Mahoe, Mora and Cypre, each climbing for a share of the sun. Passing through Turure and Guaico, they came at last to Cunapo where the Sangre Grande Post Office stood in close vicinity of the Railway Station.

Albert had explained that his house was a mere quarter of a mile from the Police Station, which was a quarter of a mile from the Post Office. Millie stated: "We're nearly there. Only a half mile to go now."

"We'll see the sea at last," Frank exclaimed.

"No," answered Millie. "We'll see Albert's house. The sea is about eight miles away." A collective groan of disappointment came from the younger ones.

A gas station was located on the left, about a hundred yards past the Post Office and the driver pulled up there to top up his tank. Opposite, at the corner of the Coalmine Road and the Eastern Main Road, the sign on a large wooden shop proclaimed: "Marlay and Company No. 2." Donkey carts crowded the thoroughfare and Indian women in saris and men in dhotis could be seen peddling wares or walking about the streets.

As they continued their journey along the main road several business establishments could be seen; among them, Bata, The Pioneer Pharmacy, Petit's, Loinsworth's, The Red Store, Baksh, and on both sides of the road, before one came to the Police Station, Marlay and Company No. 1. These two buildings were sub-let to tenants. Albert's Barber Shop was one of them.

Albert had told Millie that the Mar families owned most of the properties in Sangre Grande. Apart from Marlay, there was Marhue, Marfoe, and Marchack. He believed they were all related. Other Chinese business people were the Chows, Aquis, Tankas, Honnocks, and Chins. This prompted Millie to ask him, "What about the Akongs?" To which he replied: "The Akongs were vanquished by Mah-jong." It was sometime later that she came to understand what he meant by that statement.

Five roads emanated from the junction where the Police Station stood in commanding view. These were Sukhram Road, Foster Road, Toco Road, and Eastern Main Road, east and west. Chow-Lin-On's shop, with a bakery behind it occupied the space between Sukhram Road and Foster Road. Adjacent to the Police Station on the Toco Road was the Warden's Office, and opposite that was the Apollo Cinema. In front of the Police Station stood a large pine tree, festooned with nests of the Corn Bird (*Crested Oropendola*). Millie had never seen so many of this species in one place. On the Eastern Main Road opposite the Police Station, was Aqui's grocery, Tanka's parlour, Long's parlour, and Ng Lee's laundry. Millie was taking it all in, as this was to become her town if she married Albert. Thomas, the "ice-man" was on the left and they stopped there to buy a block of ice so they could have cold drinks on the beach. On the right, was Cumberbatch Coffins and G. Clarke, Tailor.

Proceeding from there, they passed a small cocoa estate, crossed a little bridge next to Manning's Tailoring and saw the Presbyterian church on the right. This area had many long wooden barrack type buildings which housed workers from the cocoa, coffee and rubber estates. They stopped after the Fishing Pond Road junction where one of the long wooden buildings featured a corner-shop, some dwelling rooms, and a cocoa storehouse with a cocoa drying tray above. Just opposite, was Albert's home.

This was built on posts two to three feet above the ground and had a wooden front with jalousies and a small balcony (which Albert called the gallery) typical of the period. Albert's mother and three of his sisters, Edith, Celia, and Emma, were leaning over the railing of the balcony while two excited children stood in the open doorway clapping their hands.

Albert stepped out of the cocoa storehouse where he had been talking to Attao, the Chinese proprietor, and welcomed them to his home. It had been decided that time being short, only the Browne family would alight with Millie at this point, to meet with Albert's family at his home. Introductions with the others could be made later in the bus or on the beach.

They walked over a wooden bridge and up three steps to the doorway where the two children ran from them to hide behind Emma's skirt. Before entering, Marguerite (Millie's mother), said: "May the Good Lord bless this house and all who dwell within."

James added, "Amen to that."

Isabelle then came forward and embraced each one in turn, kissing them on both cheeks. "Thank you and thank *le Bon Dieu* that you have arrived safely. I am Isabelle, Albert's mother, but please call me Belle. All my friends do."

"And I am Marguerite, Millie's mother, but please call me Meg, and this is my husband James and children Millie, Olivia, Maria and Pedro." Introductions were then made all round, including the children, Amoy and

Marla. While this was being done Albert took Millie through to see his alterations.

New curtains fluttered in the windows as they made their way through to the back of the house where two new rooms were being added on. While most of the walls were wooden, some were of tapia (adobe) and Albert explained that this was for two reasons, heat and sound insulation. Tapia walls kept one cool when it was hot outside and wooden walls let too much sound through.

While the ceiling was now extended to cover the rooms, the floors were unfinished, and Albert said that the Mahoe hardwood flooring he had bought needed another month of drying-out before it could be laid without warping. He assured Millie that their rooms would be completed in three months' time and a wedding date could then be fixed.

Millie had dozens of questions she wanted answered but was mindful of the other passengers waiting in the hot, stationary bus. They hurriedly packed the bus with more luggage and a dozen more passengers clambered aboard. Among them were Albert's sister, Celia, and her two little boys, Kenric and Cedric. They lived in one of the barrack rooms nearby. The bus was on the final leg of their journey at last.

Albert sat next to Millie and named the places of interest as they passed. First was the newly built Mutual Help Friendly Society Hall, which acted as a community center for the town. In the daytime, it housed St. Andrews High School, a private school run by Mr Eastlyn Dasent. It was also hired for important meetings and entertainment functions. Its forecourt was even used as a blacksmith's yard. A large breadfruit tree rendered shade for the smithy's work. Next, they rumbled over the Cunapo river bridge and drove through a small coffee estate, resplendent with coffee berries. Abruptly this came to an end and a cluster of houses overlooked by the Anglican church sat nestled at the bottom of a hill.

They then ascended Bravo Hill and saw the Sangre Grande R.C. School on yet another hill on the right. Albert informed them that they were now in "Sangre Grande proper," Cunapo had been borrowing the name. Passing the St. Francis Roman Catholic Church on the left (where the bus passengers all made the sign of the cross) they climbed a slight rise and the Sangre Grande Hospital came into view. The doctor's quarters were built next to it. Then came other government-built quarters for the Magistrate and the Warden.

Leaving this behind they entered Sangre Chiquito, where they crossed a smaller river than the Cunapo river but with water of the same reddish-brown hue. Sangre Chiquito boasted many fine homes of estate owners (a few of which still stand today). They then journeyed through the village of James Smart where Albert's mother Isabelle informed them that the Akongs once owned land with a house and a small shop there. (Millie would learn the story behind that later).

Passing through many cocoa, coffee, and citrus estates, the bus struggled up Mount Calabash, after which it was downhill most of the way to Manzanilla. They passed a quaint Anglican church which Aunt Marie said looked Gothic in design. (No one knew quite what that meant, other than somewhat stark and old-fashioned). A road branched off to North Manzanilla on the left but they continued on to the right past a rum-shop which proclaimed itself the "First and Last Bar" and finally saw the sea, glistening through an array of coconut trees. The excitement was palpable, as the children all clapped their hands and shouted "The sea! The sea!"

Chapter 56
The Family Picnic

The bus was driven through a wide avenue between the coconut trees where there already were a few other vehicles. As the bus parked, two people emerged from a parked jitney. "That's my sister Darvis and her husband David Petit who own the Apollo Cinema," Albert intimated. David, a slim-built Chinaman, and Darvis, who looked Chinese, were the same height. Isabella, who was seated nearest the door, began to alight first and David helped her out as he greeted her.

"We thought it best to get here early and secure a picnic spot not too far from the parking area. The children have claimed it with their towels and stuff," David announced.

"Thank you. We can always rely on you to think of these things," his mother-in-law replied.

Introductions were then made as the passengers got out. Most of the luggage was unloaded and taken a short distance away to a shady area under some Almond and Sea-grape trees. Picnicking under coconut trees was considered hazardous as the nuts or even branches could fall and cause injury. The Petit children, Harry, Antonia, and Daphne, were then introduced and David, pointing at his wife's bulge, added: "And that one is going to be called Deryck, if it's a boy, or Olivia, if it's a girl."

"I hope it's a girl," Olivia, Millie's sister, chimed in, "then when I pray for myself and my baby I'll always add: "and for my namesake," but I won't forget her name." This caused a few embarrassed titters.

The children all wanted to run to the beach but were restrained and told they would be taken soon with adult supervision after they had eaten their lunch.

"I expected May and her family to be here by now so we could all start our lunch together. Eric, Albert's older brother, was going to bring them in his friend's truck," Isabella said.

"Don't worry Ma," Albert promised, "They will be here in the next ten minutes or so; it's just that Eric is a very careful driver, especially when he has children in the back of the truck." Just then, a Bedford truck came into view. Two people sat beside the driver at the front with one adult and seven excited children in the back tray.

The truck parked alongside the bus and its occupants got out. Albert went to meet them. He introduced them as: Eric, and May, his brother and sister, May's five children, George (who sat in the front), Lorna, Dolores, Romelda and Alexander. Then came Albert's youngest brother, Verne, and his two children, Annette and Adolph (Cora, his children's mother was ill and could not come). Verne had been in the back with the children, keeping them seated and doing his best to entertain them and avoid travel sickness.

The baskets, pots and pans and various utensils having been unloaded and brought to the picnic site, Albert's mother, Belle asked Meg if she would say a blessing prayer. This she did, thanking God for bringing the families together to share His gracious gifts and pleading His blessing on the engaged couple. Enamel plates of food were distributed with families inviting each other to taste the variety of different dishes prepared. Emma, with the help of her Indian neighbours, had made dhalpuri and goat curry which was a great favourite with many. Aunt Marie's "wild meat" dishes were praised and devoured till there was none left. Darvis's sweet and sour pork was tried by nearly every one and Meg's chicken pelau was the mainstay dish, especially with the children. Baskets of fruit were then distributed and partaken of mainly by the younger ones.

A typical food carrier in the days before plastics.

Emma and May asked for help to take the plates and dishes to the sea to give them a pre-wash before packing them away and most of the children volunteered. They were just too keen to get their feet in the briny. Celia said she and her children would tidy up the picnic area as a few fruit peelings could be seen around. This the boys did reluctantly as they too preferred the sea.

Meg announced that the baskets were a gift to the Akong family and Belle thanked her saying they would come in handy for collecting chip-chip. She then invited everyone on to the beach to dig in the wet sand for this shell-fish. She had brought some buckets with her for taking them home in. They then found themselves in little groups of three or four, each with a bucket and a basket or two and began gathering chip-chip. Meg, Belle, Millie and Albert formed a foursome and chatted while they dug up the shell fish. Meg asked about the property in James Smart and Belle related the story.

Her husband, Peter, was addicted to the Chinese game, mah-jongg. Usually he played with friends in Cunapo but one week-end he was invited to Port of Spain to play with some big businessmen there. When he did not return after a whole week away, Belle became very worried. Then, to cap it all, some Chinese men came to her with a bill of sale declaring that the house and land were theirs. Peter Akong had lost it all playing mah-jongg! Where was Peter? Why did he not come home? These were the questions Belle put to the men. Their answers were vague and non-committal. In desperation, she collared the youngest of the men and forced him to tell her where to find him.

She was given a week to vacate the property. Fortunately, the two donkeys and a cart they possessed were not on the bill of sale. Belle was able to load their belongings on to the cart and take her family to stay at her sister's home in Sangre Grande. She then went on to Port of Spain with her eldest son, Rodrick, seeking her husband. From the directions she was given, she found him in what could only be described as an opium den, in Charlotte Street. He was semi-conscious. With Rodrick's, help she loaded him on to the cart and took him back to Sangre Grande. He never fully recovered and died within a year.

Millie and her mother praised Belle for enduring such an ordeal and bringing up the children without a father. Millie then enquired, "Where is Rodrick? I suppose he had to be a bread-winner all of a sudden."

"The children all helped. Rodrick got a job on a steamship and sends me money. It's how we survived," Belle replied.

When they had filled all their containers with chip-chip, they played a game of cricket on the beach. Bats were made from coconut branches and Harry had brought a tennis ball. The rules were simple. Frank had made the bat, so he batted first. Harry bowled the first ball. Anyone who fielded the ball could either bowl or elect a bowler. Whoever took a wicket batted next. Only adult men were allowed to retrieve balls hit into the sea.

Darvis and Olivia took care of the toddlers while the older ones played. Whilst making sand castles they chatted about the latest fashions in clothing. Ollie promised to make Darvis a yellow cheongsam and Darvis agreed on condition that she, Darvis, provide Ollie with cloth for two dresses, one for each of them. Emma who had just had her turn at batting, having caught a ball, then joined them and they began discussing what they would wear for Albert and Millie's wedding.

They were so engrossed in their conversation that they didn't notice Marla move away from the others and start toward the sea. Frank saw the little girl and brought her back to the group. He then said, "I've brought some toys for the little ones." Going back to the bus, he brought them a cardboard box full of egg-shell rattles. He showed them how they worked and the children were all delighted to have one each.

Aunts Camille and Pauline meanwhile, had gathered together with Belle, Marie and Meg and were discussing how to cook the shell fish they had collected. The dish of choice was *accra,* and they all agreed that the shells be soaked in fresh water overnight to remove the sand and salt. Chives and chopped green tomatoes were a must to enhance the egg and flour batter, but it was debatable whether garlic and onions improved the flavour. Meg asserted that chadon bene was the most liked herb with her own family and the others agreed to try it.

Albert and Millie, after fielding for a while, drifted a little distance away, but within sight of the family and sat under the shade of an almond tree.

"I see your family is even more mixed-race than mine," Millie ventured.

"Yes," Albert replied, "but we are mainly Chinese and African, though Ma claims French, Spanish, and even Carib blood."

"I can see the Chinese influence in everyone except Emma and little Marla, who looks East Indian," Millie added.

"Marla's father was an Indian store owner who Emma worked for. I think I told you about that. And you've met Emma's father. She's a Cezair," Albert informed her.

"Oh!" Millie exclaimed, "I get the picture now. Tony was the one who had his lunch at your mother's."

"Yes, he felt sorry for us and offered help whenever he could; but he was already married."

Emma said nothing, but compared the situation with her own. If, as she suspected, her father was already a married man, would it not cause a great disruption in his family life to admit her as his daughter? Was she wrong to try and find out who he is? Should she stop questing and hoping to find him?

Her thoughts were interrupted by a call from Aunt Camille: "Come on you lovebirds, we've got to start getting ready to go home." They dusted themselves off and went to wash the sand from their feet. Returning to the picnic area, they helped carry boxes of wares to the bus and get the children cleaned up and boarded. James and the adult men in the party were having a final drink of rum and coconut water and the bus driver, who was not allowed to drink alcohol, tooted his horn impatiently. A count of heads was undertaken and checks for shoes, towels and other belongings took up more time as the men finished their drinks. Goodbyes were said to those who travelled independently and they began the return journey home.

Chapter 57
An Unexpected Passenger

Belle sat with Meg, Marie and Camille, who related how they had escaped the volcanic eruption of Mt. Pele by sailing to Grenada. Belle told them that her parents had come from Martinique's sister island, Guadeloupe and had taught her this song which she remembered from her youth:

Martinique est brulee
Fort de France est de feu
Ceux qui sont devant sont au bien devant
Ceux qui sont derriere sont au bien derriere.

The three Martiniquan sisters remembered hearing it as children and the four women sang it together to the amusement of the other passengers.

Millie then requested *Chevalliers de la Table Ronde,* which they all sang together. Bystanders on the road in James Smart and Sangre Chiquito must have wondered where these French people had come from. Their own driver had a bemused look on his face.

They arrived at Albert's home in Sangre Grande without incident and after a round of hugging and kissing, the Akong family disembarked with their luggage. The driver was thanked and given handshakes by which means tips were passed. They promised to meet again some time before the wedding and thanked the Browne, Maclean and Le Blanc families for their goodwill and friendship. The day's outing was pronounced a truly blessed occasion.

Before the bus could continue on its way to Arima, a young man pushing a bicycle with flat tires approached. Both Millie and Olivia exclaimed in unison: "It's Carlton Cardinez!" He came to the bus somewhat sheepishly and said: "I was hoping to surprise you in Manzanilla today, but I had four punctures on the way. I had two which I fixed before I got to Valencia. I only had two rubber patches. Then when I got to Guaico my front tire went flat. I couldn't find a repair shop in Cunapo. Everything is closed for the Easter holidays."

"I can take you back to Arima," the bus driver commiserated, "and you can tie the bike on the rack at the back of the bus."

"Thank you." A grateful Carlton sighed. As he secured the cycle, Olivia prepared a seat next to hers for him. "You must think me very presumptuous," Carlton said as he sat next to her. "But the truth is that when I heard you were going to spend the day at Manzanilla beach, I had this great urge to see the sea again. I've ridden to the beach before with friends and I thought I should do it again. Only this time, no one else wanted to come with me and I didn't realize the rubber inner tubes in my tires were perished."

"I'm sorry you didn't get your wish, but at least you're safe and can go to the beach another time," Olivia responded. They then sat in companionable silence for most of the way back to Arima.

Millie sat with Julia and Helen who regaled her with their new life experiences. Looking after other peoples' children was not as easy as they thought. The expectations of city bred children were much different from those of their rural counterparts. Helen's job was with the Chans, a couple who owned a furniture store in Port of Spain. The husband was often abroad leaving the wife to manage the shop. The wife was a patient of Dr Chalfont, with whom Julia was now employed. The good doctor had recommended Helen to Mrs Chan when his patient had complained of being overworked, managing the shop and looking after the children.

The three Chan children, Arthur, Bertha, and Chrissy were quite a handful. Arthur was eleven and had just started at Queen's Royal College; Bertha, nine, was attending a private school in St. Ann's; Chrissy, four, went to kindergarten.

Helen prepared their breakfast and took the two girls to their respective schools. Mrs Chan drove Arthur to school on her way to work in Port of Spain. Helen had to learn to cook eggs in different ways which were new to her. When one child wanted scrambled eggs, another wanted poached, or fried sunny-side-up. Having asked for and been served one thing, a child seeing what was on another plate, would demand that instead, or refuse to eat. Their mother would invariably give in to their wishes and so condoned their behaviour.

Helen said she didn't mind the extra work but because she considered it a sin to waste good food, she had already gained ten pounds!

Julia's experience was different. Her two young charges adored her and did everything she suggested. Only three and four years old, they yearned for a mother-figure in their lives. She took them to the park on a daily basis (where some strangers actually thought that she was their mother). Her visits to Talparo had become less frequent especially because of their mutual attachment. She even lamented not being able to bring them on this outing to the beach.

The bus arrived in Arima in time for those going on to Port of Spain to catch the train. Helen had been given an extra day off and was going to spend the night in Talparo. This pleased her family enormously. Olivia went to help Carlton untie his bike from the back of the bus and he summoned up enough courage to ask her if she would mind him visiting her in Talparo even when he carried no work for her. She laughed and said she would be flattered. He then confessed that he had decided to ride to Manzanilla especially to see her. And so began a courtship that would lead to the marriage foretold by Rebecca and her Good Friday egg.

Chapter 58
Ollie Receives a Suitor

Alphonso was in a good mood, having backed four winners and made himself a tidy profit. He was celebrating with some friends when his passengers arrived.

"Ah hope allyou enjoy yusself as much as me," he greeted them.

"We did," James replied. "And we brought you a bucket of chip-chip from Manzanilla."

"Tanks, de ole woman will like dat. Have a drink wid me before we set off." James duly obliged as the coach was loaded with their belongings and the passengers got on board. They were all glad that their bus driver had not indulged in alcohol and were comforted by the fact that dray animals were invariably sober.

As dusk was approaching, they arrived in Talparo and the Brownes were dropped off before the Macleans. Rebecca was glad to see them home safe and sound and happy for her share of chip. "Was Albert's family nice?" She asked Maria.

"They're good people, not posh, but respectable and I think Millie will be happy among them. There's an awful lot of them though and I couldn't remember all their names," Maria replied.

"So long then, see you tomorrow," Rebecca called out as she left.

The Brownes were surprised at the amount of sand they had brought home from Manzanilla beach and had to shake off sand from every item of clothing and wash themselves thoroughly before going to bed that night. Their mother said that as a child she remembered having to wash off ash from the volcano every night for a long time when they first went to Grenada. Millie was surprised that volcanic ash could spread that far. The shellfish were put to soak in rain water before they went to bed.

The following day, as they breakfasted on accra, Meg asked Millie if they were any nearer to setting the date for the wedding. Millie explained about the need to dry the flooring boards before laying; hence they would have to wait four months to complete the extension to the house. "You know that you have to see the priests in San Raphael, and in Sangre Grande, months before to have the Marriage Banns posted," Meg asked.

"Yes Mama, I know they like to read it at least three times at Sunday Masses," Millie replied.

"That is for your safeguard. You never know what some men will get up to. I heard of a sailor who had three wives, one in Trinidad, one in Grenada and the other in Barbados. The Bajan wife's brother happened to come to Trinidad and the bigamist was found out," her mother related. They all laughed at that and Millie told them that Albert's brother, Rodrick, was the only sailor in the family. Her mother already knew of him.

That evening they had a visit from Carlton Cardinez. He brought a pot containing a beautiful orchid plant in bloom which he presented to Meg as a token of appreciation for getting him home with his bicycle the day before. For Olivia, he brought a box of chocolates. Millie and the rest of the family discretely departed leaving Olivia and Carlton sitting on the front porch.

Pedro was sent to collect a very dry coconut husk, for the orchid needed repotting to a larger container, and Millie went to search among her books to find the species of the plant her mother was given. Other than the fact that it was an epiphyte, with roots that attached themselves to trees and absorb whatever moisture they could, Millie was unable to find a name for the orchid. She wished some botanist would devote time to study the orchids in Trinidad and write a book about them.

Perhaps she could encourage her brother Pedro, who sometimes brought home unusual orchids from the forest, to make a proper study of them. One can be named after him; *Pedbrownei Macrophyllium,* she mused. Her thoughts were interrupted by Olivia who came in to say that Carlton was leaving as he had a bus to catch and wanted to say goodbye. They bade goodbye to Carlton who promised to see them again at the weekend.

A beaming Olivia then gave them the news. Carlton had proposed to her and wanted to ask her father's permission. He had heard rumours of what Desmond had done to her and found out the truth. He even wanted to marry her next month, before the baby was born so that it wouldn't be called a bastard.

They were both surprised and heartened by this but her mother asked her: "Ollie, do you love him? You are in a desperate situation now and see him as a deliverer, but are you prepared to live the rest of your entire life with him?"

"Yes Mama, he is a good man, he is a joiner, whose work is respected and I don't care for any other man as much as I care for him. He was prepared to ride all the way to Manzanilla just to be with me."

Millie thought that this reply did not answer the first question properly and wondered if her mother loved her natural father and whether she still harboured affection for him. To dig into that affair at this time, however, was not appropriate and she let the matter drop. Instead, she congratulated her sister saying: "Glad for you, Ollie, we'll now have to get your Marriage Banns read in church before mine."

"Papa will agree, I'm sure, so when Carlton comes at the weekend we'll go and see the priest," Ollie replied.

Getting her mother alone in the kitchen as they washed the wares together, Millie asked her: "Mama, you wanted to know if Ollie really loves Carlton. It made me wonder Mama, did you love Papa James when you married him?"

"Yes child, I had a great affection and respect for him. I know you are thinking of romantic love, with heart fluttering whenever he's near; but think instead of the love you have for Jesus, the gratitude you feel because He gave up His life for us. That's how it felt then and later on, I didn't just feel safe in his arms, I wanted to hug him and kiss him. The romantic side took over."

"Thank you, Mama," Millie said, blushing. "I think that's how Ollie will feel."

The following Saturday morning, Millie accompanied Olivia and Carlton to the San Rafael church to have the banns published. Although Olivia wore a loose-fitting dress so that her pregnancy was not obvious, the priest seemed to know her condition and assumed that Carlton was the father to be. They chose not to disabuse him of that notion.

He informed them of the need to have the banns read in the groom's parish of Santa Rosa as well and they assured him that it would be done the following week. Millie then apprised him of her forthcoming marriage and he advised her to see him as soon as a date was fixed. He wished them all God's blessing and said in an aside to Olivia that he expected to see her in the confessional soon.

Olivia and Carlton's wedding was fixed for the second Sunday in June and Millie was the chief bridesmaid. Their wish was for it to be a very quiet affair with no more than a dozen close family members attending. Reluctantly, their wishes were obeyed.

Chapter 59
Millie's Last Concert and a Wedding Date

Albert cycled to Talparo one evening with the news that the two rooms were ready and they could now set a date for the wedding. Millie was relieved at this, yet somehow troubled. She was organizing the school's Christmas concert which she wanted to be the best so far (and she expected it to be her last). She would be happy not to have Mr Belix overseeing everything that she did, but sad to leave the school which seemed to have become part of her, almost a reason for existence. She had not even started on her trousseau. Other wedding preparations had to be made. She tentatively suggested, "How about a Christmas wedding?" Both Albert and her mother thought that sharing it with Christmas would somehow detract from its importance. Her mother proposed, "What do you think of January 24th, your birthday?"

"That would be splendid," Millie replied and Albert agreed. Plans were therefore set in motion for a January wedding.

Millie devoted her energy to producing the Christmas concert. She wanted it to be educational as well as entertaining. *Why not invent a marriage play for Joseph and Mary? It must have happened although it's not in the bible*, she thought. The Mozart opera, "*The Marriage of Figaro*," had just been aired and Millie heard the tune, courtesy of her friend Jerome Farfan. She made up her own Christmas carol and put it to the tune of Mozart's opera. This, her choir sang during the mimed marriage ceremony. She also composed a comedy song of her own called, *The Biggest Bunch of nanas in the World*, for which she used the tune of Gracie Fields' *The Biggest Aspidistra in the World*.

Reviving the practice of calisthenics, which seemed to have lapsed with the leaving of Mr Farfan, Millie had a chorus group do something she called "*dancercise*," which included a mixture of aerobics and dance performed to the music, "*Night and Day*," danced by Fred Astaire and Ginger Rogers in their recent film, "*The Gay Divorcee.*" With this, she introduced the slogan popular in England at the time: "*Use your Vigour to Keep your Figure.*"

Albert, along with several friends from Arima, had come to attend this concert. The applause at the end of the show was deafening, and Mr Belix, who had professed grave misgivings during rehearsals, felt compelled to offer his congratulations. With this, her last concert, proving to be a success, Millie felt the stage clear to make preparations for her wedding.

Part 4
Millie's Adult Life

Chapter 60
The Wedding

Olivia had undertaken the task of making the bridal gown as well as dresses for two bridesmaids. Millie wore a long white satin gown with a high neck, nipped-in waist and vertically pleated skirt. A white veil of tulle crowned her head and flowed to the floor behind her. It was kept in place by a coronet of pink rosebuds and Baby's Breath. Borrowed pearl earrings adorned her ears and on her feet were the ivory satin slippers worn once by her mother for her own wedding. Her petticoat was of pale blue, thus conforming to the tradition of wearing "something old, something new, something borrowed and something blue."

The bride's family travelled by horse-drawn coach to San Rafael. The groom's family, along with relations and friends were already there. The Akongs had hired a car in which the married couple would travel after the ceremony. Millie was amazed at the number of people who had turned up. January 24th happened to fall on a Friday and she did not expect that many people would be able to take time from work to attend. Also, there were many who had told her that a Friday was an unlucky day for a marriage, but at 2pm. the San Rafael church was already filled to capacity. A sizeable contingent from Arima took up a quarter of the pews on one side of the church. The other seats on that side were filled with the groom's family and friends.

As James Browne led Millie up the steps of the church to the vestibule, Amoy and Annette, dressed in frilly pink frocks, stepped forth to hold up the ends of her veil. The organ struck up the notes of *Here Comes the Bride*, and they walked in procession to the altar. Her step-father handed her over to Albert and Millie felt a chill come over her. It was a warm January afternoon like any other, yet to her it felt like a cold Christmas morning. She was having stage-fright! Albert held her hand reassuringly and she could feel the warmth of his fingers. Her mind wandered. Was her biological father in the congregation?

The priest had begun the ceremony and was asking: "Who gives this woman in Holy Matrimony?"

Her stepfather replied, "I do." This brought her back to her senses as she prepared to affirm her own "I do's" to the priest's crucial questions. Her mind was a blur as the apparently automatic responses were made by herself and Albert and she came to with something of a jolt as the priest announced: "I now pronounce you man and wife. You may kiss the bride." Albert's lips on hers felt hot and she felt a warmth suffuse through her body.

From somewhere high in the ceiling of the church, the notes of the *Ave Maria* seemed to waft down on the congregation. Celia, Albert's youngest sister, had asked to be allowed to offer her talent as her contribution to the wedding. It was a contribution Millie would remember for the rest of her life. To her, Celia's singing surpassed anything she had heard from gramophone records or real life. The tonal inflection swelled and diminished; the purity of the notes seemed to pull at one's heartstrings. At its conclusion, it took a great deal of will power not to burst out in unseemly applause in the house of the Lord.

Millie turned from the altar on Albert's arm and carrying the bouquet of roses handed her by bridesmaid Marla, they processed slowly down the aisle. A surprise greeted her as they stepped out the doorway of the church. Both sides of the pathway were lined with the teachers and pupils from her school. They had been given the afternoon off in her honour and were there to throw rice grains and flower petals in her path. Mr Belix must not have been such an ogre as she was making him out to be. Their heartfelt cheers brought tears to her eyes. She felt so honoured and humbled. According to the custom, she stopped and threw her bouquet over her shoulder without turning to see who caught it. (She learned later that it was her cousin Nora.)

The best man, Jean Cezair, opened the car door for her and Millie stepped into a motorcar for the first time in her life. Albert got in from the other side and sat beside her. They cruised slowly around the little square in front of the church and horse-drawn coaches fell in behind them. The couple waved at cheering by-standers. They then set off for Arima.

The reception was arranged to take place at Apang's restaurant in Arima as this was seen as a convenient mid-point for guests from Talparo, Port of

Spain and Sangre Grande. Albert had suggested it and James agreed as long as he, as the bride's father, was paying the expenses. Music was supplied through the courtesy of Jerome Farfan who came with a large selection of records and his gramophone. The Farfans had undertaken to prepare the restaurant for the wedding and made a splendid job of it. Millie thought it looked decorated for royalty.

As the wedding party arrived, they were greeted at the door with glasses of wine or fruit juice. The newlyweds and close family were led to seats at a long table on a dais at the end of the room. James Browne asked that speeches and toasts be kept short as many had to travel long distances that day. He thanked all the guests for attending and all those who worked to make the day an enjoyable one for the couple. He asked God to bless food and guests, then called on the best man to say a few words.

Jean Cezair began by saying: "I was robbed. I saw her first." This brought titters of amusement from the crowd, many of whom knew of his initial flirtations. He went on to congratulate his good friend Albert on capturing 'a rare prize from the souk of feminine pulchritude'—a woman with brains to match her beauty. *(In those days, he would not be labelled sexist.)* After extolling the virtues of both bride and groom, he concluded with a quote from George Bernard Shaw which again brought his audience to mirthful laughter: *"Marriage is popular because it combines the maximum of temptation with the maximum of opportunity."*

Albert was asked to speak next and refuted his friend's accusation. "If two boys are walking along the road and one sees a ripe mango high up on a tree and sits down to admire it while the other fetches a rod and picks it, who deserves it more?" This elicited peals of laughter from the guests. "I was also careful to ensure that the fruit was sound. As a barber, I get customers from all over. I asked Mendoza, a Talparo farmer, what he knew of Millie. He said that there wasn't a more decent, kind, and thoroughly desirable young lady than Miss Le Blanc in all the land. I am certain I picked the best fruit from the orchard."

"Let the feast begin!" the cry arose and they tucked into the fare.

211

Chapter 61
The Honeymoon?

After the ceremony of the cutting of the cake, during which Celia sang the popular song of the time, "*I only have Eyes for You,*" Albert announced that he and his bride were leaving but the festivities should carry on. His friends supposed that they were headed to a secret honeymoon destination but the couple didn't disillusion them. As they entered the car, Olivia came up with Millie's grip containing her toiletries, nightgown and other clothing. "Don't forget this," she said. "I forgot mine at my wedding, much to my embarrassment. We'll send your other things later."

Their car, which was fairly quiet on the trip from San Rafael to Arima, rattled noisily as they took off. The driver said, "Not to worry, I'll fix that soon." When they got to the outskirts of Arima, to the area later to be known as the Wallerfield American Army Base, he stopped the car and going to the back of it untied an assortment of tin cans, old boots and a cardboard sign saying JUST MARRIED.

"That must have been done by your friends copying what they saw in the films!" Millie said. "Probably the Cezairs or the Quesnels."

"Most likely, the Aquis;" replied Albert, "they are always playing tricks on people." They were able to continue their journey without further stoppages.

Millie and Albert in the taxi arrived at their home in Sangre Grande well before the horse-drawn carriages carrying his family, just as he hoped they would. Alighting from the car, Albert picked up his bride and carried her over the threshold. He merely had to turn the knob and push open the front door. It was unusual to lock doors in those days.

Milton, the chauffeur, followed and deposited Millie's grip, wishing them a long and happy union. Hand in hand, the couple walked through to their private apartment at the back of the house, Albert carrying Millie's grip in his free hand.

(What happened next is censored.)

Chapter 62
Millie Gets Acquainted
with New Surroundings

Millie awoke with a start. She was in a strange room with someone in bed next to her. Memories came flooding back in a tidal rush. She was now Mrs Akong, Albert's wife. She felt tired but happy, remembering the events of the previous day and night. Somewhere in the distance someone was singing. It was one of the latest tunes to hit the musical world: *Night and Day.* Millie recognized the voice; it was Celia's, Albert's sister. The smell of wood smoke was also seeping into the house.

Rising gently so as not to waken the sleeping Albert, she tiptoed to the window and peeped out. Celia was putting a metal tray full of balls of dough into a clay oven. Her mother Isabelle came around the side of the house and chided her, "Celia, you're going to wake the couple. I know you have to use my oven, but do it quietly."

"But ah singin' very quiet," Celia replied. "An' anyway, it gone seven o'clock."

Millie noted that her speaking voice was coarse compared with her singing voice and wondered why this should be so. Just then a hand on her shoulder startled her. The talking voices had woken Albert and he whispered in her ear: "Let's go back to bed," Millie complied to her husband's wishes.

Later that day, Millie and Albert sat at the breakfast table with Isabelle, Emma with Marla on her lap, and Amoy. Some of the hops bread Celia had baked were on a large plate on the table. A dish of saltfish Bul jol and one full of boiled eggs stood on either side of it. With this, a butter dish containing salted butter and a slab of cheese on a plate comprised the eating menu. A jug of black coffee and one of cocoa tea (drinking chocolate) sweetened with condensed milk completed their fare.

"I hope you slept well and that crazy daughter of mine didn't wake you too early with her singing. She should have been born a bird," Isabelle apologized.

"Not at all," Millie replied, "I think she has a beautiful voice." Slicing open a hops bun and spreading butter on it, Millie added, "And she is a great baker too."

"Yes, I must admit she makes good bread," Isabelle conceded. Under her breath she muttered, "And she's too quick to have another bun in her oven." Millie's sharp ears caught this but she said nothing and passed a hops bun to Amoy whose reach was too short from her sitting position.

"Thank you, M-Miss," Amoy ventured hesitantly. "Can I call you Miss or Ma, I call grandmother Gran and my mother Mammy."

"I'd be happy for you to call me Ma," Millie responded, smiling graciously, "Miss, will make me think I'm back at school again."

"I thought you said you loved being a schoolteacher," Albert reminded her.

"I do, but there's a time and place for everything," Millie replied. "Well, I was hoping that you would help Amoy learn her lessons. She's a bit behind especially in Arithmetic."

"We can put that right, if Amoy wants to that is," Millie replied.

"Oh yes, I want to get a good job in an office," Amoy chirped.

"Then we'll start next week, shall we?" Millie decided.

After breakfast, Millie volunteered to wash the wares but Emma said that it was her job. Albert then decided to take her around and introduce her to the neighbours. They went first next door to the Hosany family, whose dhalpuri Millie had tasted on the picnic. Mr Hosany was at work on his estate in Caigual but Mrs Hosany was happy to meet her but said: "Me nah no who time papa come home." She introduced her to her children, Esau, Ushoo, Khartoun, Pauline, Hazra, and Ooshman, the baby. She offered Millie some curried baingan (eggplant) and roti which they declined, having just had breakfast, but accepted a bag of pulowrie and pepper sauce to take home. It occurred to Millie that in Talparo they had little or no contact with Indian culture and she realized that their version of English was quite different from the dialects spoken by Africans or Chinese.

After dropping the bag of pulowrie home, they crossed the road to Attao's barracks. On the corner with the Fishing pond road, he had opened a small grocery shop. In the middle section were the living quarters and at the far end, a storeroom for cocoa and coffee beans, with a traditional cocoa drying tray with a sliding roof on rails above. Attao was pleased to see them and introduced Millie to his two assistants, Ah Chee and Chin Poo. They spoke limited English but smiled and bowed profusely. Attao took Millie's hand in his and asked: "You let me be Godfadda for fus baby?" Taken aback by this sudden request, Millie was lost for words. Albert seized the opportunity and said: "Then you come to church with us tomorrow."

"But baby not born yet," Attao countered. They all laughed at this. (Attao was known as a lapsed Buddhist who loved to eat meat.) Taking leave of the Chinamen, they re-crossed the road to the smithy's.

Mr Collymore, the blacksmith, was a Bajan (Barbadian) who had married a Trinidadian and now plied his trade in Sangre Grande. He was busy at his bellows and hummed a tune to himself as he worked the handle up and down to fan the flames to a white heat. He continued his work as he greeted his guests, only pausing to wipe his calloused hands on a towel to shake Millie's hand for an instant. He had bent a length of steel into a circle and was in the process of welding the ends together to form the outer rim of a wagon wheel.

"Oi be thinking as it's me missus that'll like to meet with ye most," Mr Collymore offered. "I'm more than pleased mesself mind you."

"Oh, we're popping in to see her next. Your singing is what attracted us here first," Albert replied. "We didn't mean to disturb you."

"When oi work with a tune for company the work's easier and faster," the blacksmith explained.

"Well sing away, then," Albert declared as they turned back and went to the house next door and called out: "Good Morning."

Mrs Collymore, her hair tied in a flower-patterned scarf and a white apron around her waist, greeted them at the door. "We been expecin' to meet you for a long time; ever since we heard Albert was getting married. Sorry we couldn't accep' de invitation to de weddin' as de mistah had to wo'k." She shook Millie's hand and invited them into her drawing room.

"We know that work comes first and we were foolish to have the wedding on a Friday but it was my birthday," Millie explained.

"Ah! Now I understand. So Albert is your birthday present." They laughed at that and Millie claimed that it was the best birthday present she'd ever had. They sat in Morris armchairs similar to the ones the Brownes had in Talparo and sipped glasses of iced orange juice. The weather was already hot at ten o'clock that morning. Mrs Collymore asked Millie: "What you tink of Sangre Grande?"

"I think it's full of nice people," Millie replied and asked in her turn why Mrs Collymore had chosen to live here rather than go to her husband's island of Barbados.

"Dem Bajans too prejudice," was the reply. "De white ones call me 'usban a red nigger an' the blacks call 'im a 'bino white. Here e's just Collie the blacksmith. We have a lotta mix people here an' it doan matter what 'e look like," Mrs Collymore elaborated.

"Yes," Millie acquiesced. "I suppose we are the melting pot of all races and cultures."

"Well, I must be what the typical Trinidadian is aiming for. My mother claims she has the blood of four or five different races," Albert interjected.

"Yes, you is a proper *travesau*," Mrs Collymore agreed. They took their leave then as Albert said he had to visit his sister or she would complain forever.

They re-crossed the road and went to the long barracks opposite the Presbyterian church. There, in front of her apartment, was Celia. She was at her washing tub scrubbing away and singing as though she was the happiest person in the world. "I t'ought I'd see you dis morning. Ma said I woke you up."

"Don't worry about that," Millie reassured her. "We weren't asleep and you were singing a lovely song. We appreciated it." They were invited to sit on a long wooden bench outside her front door and offered a glass of lemonade each.

"It'll only be a quick visit," Albert said, "as we promised Ma we'd be home before twelve for lunch. I wanted to introduce Millie to her new neighbours."

"Some o' dem you could leave out or they'll cause you more trouble dan you bargain for," Celia replied.

Millie, sensing that this could lead to an argument she wanted to avoid, asked: "Where are Kenric and Cedric?"

"School yard," Celia answered. "Dey playing with friends; dey coming home for lunch jus' now."

"We want to see how Verne getting on with his house," Albert declared, "so we must leave you now."

"Thanks for the lemonade," Millie added. "And thanks for the delicious hops bread you made this morning."

Celia smiled, "Dat's nottin."

Albert led Millie up the Fishing Pond road past the Sangre Grande Government School on the left and up to a wooden house being built on the right. "This is the house that Verne is building," he informed her. The galvanized roof was up and so were the flooring and most of the walls but doors and windows were yet to be installed. Verne was at the back planning a length of wood as they arrived. "I didn't expect to see you today," he said. "I thought you'd still be in bed."

"Not everybody like to stay in bed as much as you." Cora, his pregnant wife, reproved him as she came out of the one finished room of the house. "Good morning, you must be Millie," she smiled, offering her hand. "I'm sorry I missed the picnic on the beach and your wedding."

"Don't worry about that," Millie replied taking her hand. "We'll soon get to know each other very well as you're so close." Indeed, they were close enough for Isabelle to be their handiest baby sitter whenever they needed one.

Annette and Adolph appeared at that moment and came forward to give their visitors a hug. Annette was four and a half, and Adolph just two years old. Millie had met them on the Manzanilla outing but couldn't remember their names. On her enquiry, Albert replied jokingly, "Annette is the pretty princess and the other one is the powerful Adolph Hitler. He rules this house."

Hitler was flexing his muscles in Germany that year and had just told the League of Nations to "mind its own business" when it complained about Germany's treatment of Jews. It was unfortunate that when little Adolph Akong was named, two years before, Adolph Hitler had just been declared Fuehrer and Reich-Chancellor for life. He had also gained popularity by cutting income tax for large families. The full malevolence of his dictatorship was not yet recognized. The name Adolph had therefore not acquired its unpleasant stigma.

"He's adorable to me," Millie asserted, picking up the little mite. "When you find him too tiresome you can always pass him on to me."

"I'll remember that," Cora declared.

"And Annette too," Millie added, conscious of the fact that Annette was feeling left out and had climbed on to Albert's lap as he sat on his brother's workbench. "Annette looked very special as she carried my veil at the wedding," Millie complimented. Annette beamed a beautiful smile at her then coyly hid her face on Albert's chest. "When is the baby due?" Millie enquired.

"In six months' time. If I carry it that long, that is," Cora replied.

"We'll pray that you do," Millie reassured her. The two women then went on a tour of the house.

As they stepped into the relative privacy of the main bedroom, Millie asked, "Is there a problem with any of the neighbours?"

"None at all. Why do you ask?"

"It's just that Celia hinted that I should avoid meeting some of them."

"Oh. I see!" Cora exclaimed. "That's because old Mrs Marshall is supposed to have told Louis, the father of Celia's boys, that she's carrying on with another man. The Marshalls have a little parlour next to the Hosany barracks. Mr Marshall is a shoemaker."

"Then, so that I won't be seen as taking sides, I have at least to pay them a courtesy visit," Millie declared. She wondered why Albert hadn't visited them on the way to Celia's but decided not to ask him.

On their way back home, as they reached the junction, Millie said, "Let's buy some peppermints. I can see a jar full of them on that counter in the parlour across the road." They crossed and entered the parlour where Ivy, the younger of the two Marshall daughters, was serving behind the counter. Her father, the cobbler, was cutting a piece of leather to shape at the back of the room.

"Good morning, Ivy," Albert announced. "I'd like you to meet my wife, Millie."

"Ah, so you're really married den," Ivy exclaimed. "I mus' call Ma."

There was no need for Ivy to call, because her mother appeared through the door at that instant inquiring: "Who is it?"

"Mrs Marshall, I've brought my wife to meet you," Albert answered.

"Good morning Miss. No, I should say Mrs Akong. I'm pleased to meet you. You captured the man lots of local girls were trying to catch," Mrs Marshall enthused. "Call me Millie, Mrs Marshall. And I didn't catch him, it was more like I fell into his net."

Mr Marshall had come across from his workbench and introduced himself to Millie. "I'm Malcolm Marshall, Millie, and I hope you would get your dainty feet shod by me in future."

Millie laughed at this, and Albert replied, "As she only takes size four, the children's selection you have on show will do her fine." They bought three penny worth of peppermints and took them home in a bag.

Chapter 63
Millie Goes to Her New Church

On Sunday morning, Isabelle was up bright and early. Millie could hear her bustling about the house from six o'clock. They were to attend the seven thirty Mass and Isabelle believed that nothing should pass their lips before receiving Holy Communion. Children under the age of seven only could have breakfast. Millie poured water from the ewer into the porcelain basin of the set they had received as a wedding present and washed herself. She brushed her teeth; then having checked through the window that the outhouse was vacant, hurried out to do her business.

Albert rose himself out of bed as she re-entered the house and Millie poured water from the refilled ewer into the basin for him. "Are you going to shave?" she asked.

"No need to, it's the Chinese in me. I shave once a week. We are not a hairy people." They were both dressed and ready for church when Isabella knocked on the interconnecting door at seven o'clock.

"We are ready Ma," Albert said. "I know it takes you half an hour to walk to church."

"It's that Bravo Hill, it troubles me rheumatic knees," his mother admitted.

The walk to church was pleasant in the early morning air. A few people caught up with them and lingered to exchange a few words on their way to church. They arrived as the last bell was ringing the stragglers in. As they blessed themselves in the vestibule on entering, Millie noticed a sign which said that baptisms of legitimate children would take place on Sundays and illegitimate ones on Saturdays. She wondered what Christ would think of that and thought about discussing it with the parish priest. The Akongs went to a pew with their name on the front railing and knelt to pray. The organ struck up the notes of the entrance hymn and people rose to sing: *"Lord of all*

Hopefulness, Lord of all Joy." It was a hymn Millie knew and sang lustily. The words gave her comfort in this new stage of her life.

In his sermon, the priest, a first-born Irishman like so many others, thanked the Good Lord for adding Millie to his flock. She was surprised that he recalled her name, then remembered that he must have read it out three times in the marriage banns quite recently. Many heads in the congregation had turned to look at her and Millie smiled back graciously. She recalled what Mrs Marshall had said about the local girls "trying to catch" Albert and wondered if any of those present were envious of her.

As they left the church after Mass, a few people approached to offer best wishes and congratulations. Among them were the Charleries, who invited them in for coffee on their way home. Fiette Charlerie was Isabelle's widowed sister who lived at the foot of the hill where the Sangre Grande R.C. School was built. She and her husband had taken Isabelle and her family in after they had lost their home in James Smart. Fiette had three grown-up sons, Aldon, Joseph and Farrell. Aldon lived at home and was a tailor.

Water from an earthenware goblet was their first drink of the day, as was the custom after receiving Holy Communion. The coffee, served in what they called *demi-tasses,* was strong and bitter. Isabelle was especially glad to have the coffee, without which, she said, she would have fallen by the wayside. Fiette apologized for not being able to attend the wedding ceremony, but Aldon had made it to the church. Millie had only vaguely remembered meeting him, there were so many different names to remember and faces were just a blur.

Chapter 64
Lunch and an Impromptu Party

When they reached home, Celia was there. She had gone with her children to the six o'clock Mass. Millie wondered how she managed to get the children and herself ready so early, without anybody to help her. Celia had come over to help prepare lunch for them. They invariably had chicken on a Sunday and she had cut up and marinaded the chicken ready to be made into a pelau. She often had Sunday lunch with the family. Millie tried to help but was told that she was the guest of honour and the best way she could help was by keeping the children amused. This she did by teaching them to sing *Frere Jacque*. They enjoyed it.

Albert went out the back to pick coconuts so they could have coconut water with their lunch. He also came back with two ripe Avocado pears which were about to be pecked by the birds. Their backyard was a mini orchard which also boasted two mango trees (Julie and starch), a cherry tree and a pomme-cythere tree. A few Rhode-Island and Leghorn hens ruled over by a strutting Rhode-island cock, roamed the yard. Millie was to spend many an hour there in quiet solitude in years to come.

Their Sunday lunch was a garrulous affair, with questions being asked (mainly by the children) about life in Talparo (which they thought of as being in the bush). They, in turn, were happy to chat about the films they were allowed to see in the Apollo cinema. Kenric and Cedric were in raptures describing the exploits of the masked crusader, Zorro. The adults wanted to know all about Millie's family and how they had escaped from Martinique. She told them as much as she knew.

After lunch, they decided to play games and two packs of cards and a jigsaw puzzle were brought out as well as the chess board and pieces. Albert invited Millie to learn the game of chess which he was teaching Kenric. She agreed to watch as he explained the game to his young nephew. The names of the pieces she already knew, but the movements, of the knights in particular, she found perplexing. The other adults in the room were engrossed in games of All-fours.

Relatives popped in to visit from time to time so that by tea time there were over two dozen people in the house. The remnants of the wedding cake were finally distributed and so were the sweet-bread and other cakes and pastries that some of their visitors brought. This was the at-home Sunday evening wedding party that many of them had expected. Wines and other liquor were consumed by the adults while the children were allowed a little Cherry Brandy along with their fruit juices and coconut water.

One of Albert's apprentice barbers turned up with a violin and two other guests brought guitars. To Millie's surprise Albert produced a mandolin, and music and singing filled the room. There was no room for dancing unfortunately.

Chapter 65
A Visit from Talparo

On the Monday morning, Millie received a visit from her two sisters and her brother, Pedro. They brought with them a sea chest containing most of Millie's belongings. They had hired a donkey cart from the railway station to take them with their luggage to the Akong's home. The cart driver promised to return for them at twelve. As Olivia brought her baby, Maurice, with her, they needed Pedro to help Maria carry their luggage. Pedro had also brought her a wedding present of an ice-box he had made for her. This could hold a twenty-five pound block of ice which would normally last two days. They were impressed with Millie's apartment and Olivia invited Millie to visit her new house which her husband Carlton had built in Raglan Street, Arima.

Marla, Emma's toddler, wanted to play with Maurice the baby who held her finger in his chubby little hand. Emma and Olivia went into Emma's room where they put Maurice on the bed to play with Marla while Maria and Pedro helped Millie unpack. The sea chest, which belonged to Uncle Ian, had to be returned that day. Olivia and Emma had much in common to talk about although their babies were a year different in age. By the time Millie's bits and pieces (mainly books and handicraft materials) were stored away, the transport had arrived to take her siblings and the baby back to the station.

"But I thought you would stay for lunch," Isabelle complained.

"Sorry, we should have said. Because of the train times we can't," Maria apologized.

"Then you must take some with you. Because you liked the curry and roti we took to the beach so much, I made you some. But this one is only Sada roti," Isabelle insisted.

"Thank you, you've been very kind," Olivia responded.

After her visitors had departed, Isabelle scolded Millie for not getting them to stay at least for lunch. Millie assured her that no disrespect was intended as the transport arrangements were at fault and after all the roti was gratefully accepted. That appeased her somewhat and they sat down to their own lunch. They were joined by Amoy who came over from the Government School nearby for lunch as she usually did.

"You'll come over after school for our first lesson, won't you?" Millie asked her.

"Oh yes," Amoy replied. "I wanted to come yesterday too but Mammy said you were having a private party and anyway, I should spend more time with her at home."

"You would have been welcome, but your Mammy is entitled to spend time with you too," Millie conceded. Whether Amoy agreed with her Millie was not sure, but she felt determined to give Albert's daughter the best chances in life she could.

At lesson time, Amoy confessed that remembering her multiplication tables was one of her biggest problems and Millie encouraged her to write them out and look for patterns. This she did. Not all of them had discernible patterns but she soon noticed that the sum of all the digits in the three times table always added up to three, six or nine and the five times table always ended in a five or nought.

The nine times table which she had always found difficult, revealed two secrets. Apart from always adding up to nine, the units digit decreased by ones from nine to nought while the tens digit increased from one to nine! Amoy was thrilled with this discovery and told Millie that she should come and teach at her school. Millie suggested instead that Amoy become a pupil teacher and Amoy agreed to think about it.

She claimed that she normally found schoolwork too boring. Millie tended to agree with her but said instead that it could be made interesting and turned into fun. Millie remembered the hours of tedious mechanical recitation she herself had to endure as a child and decided to present a new way of learning to Amoy. Amoy had expressed admiration for Millie's script/cursive hand-writing and Millie made penmanship one of her first lessons.

Chapter 66
Millie's Introduction to Cunapo

The next day Millie thought she should visit the town of Cunapo and get a feel of the neighbourhood. Albert had left for work early as he normally did. Emma wanted to accompany her but Millie said she wanted to see how the townsfolk would react to a complete stranger.

She walked at a brisk pace and was soon at the crossroads by the police station. Entering Aqui's shop, she bought a packet of salted prunes. The proprietor looked at her carefully and said that he felt sure he had met her before. Millie had no recollection of him but told him that she had been at an Aqui's wedding in Arima some time ago. He immediately remembered and said: "You were dancing with Al Akong! You must be the new bride! I heard he was getting married!"

"You know my husband then."

"Of course, everybody know him, he's my barber," the shopkeeper expostulated. He made it sound as if it would be a heinous crime for anyone in Cunapo not to know Al Akong. Taking her leave of him, Millie wandered as far as Andre Street before crossing the road between a parade of donkey carts and came to the end of the longest building in Cunapo, the Marlay building. Walking past the haberdashery and grocery shops she came upon the rum shop where Albert must have worked before he became a barber.

As she was tempted to look in, a wolf whistle from a group of young men made her avert her gaze and walk on. Coming to the barber shop with its red white and black painted pole outside, Millie marched straight in and saw Albert shaving an elderly gentleman. He was deftly shaping the man's sideburns as conversation in the saloon suspiciously stopped and Albert looked up to see Millie smiling at him. "What a surprise! I didn't know you were coming today." Albert grinned. "Everybody, this is my wife, the reason you didn't see me here most Saturdays. This is the lady I was courting."

"Congratulations!" The hearty collective response sounded loud in the narrow barbershop. One of the waiting customers offered up his seat to Millie as Albert finished by swabbing Limacol on the cheeks of his client. The gentleman was encouraged to examine his newly shorn features in the mirrors before he departed. The barbershop boasted four pairs of large mirrors which faced each other, two at each barber's station. There were three other barbers at work. One was Mr Valdez, who had visited on Sunday with his violin, another was Alexander, Albert's nephew, and the third a Mr Johnson, who because he was a new apprentice, occupied the station next to Albert.

"Please carry on with your work," Millie exhorted. "I didn't come to be a distraction."

"You can be a most welcome distraction anytime," Valdez retorted. The only other time women visited this bastion of masculinity was when mothers brought their sons in and waited with them. The conversation among the clients which was jocular at first now sounded subdued. Millie decided not to make it a habit of visiting.

She intended to make the most of this visit, however, and observed her surroundings carefully. Above each mirror was a different motto. Most of them had to do with time:

Time and tide wait for no man. Do not put off for tomorrow what you can do today. Time, you old gypsy man, Will you not stay, Put up your caravan, Just for one Day? "The time has come," the Walrus said, "to talk of many things: Of shoes...and ships...and sealing wax...and cabbages and kings." There is a tide in the affairs of men, which, taken at the flood, leads on to fortune; omitted, all the voyage of their life is bound in shallows and in miseries.

Finally, Millie noticed a grandmother clock at the end of the room. On the face of it, in gold letters was written: *TIME IS MONEY.* She thought to herself: *I have learned a little today about my philosopher husband by coming here.*

Albert dispatched his last customer just as the clock was striking twelve and Millie rose to walk home with him for lunch. "You have a good clientele." She complimented him.

"Yes," he agreed, "the numbers swelled when my brother-in-law, who was also a barber, left and went down south. There is more money in the oil-fields."

Millie wondered which brother-in-law, but decided not to ask him. She would find out in due course. She asked him instead, about the writings on the wall and he admitted that having inherited the first two from Tony Cezair, he began his own collection.

"I thought you two would be coming home together, and I was right," Isabelle said as she saw them. "The food is on the table as soon as you wash your hands."

During their meal, Millie made it clear that she would not make it a habit to visit the barbershop, just in case Albert got the wrong impression.

Chapter 67
Some Women Are Luckier than Others

After Albert had returned to work, Millie found herself alone with Emma in the drawing room. "Your sister Olivia is a very lucky woman," Emma said to her. "We had a long chat the other day. To get a good man to marry you when you have another man's baby is not easy."

"Well, I suppose we are a lucky family," Millie replied. "It happened with my mother too."

"I could see that James Browne is not your real father. Do you know who your real father is?" Emma asked.

"No. my mother would never tell anybody. When I was younger, I desperately wanted to know, but now, sometimes I feel almost afraid to find out. I'm sure it would cause unhappiness," Millie explained.

"But it already caused unhappiness," Emma argued. "No woman is happy to be raped; and is a child without a father happy? The man responsible should pay for his sins."

Millie pondered this for a while then asked, "Did you tell Marla who her father is?"

"Yes. I can't afford everything for her so I took her to him one day when his wife wasn't around and told him what I wanted. I got him to help."

"How did he react to Marla?" Millie wanted to know. "He actually held her and said she was a pretty little girl. Marla giggled at him and he kissed her." Millie considered this situation and reflected that it was quite different from hers. Each situation is unique; different players with different characteristics are cast in every scene. Would her father be fond of her? She somehow doubted it. He might be too full of recriminations.

Marla was having her afternoon nap and they went quietly into the bedroom to see that she was all right. As she lay on her side peacefully sleeping

Millie envisioned her as a grown teenager with long black plaits; her large dark eyes twinkling with humour. She would attract men like flowers in bloom attract bees. Would the same type of fate befall her? Illegitimacy seemed to run in some families. A feeling of inferiority was somehow branded on its victims. It was a stigma which was perpetrated even by the Catholic Church. She remembered her priest telling her that if she was accepted as a nun, she'd never be Mother Superior, because of her birth. Martin de Porres couldn't become a priest because he was illegitimate. Men of social standing would shy away from marrying an illegitimate girl. She, Millie, was indeed lucky to be a respectable married woman today.

Millie kept her thoughts to herself and complimented Emma on bringing up Marla to be a well-behaved, well-adjusted little girl. Emma said that her mother deserved the praise. Without her help and the help of all the family, she just wouldn't have managed. Even now, it was only by doing her sister Darvis's laundry that she was able to feed and clothe her daughter. Millie said to herself: "And, by living in the house that Albert built." She immediately chided herself for thinking the uncharitable thought. "God helps us carry our burdens," she said, "so let's give Him the praise due to Him also."

"I say Amen to that," Emma replied.

Chapter 68
Preparations for Carnival

The following month saw preparations being made for Carnival. It seemed that in Sangre Grande most families had at least one member who took an active part in it. Albert's brother, Verne, wanted to portray a *Mid-night Robber*. His wife Cora needed some help with making his black velvet costume. Millie volunteered to help sew on the sequins. Verne wanted a honey-comb pattern across his chest which neither Cora nor Millie felt capable of executing, so they suggested going to Arima to seek the help of Olivia. Leaving the children with their grandmother, Cora, Verne and Millie took the train to Arima one day.

Olivia was delighted to see her sister and to show her the house Carlton had built for them. She was also happy to show her skill in pleating the material and producing just the pattern Verne wanted. She had the basic costume assembled in short time. Her toddler Maurice was delighted to have Aunts Millie and Cora and Uncle Verne play with him in the mean while.

Carlton had also had lead piping laid from the standpipe at the corner of the road to his home, so they had a tap over his kitchen sink and didn't have to carry water from the standpipe. It came through a meter, however, and he had to pay for what he used. Millie thought she should get Albert to do likewise. Olivia mentioned that her next project would be to get an indoor toilet built as they had seen in St. Ann's, so that they wouldn't have to use latrines. Verne also showed interest in the indoor plumbing.

When they returned to Sangre Grande, they told Isabelle and Emma of the metered water tap indoors and they all agreed to ask Albert to make it a priority. Carrying buckets of water from the standpipe had been a daily chore they had become accustomed to doing, but one they would not be sorry to lose. Albert had one objection. He had read somewhere that lead pipes caused poisoning especially in warm climates. He promised that when he could acquire cast-iron piping, which was just being made available, he'd get the pipes laid.

Verne, on the other hand, went ahead and was one of the first people in the area to install indoor plumbing. This meant that his children no longer underwent the indignity of being bathed in full view of the public as many other children in the neighbourhood were.

Carnival was celebrated with much gusto that year. Rumours of a looming world recession did nothing to dampen the festivities. If anything, people seemed determined to have "a last fling" before tightening their belts. Masqueraders went to great pains to have their costumes as authentic as possible. World leaders were depicted in burlesque fashion; strutting Mussolinis, imperious Hitlers, a gilded Aga Khan, and a muscle-flexing Anthony Eden, were all portrayed by ingenious revellers. Thanks to Pathe News, the forerunner of modern-day television, cinema patrons were made aware of the goings-on all over the world and in Trinidad, carnival was a medium for spreading the news. The popularity of Charlie Chaplin, whose latest film, "*Modern Times*," had just been released, was instrumental in getting the masses aware of world events.

Mussolini had conquered Abyssinia, Hitler had occupied the Rhineland, the Aga Khan in India was weighed in gold, and Anthony Eden, in his first speech as Foreign Secretary, was advocating "Peace through Strength." The art of caricature comes into its own at carnival time, and costume designers were given free rein to exercise their talents. Verne had recommended Olivia to his friends so she sewed many costumes. Millie's talents also were made use of: the colourfully menacing speeches made by Midnight Robbers had to be artfully composed, and Millie was coerced into helping Verne and his friends write speeches.

The merchants had been approached and inveigled into playing their part in making carnival a success by donating prizes. Competitions were held for various categories and to Millie's surprise, Verne was awarded a prize.

Chapter 69

The Observation of Lent and News of Pregnancy

Lenten devotions were a solemn affair in the Akong household. No singing or dancing was allowed, except for religious hymns. Fasting and abstinence days were strictly adhered to and all church services attended religiously. Isabelle wore black or white clothing most of the time and kept the curtains drawn throughout the house. In the neighbourhood, children "cut lent" with each other so that if one was caught singing a calypso, using a swear word, or eating something that was "given up for lent," the other was entitled to deliver a cuff as punishment.

Millie thought these customs amusing but went along with them. When she saw Kenric hitting Annette one day, however, she admonished him saying, "Boys should never hit girls."

"But she was singing: *De ole lady run a mile an' a half an' she taylaylay*," he replied. "An' she cut lent wid me." Millie couldn't help but smile at this and suggested instead that boys "cut lent" with boys, and girls with girls.

It was fortunate that fried foods were not on the breakfast table during lent for Millie discovered that she was having "Morning Sickness," that dreaded illness that's a give-away to pregnancy. Emma and Isabelle were quick to notice and to offer several remedies; none of which worked. Bananas seemed to be the only thing that her stomach accepted. When she told Albert that he was going to be a father again, his reply was that he had already been told by Emma and was waiting for her to confirm it. Millie was not very happy at this and wished they had more privacy. Fortunately, Albert was coming to the same conclusion.

His older brother, Eric, had bought a lot of land in Sukhram village and had started to build a house where he claimed his mother would be happier;

she had complained every November when the Cunapo river burst its banks and flooded the area. Albert decided to help him complete it so that both his mother and youngest sister could live there. Millie had long expressed the desire to do her cooking for herself and Albert and had bought her own coal pot and other cooking utensils. This was a source of some contention as Isabelle had remarked: "So our cooking's not good enough for you."

With a new addition to the family imminent, it was expedient to have his mother and sister move elsewhere. Albert and Millie discussed their plans secretly and decided to keep quiet until the rainy months when Isabelle herself might suggest a move. To broach the subject too soon could result in bitter acrimony which they wished to avoid.

As Lent drew to a close, Millie made some egg-shell rattles for the children on Good Friday, which even the adults enjoyed playing with. They talked about the previous Easter which was spent on Manzanilla beach with fond memories. Because of an invasion of jelly-fish this year, however, a repeat was not advisable. The sting of a Portuguese Man-of-War could leave one incapacitated for days. They opted instead for a large Akong family Easter Dinner party.

Millie was permitted on this occasion to make a dish and she prepared a chicken pelau, Browne style, with pumpkin and pigeon peas added. She was complimented by everyone not only on her cooking but on "the bun she had in her oven."

Chapter 70
Sisterly Love

On paying a visit to her sister-in-law Celia one morning, Millie found her retching into a bowl. Realizing that something was wrong with her, she ventured to help her, Celia, however, said: "Go away! I don't want anybody 'round me now."

Millie turned to go, then changed her mind. "Look here, Celia," she said. "I haven't come to criticize, or find fault, or tell tales on you. I care for you as a sister and want to help." She then took the bowl and emptied it in the outhouse and washed it at the rainwater barrel. Celia, mollified, motioned her to sit on the bench next to her and explained her predicament.

A nosey neighbour had told Louis Lamont, her children's father, that she had been receiving visits from a "man-friend" in his absence. Louis, an inspector who worked for the Ministry of Agriculture, stopped visiting her and supporting his children. He had paid the rent for a year on her apartment and that was all she'd get from him. She was forced then to ask the said "man-friend" for help and that resulted in her getting pregnant. She was too ashamed to turn to her mother or brothers for help and just wanted the nightmare to go away. Death would be welcome.

Millie put her arms around her and let her cry into her shoulder. When Celia had stopped sobbing, Millie asked her, "Does the baby's father know you are carrying?"

"No, that might chase him away," Celia said.

"Sooner or later, everyone will know. We have to face up to reality. You should give him a chance to show what sort of a man he is. I'll tell your family for you and I'm sure they'll sympathize."

"I suppose you're right," Celia conceded.

It turned out that Alan Badow, the "man-friend," was prepared to shoulder his responsibility and gave support to Celia and her children. Four months later, his daughter, Sylvana, was born.

Chapter 71
The Trials of Pregnancy

The remainder of Millie's first year in Sangre Grande progressed quietly as her baby grew in her womb. Cora had suffered a miscarriage and suffered a depression which made her refuse to see anybody. Her other sister-in-law, Darvis, however, had given birth to Derryck, a healthy, plump little baby boy and Millie loved to visit them so she could hold the baby. Darvis allowed her to practice bathing him and changing his diaper so that she'd do these things comfortably when her own baby arrived. Thus, Millie developed a close friendship with Darvis which was to be a great comfort to her in later years.

While Millie considered the half-a-mile walk to visit Darvis to be good for her health and that of the baby she was carrying, her mother-in-law thought it too much for a pregnant woman who should be resting as much as possible. It was impossible for Millie to be mistress in her own home. That October, the rains came as usual and floods threatened, but although the house that Eric built was ready for occupancy, Isabelle found another excuse to remain in Albert's house. She wanted to help with the baby that was shortly due.

During one of her brief visits to Talparo, Millie had unburdened herself on her mother telling her of her problems with Isabelle. Meg understood the situation very well and tried to explain that Isabelle's interference came from over caring and had no malicious motives behind it. That did little to ease the feeling of frustration that enveloped Millie. Conscious of the fact that she would need help when the baby was born, Millie decided to let matters be for the time being.

One of her biggest problems was that she had developed an intolerance for the smell of garlic and onions. The Akong family had fried onions or garlic with every meal it seemed, and while pregnant, Millie's stomach retched at the slightest aroma of these pungent smelling members of the allium family of herbs. She therefore went for a walk as soon as anyone began preparing a meal. Isabelle noticed this and kindly made allowance for her actions, even going so far as to warn Millie before frying or even peeling onions. It was thus very difficult to fall out with someone who quite innocently, smothered you with good intentions.

As the time for the baby's birth grew closer suggestions for its name were made by family members. If it were a boy, Albert was in favour of naming him after either the Governor, Arthur George Murchison Fletcher, or the Home Secretary, Howard Nankivell. Both of these men of high position were philanthropically inclined toward the working classes. They held the view that *"Industry has no right to pay dividends until it pays a fair wage to Labour."* Wary of choosing a name that might fall into disrepute, like Adolph, Millie said she would name the baby on the saint's day of its birth.

On the evening of the ninth of November, Millie's labour pains began and the midwife, a Mrs Henry, was called in. Albert was very anxious and paced up and down in the tiny gallery at the front of the house. At nine o'clock, his mother told him to go out for a drink with his friends lest he wear a groove in the floor. His favourite recreation club was near the Post Office and it was there that he learned, at one o'clock the following morning, that he had a son.

November tenth happened to be attributed to St. Andrew, so the boy was named Andrew. For a while, everything in the house seemed cantered around the baby. Both Isabelle and Emma wanted to tend to him. Even little Marla made it her business to inform the adults as soon as the baby woke or whimpered. Millie felt *post-partum* tiredness but was otherwise fit. She did not want all the extra help being tender

Chapter 72
The Christening

Isabelle had a childhood friend, Juanita Hodgkinson, with whom she still communicated. This friend had married a Port of Spain businessman and now lived in Belmont but on being told of Andrew's birth, offered to be godmother in order to continue the bond of friendship with the family. Millie was constrained to accept the offer, although she would have preferred her aunt Pauline as a godparent. Furthermore, Albert had agreed to Attao's request to be godfather, although he was a Buddhist. This meant that Verne acted as proxy godparent and baby Andrew had two godfathers present at his baptism.

Millie got her own way with one issue, however. She disliked the Church's ruling on having Sundays for legitimate babies and Saturdays for illegitimates. Her niece Sylvana was also due to be baptized and the priest insisted that it be done on a Saturday. Millie then asked that Andrew be christened on the same day, saying that Jesus, as a Jew, observed Saturday as the Sabbath and that her legitimate child, Andrew, being baptized on a Saturday would be no less blessed. Not wishing to get into a theological argument, he consented to perform the two baptisms on the same Saturday (somewhat to the consternation of a few Catholics).

A joint Christening party was held at which the families who had got together for the Easter Monday beach outing two years before were reunited and had a great time of rejoicing once again. Albert had installed indoor plumbing and built a shower annex to the house, so it was much improved from the time they had last seen it.

The Petits had brought their ice cream churn and the older children took turns at turning the handle. The icebox made by Pedro had been placed inside the Akong's old icebox and this proved to be a more efficient way of storing ice. A twenty-five pound block of ice lasted twice as long. This, Albert deduced, was because of the layer of insulating air trapped between the sides of the two boxes. There was enough ice for making ice-cream which the children enjoyed and for adding to drinks for the adults.

Chapter 73
Mistress in Her Own Home

After a year of putting up with the interference of her in-laws, Millie said to Albert: "I am fed up to my neck with your mother and sister telling me what I must and what I mustn't do. I think we should move to Eric's house in Sukhram village."

"But Eric has already registered the house and land in Ma's name," Albert replied. "We'll have to beg both Eric's and Ma's permission to do that. I think we should try and talk to Ma about this."

This was easier said than done. Hints had gone unnoticed and suggestions swept aside in the past. It appeared that Isabelle, having spent her life moving from house to house, from Arima to James Smart, from there to her sister's in Upper Sangre Grande and finally to her present abode where she felt that she had at last put down permanent roots, just didn't want to be uprooted again. When confronted with the fact that Millie needed to be mistress in her own home, she finally agreed not to interfere but promised to keep to her own room and let Millie run her house as she saw fit. Emma and Marla would go and live in Eric's house. Eric promised to contribute to his sister's welfare.

This arrangement lasted for just over a year, by which time relationships were strained to breaking point. Millie discovered that Isabelle's silence could be more unpleasantly poignant than sharp words. When Albert was around, his mother was as pleasant as could be. In his absence, her aloofness was a weapon more effective than the mustard gas that the Italians were using against the Abyssinians at the time. This took such a toll on Millie that were it not for the long walks she took to visit Darvis and the comfort she received from her sister-in-law, she thought she would lose her mind. Teaching Amoy had been a welcome distraction, but that young lady had done so well that she was able to gain employment as a railway clerk. Her Elementary School Leaving Certificate showed she had received top grades in every subject.

A significant change in Isabelle's behaviour came about when it was discovered that Emma was expecting another child. One of the village Romeos was reported to have been visiting Eric's house on occasion. Isabelle blamed herself for not being there to take care of her daughter's moral welfare. She cried on Millie's shoulder and said: "I'm sorry I will have to leave you here alone with the baby and Albert, but that last daughter of mine can't manage on her own." That very week, Isabelle left and Millie breathed a sigh of relief.

Chapter 74
A Most Auspicious Year

Albert, Millie and baby Andrew at last had the house to themselves. From the time of Andrew's birth, Millie's aversion to onions and garlic had passed and she could cook whatever Albert fancied. She thought it was time she improved her culinary skills and asked Albert to buy a pitch-oil (paraffin) stove as she had seen being used in her sister-in-law Darvis's kitchen. It was much easier to light and to control its heat than the coal-pot and charcoal she had been accustomed to use. Also, the clay oven at the back of the house needed a lot of charcoal or wood and was not economical unless a great amount of baking was being planned. It was in the bakery department, however, that she chose to experiment. A large box-like biscuit tin had been fashioned into an oven that sat on the pitch-oil stove. She tried her hand at making coconut sweet-bread, tea muffins, fruitcake, and a sponge cake with cherries which was baby Andrew's favourite.

Annette and Adolph, Kenric and Cedric, as well as a few of their friends became regular drop-in visitors after school. (Millie believed it was the smell of her baking.) Kenric enjoyed a game of chess and taught Millie to play when Albert was at work. Albert was pleasantly surprised at her improvement when he played with her.

Another game called Lexicon, had just been invented and was being sold for half a crown. Millie considered this game an invaluable tool for encouraging children to learn to spell and to improve their vocabulary and invested some of her savings in buying a set. The children took to it so much that her house was usually filled with children's laughter after school. This sound of merriment proved to be the best medicine for Millie's depression.

When Albert came home from work and the children were dispatched to their homes, the house often seemed unnaturally quiet. Albert and Millie would talk over the events of the day while Andrew "rode horsey" on Albert's knee. On one such day, Albert said to her: "A friend at work told me that the year we got married was one of the most auspicious years the world has ever seen."

"Surely he couldn't have meant that we had anything to do with it," Millie replied.

"No, but these are some of the things that got mentioned:

King George of England and one of Britain's greatest authors, Rudyard Kipling, both died. Charlie Chaplin could be heard talking on the cinema screen for the first time, and the BBC added sound to television pictures. Hitler launched Germany's people's car, the Volkswagen. England produced a new "Spitfire" fighter airplane and the Queen Mary, Britain's super liner, made its maiden voyage from Southampton to New York. Mussolini proclaimed victory over Haile Selassie's Abyssinia (Ethiopia).

The fascists under Franco sparked Civil War in Spain. An Englishman called Fred Perry completed a hat-trick at Wimbledon. Jesse Owens, a black American, won four gold medals at the Berlin Olympics. A British woman, Beryl Markham, became the first woman to fly across the Atlantic. And King Edward VIII abdicated his throne for the love of a twice-divorced woman. I don't think we can add anything to that."

"Besides us getting married and having a baby, the only thing I thought of was the invention of a game called Monopoly, which I hear is all the rage in America," Millie added.

"When it comes over here, I'll buy it for you," Albert promised.

"Thank you," Millie replied, "but I'm expecting that gramophone you promised first."

"Ah, my friend Salim has that in hand. He's expecting a shipment of goods any day now," Albert announced.

Chapter 75
Millie Gets Her Gramophone

Apart from at the cinema, which Millie had stopped going to since Isabelle had left, the only occasion she heard the latest songs was on her visits to her sister-in-law Edith, whose husband Emry had bought her a radio. This was a brown Bakelite box with knobs and dials which fascinated Millie. It could be tuned in to BBC London, or faraway places like Tel Aviv or Hong Kong. It was powered by a lead-acid accumulator (battery) which had to be topped up periodically with distilled water and recharged by a generator at the "Wicko." Millie did not think this suitable in a house with little children however. She would be content to listen to Albert playing the mandolin in so far as music was concerned for the time being.

During a visit to Edith, Millie was intrigued to hear a BBC broadcast account of Prince Albert's accession to the throne. When his brother Edward VIII abdicated, the mantle of kingship was thrust upon "shy Bertie" as he was known to family and close friends. He was an RAF pilot and had taken part in the Battle of Jutland. He loved tennis and had played at Wimbledon, was married to Elizabeth and had two daughters, Princesses Elizabeth and Margaret-Rose. He would become the head of the British Commonwealth as King George VI. This she related to her own Albert as she got home.

"We knew most of that," Albert replied. "I just didn't know that he fought in the war or played tennis."

"I might call you King Bertie from now on," Millie jested.

"Well, with me as king of the household, you'd be Queen Lizzie and Andrew we'll call Governor Murchison." Albert laughed. (These monikers were to persist for far longer than anyone suspected.) "There is already another Governor Murchison in Sangre Grande, by the way, my friend George Clarke the tailor, named their baby, Murchison." Millie merely smiled affably at that.

The following month the gramophone arrived. It was called a Victrola and a packet of some of the latest records came with it, the most popular being: *The Way you Look Tonight, When I'm Cleaning Windows, September in the Rain, The Folks who Live on the Hill,* and *A Nice Cup of Tea.*

Millie was overjoyed to have it. She picked up Andrew and danced with him in her arms when Albert was not at home. Celia was invited over and became the most regular visitor thereafter. She learnt the songs quickly and could be heard singing them in her own home.

Chapter 76
A Resemblance Noted

Celia's boys continued to visit Aunt Millie after school as they were assured of some small treat or other and there were always games to be played. On one afternoon, as Millie played a game of chess with Kenric in the front gallery, the principal of the St. Andrews High School stopped on his way home and addressed her. "Good afternoon Mrs Akong, might I have a word with you?" "Of course," she replied, "I'm just having fun with my nephews as usual, but my time is my own."

"Your nephews?" Mr Dasent, the principal, replied. "But I thought they were your children. You look so alike!"

"They are my sister-in-law's," Millie affirmed. "If what you have to say is confidential, I can send them indoors."

"Not really, it's just that I'm opening a new branch of my school, a primary and kindergarten department, and I wondered if you would consider sending your children there. But as they are not yours, I've made a faux pas."

"You have not blundered," Millie replied, "I might send my own son next year, when he is four. He is having an afternoon nap at the moment, as I took him on a long walk today."

"Thank you, I'll look forward to that," Mr Dasent replied as he took his leave.

Millie knew that Celia was in no position to afford to send her children to a private school and had therefore not suggested that they be considered. Instead, her proposition to enlist her own son, Andrew, served to satisfy Mr Dasent's solicitation. His observation of the likeness between herself and Celia's boys, however, gave her food for thought. Could they be blood-related? She decided to find out more about the boys' father when next she spoke with Celia.

It so happened that her mother-in-law, Isabelle, was the one who provided her with the information she wanted. Isabelle dropped by on her way to confession that Saturday afternoon and Millie asked her if she knew the children's father. "Their father! Of course, I knew him. I even knew Louis Lamont's own father, Kenneth Lamont." She chuckled. "He was quite a man! He charmed the ladies everywhere he went. They say he fathered children in every town and village in Trinidad. I was afraid the son, Louis, would turn out just like him, so I forbade Celia to see him, but she ran away with him nonetheless."

"How could he have children all over the island?" Millie asked. "Traveling around isn't easy, even now."

"He too was an agricultural inspector and he had his own buggy with two fine horses," Isabelle informed her. "But I shouldn't be telling you of other people's faults, especially when I'm on my way to confess my own. I must say goodbye, I've rested enough to tackle that Bravo Hill now."

After her mother-in-law's departure, Millie pondered her situation. Should she ask her mother if she knew Kenneth Lamont? What if it turned out that Kenneth Lamont was indeed her father? She didn't even know if he was still alive or dead. Would he acknowledge her? Would she really want him to do so? There were too many things to consider. She must find out a lot more about the Lamont family first. If Kenneth Lamont turned out to be her father, then Louis Lamont would be her brother and she'd be Kenric's and Cedric's aunt twice over. They seemed to like her very much, or was it her cakes they liked? She smiled to herself.

Then she had another sobering thought. I must have dozens of brothers or sisters out there and we don't know each other. I could have married my own brother! Part of her still wanted to know her father and another part didn't want to know. She was in a dilemma that had no obvious solution, the type that her mother always said "was best left in God's hands." The quest to discover her real father had been on the back burner in recent years, perhaps it was time to take it off the cooking range. She decided, however, to let it simmer as she got on with her life.

Chapter 77
A Visit from Maria

Millie wrote every month to her parents in Talparo and received replies regularly. Her parents were worried that all their children were leaving the roost one by one. Pedro wanted to go and work in the oilfields where trade unionists led by Tubal Uriah Butler had at last managed to secure better wages, much better than those earned by agricultural workers many of whom worked for just a shilling a day. She learnt that Maria had been visiting relatives in Cascade very often and had met a young Tobagonian who had gone as far as Talparo one weekend to meet her parents. Millie thought this a sign of impending matrimony. She wanted to find out more and wrote inviting her youngest sister to spend a weekend in Sangre Grande.

Maria arrived one Friday evening much to Millie's delight. The two sisters had so much to talk about that Albert felt left out in the cold. He went off on a long cycle ride claiming that he needed the exercise to get rid of the weight he had put on since getting married.

Norman Francks, the young man who was courting Maria, worked on the boats that plied between Trinidad and Tobago. He had been invited home to tea by Aunt Pauline's husband, Jose, and met Maria there. Maria had not encouraged his attentions but he was very persistent. Jose had recommended him as an industrious hard-working seaman who was not given to drinking and gambling as were the majority of young men who worked on the steamships. Millie sensed that there was something about him that bothered Maria nonetheless and asked: "Is he ugly or fat or has some unpleasant characteristic that's putting you off?"

"Oh no," Maria replied, "he's quite good-looking and is slim-built. It's just that I always imagined if I got married it would be to a farmer and we would live in the country. Norman wants to get away from working on the land. His family owns agricultural land in Tobago, but he says that's not for him. He wants to buy a plot of land and build a house in St. James."

Millie considered the problem for a moment, then asked: "Wouldn't you be able to grow crops around your house in St. James?"

"I suppose so, I could grow peas, ochroes, peppers, and even the odd breadfruit and zaboucca tree, but I'm accustomed to cocoa, coffee and citrus on a large scale," Maria responded.

"And does Norman want to work on boats all his life?" Millie enquired.

"No, he intends to be a painter and decorator when he leaves the ships."

"Well, it's something you'll have to decide for yourself. I think if you love each other enough you'll live anywhere you can be together." Millie let Maria ponder on that reflection.

Little Andrew who had been playing quietly on the floor with some alphabet cards announced: "I love you, tantie Maria. You mus' come and live with us."

Maria laughed at that and said, "You will come and spend holidays with me when I'm married." Millie then knew that Maria's mind was already made up. She just needed reassurance that she was doing the right thing.

Chapter 78
War Is Declared

The Trinidad Guardian was the first and only West Indian newspaper to install its own wireless receiving plant. Millie occasionally bought a Guardian newspaper from the Marshall's parlour for four cents, but Albert more often than not, would bring home a newspaper left in his shop by one of his customers. (Most of these were consigned to the outhouse where they were perused while attending to nature's calls.) They were therefore conversant with news of what was going on in the wider world. Hence it was no big surprise for Millie to learn that war had been declared in Europe.

The newspapers had aired the concerns of sceptics who were openly critical of British Prime Minister, Chamberlain. He had returned from a meeting with Deladier (the French Prime Minister), Hitler, and Mussolini, in Munich the year before and announced: "I believe it is peace for our time." They had agreed to hand over the Sudeten region of Czechoslovakia to Germany. To appease the Czechs, the Bank of England had given them a loan of ten million pounds. Many British M.P.s considered it "a sell-out to Hitler."

Precautions in Britain, however, were being carried out. The R.A.F. was taking delivery of four hundred new aeroplanes per month and hoped to have two thousand eight hundred and forty by the following March. Five thousand eight hundred trained pilots were in action and employers were being urged to release reserve and volunteer fliers for six-month training periods. In addition, thousands of air raid shelters were being built and distributed in the towns and cities and plans were made to evacuate two and a half million children. All this disturbing news was circulated to colonials around the empire on which "the sun never sets" by means of wireless technology and the printed media.

On the 1st of September, 1939, Germany and Russia invaded Poland. The German Luftwaffe knocked out the Polish railway system and were shooting the Polish Air Force out of the sky. Britain and France having pledged to defend Poland, declared war against Germany on September 3rd, 1939.

"I'm going to shoot the Germans!" Andrew declared as he marched into the room carrying a broom on his shoulder as he had seen the marching soldiers do in the cinema. Andrew had been taken to see Walt Disney's *Snow White and the Seven Dwarfs,* a cartoon film which had recently been released. He seemed, however, most impressed by the Pathe News and the trailers. A film clip of soldiers marching in columns stuck in his mind and he loved to imitate them although Millie tried to tell him that war and fighting were not good things. Albert smiled at the child's antics and said: "When you're old enough to fight, this war will be long over. They said the last war was the war to end all wars but I think as long as there are men like Hitler and Mussolini, there'll always be wars. You might be called up for a different one."

Chapter 79
The Young Men Are Volunteering

Millie took Andrew across to visit Celia and ask her if she had heard the news of the war. Celia, who was at her laundry tub, had heard of it and moreover was disturbed by the fact that many young men (including Sylvana's father, Alan Badow) wanted to join the West Indian Regiment or even the Royal Air Force. Millie asked her if she had heard any news of Louis Lamont, the father of her boys.

"That scamp!" Celia replied. "I hear he's got a girlchild in Belmont. He doesn't even send me a shilling to feed his children!"

Millie refrained from reminding her that she too had a girl child, Sylvana, from another man. Instead, she sympathized with her saying, "Many men aren't interested in bringing up children, they are only interested in indulging in the act that makes babies. They are then applauded by their fellow men while the poor women who have to bring up the babies are looked down upon by society."

"Yes girl, that is so true," Celia added. "We poor women are taken advantage of."

To change the subject, Millie asked: "Have you heard the latest song to come out of Britain, *Hang out your washing on the Siegfried Line*?"

"No," Celia responded, "but I learnt this one." And she sang:

Pack up your troubles in your old kit bag and smile, boy, smile. Borrow a Lucifer to light your fag and smile boy, that's the style. What's the use of worrying? It never was worthwhile. So! Pack up your troubles in your old kit bag and smile, boy, smile.

"Songs like that'll buck-up the morale of the soldiers, I'm sure," Millie replied. "It made me smile. If you lived in England, you could sing for the soldiers like that Vera Lynn woman who I hear is making a great name for herself."

"Chance would be a fine thing," Celia muttered.

The boys who were playing peek-a-boo with Sylvana from behind a water barrel, stopped their game as Celia was singing. "Mama," Kenric asked, "can you sing the one about the German balls that Uncle Alan taught us?"

"Oh no. That's not suitable in polite company," their mother replied.

Intrigued, Millie asked, "Why not? If the children can hear it, I can hear it too."

"Well, they don't understand you see, so it didn't matter that they heard it, but you will know what it means." She sang the first line: *Hitler has only got one ball.*

"Oh, I see what you mean." Millie laughed.

"The rest of the song is about Himmler and Goebbels, his generals," Celia explained. "The children think it's about cricket balls." The two women then had a conspiratorial chuckle.

"I must leave you now to do my own laundry," Millie apologized as she took Andrew's little hand in hers and turned to go home. As she went, she could hear Kenric and Cedric singing: *Himmler, has something sim'ler, but ruddy Goebbels has no balls at all.*

Chapter 80
Millie Is Offered a Job

The following week, Mr Dasent again stopped by. "Good afternoon, Mrs Akong. I wonder if you can do me a favour."

"Ask away; if I can, I may," she replied.

"I heard that you were a very good teacher," he continued, "and I have just been let down by one of my prospects. I was wondering if you would take his place. Winston Harper is going to join the R.A.F."

Taken aback by this request, Millie replied, "But who could have told you that I was a teacher? It wouldn't be Albert, because he doesn't want me to work."

"I have my confidential sources and this man is confident in your ability. I'd like you to consider my offer. The pay is small to begin with but will increase as the school grows. Every good teacher knows that teaching has far more than monetary rewards." Millie felt flattered by his implied compliment and said, "I'll have to talk it over with my husband, but I'm almost certain that the answer would be no."

Mr Dasent somewhat ruefully admitted, "I was afraid that that would be the answer I'd get, but at least I tried. Good day to you, and please let me know at your earliest convenience."

As he departed, Millie mused, "I'll bet he knows Mr Farfan."

That night she related the encounter to Albert who said, "That's all very flattering and perhaps tempting to you, but who will take care of the house and the livestock?"

"What livestock?" Millie asked, "We've only got a few chickens."

"You'll see. We'll have more. The government wants us to be self-sufficient," Albert announced as he turned over to sleep.

Chapter 81
Helping the 'War Effort'

The following week, Albert built a pig pen at the back of the house. It was made of sturdy clay bricks and had a concrete floor sloping slightly to a drain that would make it easier to clean. The drain, unfortunately, ran alongside the house to a canal which ran in front of the houses and emptied into the Cunapo river. Millie voiced her objection to this arrangement saying that the stench in the house would be unbearable but was overruled. The War Effort had to be supported. It would only be for a short while, until the Germans were beaten again.

Two suckling piglets, recently weaned from their mother, were delivered by Eric, Albert's brother, a few days later and Millie was given charge of them. Andrew was delighted with the little squealers and wanted to play with them. He named them Porky and Bess. Millie did her best to discourage his attachment to them as she knew that Porky, the young boar, would be consigned to the butcher's shop as soon as he had put on the required weight. Andrew would not want his pet to be slaughtered. The sow, Bess, would be kept for breeding.

It was perhaps unfortunate that Andrew's first acquaintance of pigs came as a result of being introduced to Chanka, the pet pig of a Mrs Maingot, a rich, eccentric woman who lived on the Fishing Pond Road. Millie had been invited in for a cup of tea by her on one of her walks with Andrew. Mrs Maingot let Chanka roam all over her house and claimed that he was smarter and cleaner than a dog. Chanka certainly showed intelligence and would go under her bread basket (which was hung from the ceiling out of his reach), and snort twice when he wanted to be fed. Chanka let Andrew pat him on the head and rub him under his chin. The little boy wanted to have one of his own.

Now that they had piglets, Andrew wanted to take them into the house but was strictly forbidden. The smell of their droppings helped to convince him that it wasn't a good idea. He nevertheless was allowed to put food into their trough and watch them eat greedily. Their droppings and wet straw were put into a barrel in the farthest corner of the yard, later to be dug into the soil as manure. Thus, the smells that came from the drain running alongside the house were not as bad as Millie had predicted.

In due course, one day Porky's place in the stay was vacant and Andrew was told that the money he fetched would be spent on a tricycle. A month or two later he not only got his tricycle but was further promised that when Bess (who had been taken to a farm for servicing) delivered her litter, one third of the litter would be his. That made him a happy little boy. The War Effort was proving to be of benefit to all.

Chapter 82
Andrew Goes to School

Millie taught Andrew to read and write as soon as he showed the inclination to learn; and learn he did quite quickly. However, he did not get on well with his cousins who visited from time to time. She thought that if he went to kindergarten, he would learn to give and take and be more sociable. Killing two birds with one stone, Millie declined the offer of a teaching post and enrolled Andrew at St. Andrews Primary.

For the post of Head Mistress, Mr Dasent had secured the services of Miss Louise Matthews, sister of Dom Basil Matthews, Trinidad's first locally ordained priest. She was a kindly and competent teacher whom Andrew took to immediately. His fellow pupils, however, were another matter. On his very first day at school, when Lennox Marhue, a boy of his own age, put his arm around his neck pretending to wrestle with him, Andrew, unable to duck out of the hold, bit him, drawing blood. Lennox screamed as he saw the red blood pouring on to his shirt. Everyone was upset by this, including Andrew, who burst into tears. Miss Matthews spoke to him sternly, telling him that it wasn't gentlemanly behaviour and the purpose of the school was to bring up educated, well-behaved gentlemen and ladies. She would have to report his behaviour to his parents.

After Lennox's wound had been seen to, Andrew went to him and told him he was sorry and wouldn't bite again. Lennox, for his part, was more worried about how he would explain the blood on his shirt to his parents who had warned him about getting into fights. He was too often wrestling with his brothers at home and getting his clothes torn.

Millie went to collect her son from school that afternoon and was dismayed to learn what had taken place. Phyllis Manning, an older pupil who had witnessed the entire incident, spoke up for Andrew and told her that he was being strangled by the other boy. She was about to separate them but Andrew acted in his own defence before she got to them, Millie nevertheless gave Andrew a proper scolding when he got home and threatened to take his toys away if he ever did it again. As it turned out, Andrew never got into trouble at that school again for Phyllis made it her duty to watch over him, even taking him to and from school on a regular basis.

Chapter 83
The Yanks Come Over Here

The war in Europe was causing considerable repercussions in Trinidad and Tobago. In England, the placid-natured Chamberlain was replaced as prime minister by the somewhat bellicose Winston Churchill. The combined European forces aligned against Germany could not withstand the ponderous might of the Fuhrer's military power and Churchill courted aid from the U.S.A. On September 2, 1940, he signed an agreement with the Americans permitting them to establish military bases in the Caribbean with a lease of 99 years, in exchange for fifty American destroyers.

On October 10th that year the then Governor of Trinidad, Sir Hubert Young, received a memorandum from Admiral John W. Greenslade of the U.S.A. stating that he would be visiting Trinidad for the purpose of investigating suitable locations for establishing military bases. American bases were quickly developed at Chaguaramas and Wallerfield (an area between Arima and Sangre Grande.) This brought a great deal of employment to native workers. Within six months, some 15,000 workers were employed by the Americans. Not only carpenters and masons, but clerks, teachers, and even policemen. Agricultural workers left the estates in droves as they could earn four and five times as much doing unskilled jobs, such as security guards for the Americans as they did for working on the land. As a popular calypso announced, they were now "*working for the Yankee dollar*."

As the American officers were allowed to bring their families with them, even schools and cinemas were built on the bases. Teachers who were paid $30 per month by the government could now earn $80 to $150 per month from the Americans. The economy of Trinidad was thrown into turmoil.

Prices of goods began to escalate as people who once worked for shillings now flaunted dollars. Even the price of a haircut went up from 15 cents to 20 cents. Millie asked for an increase in her housekeeping allowance, but was met with reluctance from Albert. He claimed that it was a time for tightening belts, working harder and sacrificing. On enquiring what he was doing with the extra money, she knew he was now getting, she was told that it had to be saved for the little governor's education. He might even want to go on to university! She managed, however, to get Albert to buy her a hand-sewing machine so that she could sew their own clothes.

She had been able to buy cloth from a Jewish traveling salesman by the name of Hoffmann at much cheaper prices than the local shops charged. This, however, changed as Hoffman, a refugee from Germany, was ordered to be incarcerated during the war. She had to pay twenty percent more at the local shops for cloth to make Andrew's khaki pants for school.

Chapter 84
Millie Finds Accommodation for Relatives

Millie's letters from her mother kept her abreast of how her extended family members were getting on. Aunt Marie was happy and very busy with Irene, her last child, who was proving to be quite a handful. Helen, was "in the family way" and had been dismissed by the woman she worked for. Her husband was suspected of being the father. Aunt Pauline had offered to take care of her and the baby. Maria had gone across to Tobago where she had a quiet wedding without family involvement. Mother's brother, Uncle Gerald, had died in Grenada and his wife Cecile was bringing her family over to Trinidad as it was desperately hard to find work in Grenada and Cecile also had a sister, a Mrs Anna Baird, who was a seamstress in Sangre Grande. Meg wanted to know if Millie had met her.

Millie immediately began making enquiries about Mrs Baird and was told by Celia that Mrs Baird, a Grenadian, was practically her neighbour. Mrs Baird lived next to the Presbyterian church in a little house set back about thirty yards from the road. Millie was delighted to hear this and decided to pay Mrs Baird a visit.

Millie took Andrew with her and walked down the gravelled track that led to Mrs Baird's house and called out, "Good morning, Mrs Baird." A short, light complexioned woman of indeterminate age came to the door and said, "Good morning. Is it sewing you come to collect?"

"No," Millie replied, "I've come to see Mrs Baird, who I believe is a sister of my Aunt Cecile from Grenada."

"Is me you lookin' for den. But I didn't know Cecile had any relation here odder dan me."

"Well, I'm an in-law relation, because Aunt Cecile was married to my mother's brother, Gerald."

"Den you mus' come in an' tell me all about it. I jes hear dat she 'usban' dead an' she want to come wid she chilren an' live in Trinidad," Mrs Baird acknowledged.

Millie entered the house with Andrew clinging to her skirt and was invited to sit on a chair which was quickly cleared of some sewing material. A treadle Singer sewing machine took pride of place in the living room, while every surface was covered with bits of cloth, paper patterns and other paraphernalia. It reminded Millie of her sister Olivia's first home in Arima. "You does drink tea or coffee?" Mrs Baird asked.

"Either," Millie replied, "But you needn't bother on my account. I've just had breakfast and I only live four doors away. I'm Millie Akong, wife of Albert the barber."

"Ah, I see," said Mrs Baird, "You can call me Anna. I don't go out much. People come to me an' I hear he get marrid but I nevah concern meself in odder people business."

Anna seated herself in the only other vacant seat behind the sewing machine and smiled at her. "With your sister coming to Trinidad, I suppose she will stay with you," Millie opined.

"Oh no. She cyah stay here. Since me 'usban dead I have he sister an' she son Arnim livin' wid me an' is a small house. We ent have de room," Anna explained. "I been askin' aroun' if anybody have a house to rent but I cyah fine one yet."

Millie thought about this problem and asked: "Will she stay in a barrack room? I believe Attao has two rooms vacant as two of his tenants recently moved out."

"If dat is all she can get, she'll 'ave to take it. She suppose to lan' nex' week."

Chapter 85
The Le Blancs Come to
Reside in Sangre Grande

Aunt Cecile and her children did arrive the following week. Her children were, to Millie's eyes, grown up. Sebastian was eighteen, Eric, sixteen, Joan, fourteen, and Cuthbert eleven. Millie had provisionally booked the two rooms for them with Mr Attao, who was willing to accommodate a widow in distress.

Having travelled by train from Port of Spain to Cunapo, they left most of their luggage at the railway station and took a buggy to Mrs Baird's home. Cecile was delighted to meet her sister, Anna, but dismayed to learn that she would have to live in barrack rooms. Although she did not regard Trinidad as "a land of milk and honey," as some "small-islanders" did, she had expectations of being accommodated in something better than what she regarded as "slave quarters." On hearing from Anna that she had a niece, Millie, living nearby, she asked to be taken to see her. That wasn't necessary as Millie was already on her way over to offer whatever help she could.

Having introduced herself to her aunt and cousins, Millie arranged for a mule cart to fetch the Le Blanc luggage from the railway station. The mule had just been shod at the blacksmith's and the owner was glad for the work. Sebastian went with him and they unloaded the grips and boxes into one of the rooms Millie had procured for them.

Millie, in the meantime, was assuring her aunt that it was only a temporary measure until better accommodation could be found. Aunt Cecile was somewhat appeased after several cups of Red Rose tea and coconut buns. Millie had heard of a project called The Brooklyn Land Settlement Scheme. This initiative was a result of the Moyne Commission, 1938–1939, which sought to establish small holdings among the poorer classes.

In the Brooklyn area of Sangre Grande, roads were laid down and houses built on plots of land measuring about two acres so that mixed farming could be carried out. Applicants had to be landless, within the lower income earning bracket, and willing to practise agriculture. A small monthly fee had to be paid, but the house and land would be considered owned after twenty five years.

Aunt Cecile was attracted by the idea and asked Millie to find out more about this scheme. If she and her children could somehow qualify for it, the sacrifice of living in the poor conditions being offered at the moment would be worth it. She decided to make the rooms as comfortable as possible and bide her time until better could be afforded. So it was that another branch of the Le Blanc family became established in the Sangre Grande area.

Chapter 86
Hello Joe

American soldiers could now be seen in Sangre Grande on a regular basis. Those off-duty seeking recreation were often opportuned by young women who openly flirted with them in the expectation of being bought drinks or given expensive presents. More often, the soldiers were passing through in a convoy of large trucks taking them to practise what they considered to be "jungle warfare" in the surrounding forests. These were hailed by small children who stood at the side of the road and shouted: "Hello Joe!" In return, the soldiers threw them packets of Wriggly Chewing Gum which was much better than the "laglee" they got from slicing the bark of breadfruit or sometimes called breadnut, trees and extracting the milky gum.

Andrew was encouraged by his cousins, Kenric and Cedric to stand and shout "Hello Joe!" at the soldiers and was rewarded not only by chewing gum, but by coins which he and his cousins scrabbled for in the dust at the side of the road. There were copper pennies and cents and even tiny silver six cents coins which were thrown to the children as the soldiers simply emptied their pockets of loose change. Andrew found a silver coin but Kenric exchanged it with him for three pennies. Kenric was collecting silver coins in a metal tube which once contained a cigar.

Going into the Marshall's parlour after the military convoy had gone, the boys bought paradise plums (lemony tasting sweets, red on one side and yellow on the other) at two for a cent (i.e. a farthing each), Kaiser balls (hard, red coloured sweets the size of a golf ball) at a penny each, and toolums (dark brown sticky pyramid-shaped cakes made from ground dried coconut and molasses), which also cost a penny. Andrew took home four paradise plums and a toolum. Much to his dismay, Millie confiscated his spoils, allowing him just one paradise plum, and forbidding him from standing with other children to shout at passing convoys of soldiers. (Mothers can be such spoil-sports!) "Only beggar children do things like that!" She scolded. Andrew was about to protest that his cousins were encouraged to do it but thought better of it. He didn't want to get them into trouble and they at least would share their sweets with him.

Chapter 87
Employment for Everyone

So many people from Sangre Grande had found work at the Wallerfield base that a transport system was established for taking workers to and from the base. Sebastian, Aunt Cecile's eldest, got on with the workers one morning hoping to get a job. He returned that afternoon saying he had been hired as a security guard! Great was the joy at this news in the Le Blanc household. He was issued with a khaki uniform which made him look like an American soldier. In a short time, many girls became attracted to him, much to Aunt Cecile's disapproval. The money he earned was vital to the family's upkeep.

Cuthbert was enrolled at the Government school nearby and Joan became apprenticed to her seamstress aunt, Anna. Eric was employed as an odd-job man by Attao, who needed help in the cocoa store. The Le Blancs were thus managing to keep their heads above water while they waited to be time-qualified as residents in Trinidad before they could be allocated house and land in the Brooklyn Land Settlement scheme. Millie had been instrumental in getting them registered as prospective small farmers and was confident of the success of her efforts.

Andrew was delighted to have an older cousin who could climb trees and pick fruits such as balata, caimite and chennet. Cuthbert could also catch fish in the river using shop twine and a bent pin. He was not allowed to accompany Cuthbert to the river, however, but was able to share in the fish broth as he helped to de-scale and clean the fish. The catch was often varied, wabeen, coscorob, matawal, and the occasional catfish. Cuthbert also taught him to grow topi tambu and cassava, which they cooked with the fish.

Millie was happy to have relatives from the maternal side of her family living close by. Apart from Aunt Cecile, Eric was a frequent visitor who, like the children, would pop in to sample her coconut drops and have a cup of tea or coffee. His main place of employment was across the road and as his mother was often visiting her sister, Anna Baird, Millie's house became his second home. He too had taken a liking to the children whom he considered "family." Millie had already decided that Kenric and Cedric were blood relations from the obscure paternal side of her family and hoped that her intuition would prove correct. Even an outsider like Mr Dasent could see the resemblance!

Chapter 88
Millie as Agony Aunt

Millie received a surprise visit from a distressed looking Dolores, one of her sister-in-law May's daughters, one day. After the usual pleasantries were exchanged, they entered the kitchen where Millie had just made a pot of coffee. "Millie, I in big trouble," Dolores confessed. "I'm pregnant, and the Yankee scamp say he cyah marry me, he marrid already."

Dolores, who had worked as ticket seller at her uncle's Apollo cinema, had left that job to work at the Wallerfield cinema for much higher wages. This brought the attractive teenager in close, unsupervised contact with the American soldiers and airmen. Her brother George, who had taken up his father's trade as a barber, also worked at the American base and was expected to keep an eye on his sister. But, as is usually the case, young people in love, or lust, will find a way to be alone together. "Have you told your mother?" Millie asked solicitously.

"No, not yet," Dolores replied. "I just don't know what to do. The scamp tellin' me to get rid of it. He hear people in this country know bush medicine to use for that."

Millie was astounded. How could they so casually think of snuffing out a human life just like that? "Well, I think that is out of the question!" Millie replied. "Your family will support you and the baby. You are only eighteen years old. Am I right?"

"Next month I'll be eighteen. But I told them I was twenty-one in order to get the job." Millie was unhappy at this answer as it would rob Dolores of credibility with the American authorities. She thought, *however, that big brother George, might be able to salvage the situation, if only to get the American military to pay for the upkeep of the baby*. She had read somewhere of British women being paid child maintenance by the American forces occupying Britain at the time.

"Why not get George to talk to his commanding officer?" Millie suggested.

"George doesn't know about this yet. I only told you because you from the country and know bush medicine," Dolores lamented. Millie was flabbergasted at this.

"You have to tell him and your mother, and don't ever think of getting rid of it. That child is probably the one who will support you in your old age," Millie admonished. "The more you are open and honest about this, the more help you'll get. You're not the first girl to get into trouble this way and you're not going to be the last."

"I suppose you're right," Dolores admitted. "I feel so terrible about this, I wish I could die." The tears that were welling up inside of her forced their way out and Millie hugged her in a comforting embrace as she sobbed.

When she had composed herself and dried her eyes on one of Millie's handkerchiefs she said to Millie: "I feel as if a burden has been lifted from my shoulders after talking to you. You don't know how awful it is to find out you pregnant and you cyah get marrid."

"No, I don't," Millie agreed. "But I do know what it's like not to know one's own father. Promise me one thing, that you'll tell the child who his or her father was as soon as it's old enough to want to know. That's something that everyone has a right to know."

"OK, I'll do that," Dolores agreed.

As it happened, when George was told about his sister's predicament, he accosted Sgt Coleman, the seducer, and told him that he was going to inform his superior officers about the incident and tell them that his sister was only seventeen. The sergeant, not wishing to be disgraced, and also fearing that the captain in charge of his squadron who knew his family back in Texas would tell his wife, promised to pay a monthly sum of forty dollars as child maintenance. This amount was more than acceptable as it was enough to feed and clothe a family of four at the time. The matter was therefore laid to rest.

Chapter 89
Food Is Rationed

Especially in the larger villages and towns, flour, rice and potatoes were the main ingredients of the staple diet. All these items were imported and therefore became scarce due to the war. A popular calypsonian, Growling Tiger, at the time sang:

Before the war I was livin' nice
Hot potato wid me beans stew-pork an' rice
Toast bread wid butter an' jam
Seven eggs in de mornin' wid chunk o' ham
Today ah livin' like a wand'ring bird
If ah see a pot for seconds ah cyah fine me food
Ah livin' by guess. Oh have sympathy!
Since war declare wid England and Germany.

Millie was happy to receive a ration book from Albert one day. He had queued up at the Warden's Office for it and was told that it entitled him to a year's ration of flour and rice. Each family was allowed to buy a weekly ration of flour and rice. The ration book was to be handed to the shop keeper who would then stamp an X in the ration book for each item bought.

TRINIDAD AND TOBAGO

CONSUMER

REGISTRATION BOOK

A	FLOUR							A
1	2	3	4	5	6	7	8	9
10	11	12	13	14	15	16	17	18
19	20	21	22	23	24	25	26	27
28	29	30	31	32	33	34	35	36
37	38	39	40	41	42	43	44	45
46	47	48	49	50	51	52		

B	RICE							B
1	2	3	4	5	6	7	8	9
10	11	12	13	14	15	16	17	18
19	20	21	22	23	24	25	26	27
28	29	30	31	32	33	34	35	36
37	38	39	40	41	42	43	44	45
46	47	48	49	50	51	52		

This alleviated the situation considerably. Other items, however, were still in short supply. Salt fish, tea, cheese, butter and even sugar became scarce. Although sugar was produced locally, the bulk of it was shipped overseas to help the "War Effort." Albert improvised his own press for squeezing the juice from ripe sugar cane and by boiling this, could reduce it to make sugar or use it as a liquid sweetener.

Andrew loved to help by feeding the cane into the press which was built into a hole about three feet off the ground in an old pomerac tree. He was usually rewarded for this by being given a piece of fudge made by Millie who boiled the cane sugar with cocoa powder made from ground, parched cocoa beans.

Chapter 90
Children Are Conceived Despite
the Hardship of War

Shortly after her chat with Dolores, Millie discovered that she too was expecting another baby. She hesitated to tell Albert who had become more grumpy as the war in Europe wore on. The German blitzkrieg had captured Yugoslavia and Greece and English cities were taking a cruel battering from the German bombers. It was reported that in a single night London's casualties were 20,000 dead and 25,000 badly injured. The Royal Air Force, however, though vastly outnumbered, managed to shoot down 29 German bombers. This prompted Winston Churchill to quote those memorable lines of praise to the R.A.F.:

"Never, in the field of human conflict, has so much been owed by so many to so few."

Other British cities, such as Coventry, Liverpool, Hull, Clydebank, Portsmouth, Plymouth, and Southampton, had also been heavily "blitzed," with massive damage and loss of life. The Nazis, who had previously signed a non-aggression pact with Russia, were even taking over Russian territories. It didn't seem to be a favourable time to be bringing babies into the world. Thousands of British West Indian volunteers were joining the British Army, Navy and Air Force. Some considered them mere fodder for the war machine.

Albert's oldest brother, Rodrick, was in the merchant navy serving on a motor vessel of the Prince line. Belle wasn't sure which of them. News came of the sinking of the Cyprian Prince by the Germans. She felt in her heart that she had lost her eldest son and even offered up a Mass for him. The Akong family attended to mourn their loss. The remittance that Belle had come to rely on was no longer forthcoming.

As they lay in bed one night, Millie broached the subject of an addition to the family.

"Albert," she began, "what do you think of us having a baby brother or sister for Andrew?"

"He's got cousins who are always around, and friends at school. It's not as if he's a lonely child," Albert replied. Millie sensed that he was not in favour of more children at this time. However, she persisted.

"God is the one who decides on the size of a family. What if he gives us a daughter?"

"If he does, he does. We'll face that when the time comes. I'm tired now, so let's go to sleep, all right?"

"Well, the time has come," Millie declared.

Albert turned over and sat up. "What do you mean by that?"

"What I'm trying to tell you, is that I'm pregnant," Millie sobbed.

"Why didn't you just say so instead of beating round the bush?" Albert asked, irritated.

"I was afraid you wouldn't be happy to have another child just now," Millie admitted. "What with you having to help support your sisters and giving handouts to other people's children as you do."

"Well, what's done is done. You should know that my children would come first. If God gives us another one now, so be it." Albert lay down again, but Millie sensed that he wasn't as pleased as she hoped he would be. She had hoped that he would hug her and say that it was all right. She settled down and prayed herself to sleep.

Chapter 91
Darvis Warns Millie to Be Wary

This time, her pregnancy did not induce morning sickness and the scent of onions or garlic being fried did not cause her nausea. *It could be a sign that the baby would be a girl rather than a boy*, she thought. Without a mother-in-law in the house controlling her actions, she determined to keep fit and took long walks with Andrew (sometimes on his tricycle) to visit her sister-in-law, Darvis, who was also pregnant at the time. She would go along the Fishing Pond Road past the Maingot's house, then turn left along the El Reposo road which took her to the Toco road where she turned left again towards Cunapo. This took her through a citrus estate owned by the Marlays. Tall Immortelle, Poui, and Pomerac trees provided shade in some places and their orange, pink and yellow blooms painted a scenery which gave her a sense of serenity much needed in that turbulent time. Kiskadees, Semp and Mockingbirds serenaded her along the way.

She arrived at the Petit's on this particular day feeling nicely tired physically, but mentally and spiritually refreshed. Darvis, who thought that walk excessively long, invariably offered them a welcome cold drink. No sooner than Andrew had downed his glass of sorrel, he went off to play with Derryck who was making a chickichong kite behind the house. This left the ladies free to talk to each other without being overheard as David had gone to Mayaro with his pigeons. Harry had gone with him but Antonia and Daphne had remained at home and were at the pigeon coop at the back of the house with watch and notebook ready, to time the arrival of the pigeons. David was reported to have some of the best homing pigeons in the country and liked to race them.

"Has Celia spoken to you lately?" Darvis asked.

"Not since last week," Millie replied. "Why do you ask? Is she in some sort of trouble?"

"No, but she thinks we should be keeping an eye on our husbands' whereabouts. She saw David and Albert in David's pickup with two Indian women who were putting their arms around them in a very familiar way. The men looked very embarrassed when they saw her and edged away from the women," Darvis divulged.

"I suppose there could be perfectly innocent reasons for their behaviour," Millie countered. "They might have done some sort of charitable act for the women who were grateful to them. Albert is always helping those in need."

"I hope you're right," Darvis acknowledged. "But I think we should find out what it was about. I asked David if he gave Coolie people lifts in the pickup and he just said, "All the time, I don't discriminate." That was against me for calling them Coolie. The Chinese think Coolie is a very degrading word."

Millie tried to rationalize the incident but it nevertheless left her with a very uneasy feeling. Since she had told Albert about her pregnancy, he was not very amorous at night.

"I'll ask Albert about it somehow and find out who the Indian women were. I don't think it's anything to worry about." Millie tried to sound reassuring. She nevertheless entertained a soupcon of doubt herself.

Antonia and Daphne came rushing in shouting: "They're home!" Three of the pigeons released in Mayaro had made the journey home in what might be a record time. They would only know the precise release time when their father returned. Andrew was as excited as the other children and wanted to stay but Millie excused herself and took him home, this time by the shorter route.

Chapter 92
Millie Finds Out About Indian Customs

Having been taught to make sada roti by Khartoon, her neighbour's daughter, Millie made roti and curried chicken with bodhi peas for their dinner. Albert was pleasantly surprised and seemed to enjoy his meal, which was tasty enough for him once he had added some pepper sauce. Millie made mild curries for the sake of the children. (Andrew's cousins frequently dined with them.)

"Do you prefer Indian cooking to other kinds?" Millie asked.

"I like all kinds. It's just nice to have a change from time to time," Albert replied.

"If you tell me what you want for dinner, I would be happy to make it. I like to experiment," Millie added.

"I quite like having a surprise; you can go ahead experimenting," Albert re-joined, somewhat unhelpfully from Millie's point of view.

"Do you have many Indian friends?" Millie persisted.

"You know Razack Khan," Albert replied. "We went to school together. He comes here occasionally to play chess. And there's Boysie Sinanan, I suppose that's it."

Millie thought that she was getting nowhere with her line of questioning and decided to change tactics but Albert demanded: "Why this interest in Indian people?" Millie thought for a moment then answered. "Khartoon, next door is getting married and we are invited to the wedding. I don't know who else will be there or what we should wear or anything. Actually, they are the first Indian people I've ever spoken to. We didn't have Indians in Talparo. Have you been to Indian weddings before?"

"Yes," Albert replied, somewhat relieved. "The whole village is usually invited to an Indian wedding; their culture is different from ours. I'll tell you a little about it." He related:

"First difference: The bride and groom do not choose each other. Their parents do that. The parents of boys are usually on the lookout for suitable brides for their sons. They look for a family with land and cattle or a profitable business place. This is because the girl's family has to provide a good dowry. They then talk to the girl's parents and let them meet their son and see that he can take care of their daughter. The girl doesn't usually see her intended husband until the wedding day. The boy would often contrive to sneak a peek at the girl to satisfy himself that he could live with her.

The next important consideration is the size of the dowry. This is actually not known until the feast day. Drummers play their music and guests are assembled in a tented area in the open air. A tarpaulin is sometimes spread on the ground in the dining tent and barefooted guests sit on it to eat. Nowadays trestle tables are provided. Food, usually boiled rice, parathas, dhal, curried baigan, goat etc. is served on leaves placed in front of the guests. No one eats before the groom begins to eat, but before he does, he has to be satisfied that the dowry is sufficient. The bride's family would give him sums of money, land, cattle, all of which he gratefully accepts. When he is satisfied, he begins to eat and everyone breathes a sigh of relief and tucks into the feast which is eaten with their fingers. The only cutlery used is wooden ladles for serving the food. They eat one-handed, for the other hand is reserved for cleaning their nether regions. That's it in a nutshell."

"Wow!" Millie expressed her surprise. "I didn't know half of that. You mean Khartoon wouldn't have seen the man she's going to marry?"

"That's right," Albert acknowledged. "She has to trust that her parents, mainly her father, will make a good match for her."

"Let's hope for her sake that he has chosen well. I don't know any woman who would willingly consent to that," Millie replied.

"The old customs are gradually changing," Albert admitted. "As the children become educated in our Western culture many are rejecting the old ways and want to choose partners for themselves."

Millie was aware that the conversation, though enlightening in some respects, shed no illumination on the goings-on between Albert, David, and the

Indian women, if indeed there were any. She determined therefore to take up the matter with Celia at another time.

As Celia came across to bake bread the following week, Millie enquired of her: "Have you seen Albert in a compromising situation with another woman?"

"What you mean by compromising situation?" Celia asked.

"You know, having an affair," Millie explained.

"Oh, Darvis must have told you," Celia replied. "Well, I saw them with these two Coolie women in David's jitney. The women were laughing and put their arms around the men's necks. Then David saw me and the men pulled away. I just wondered if there was something fishy going on."

"Did you know the women?" Millie asked.

"Not really, although I thought one of them might be Poolsie, a girl Albert went to school with."

"Thank you," Millie offered. "There doesn't seem to be cause for worry. The women must have been glad to get a lift." Millie tried to put her suspicions to rest and let the matter die a natural death.

Chapter 93
Millie and Andrew Visit Talparo

As her pregnancy progressed Millie became quite restless. Her visits to her sisters-in-law failed to satisfy the need for familial companionship she felt. They provoked instead a feeling of insecurity which sapped her confidence and tainted her view of mankind. Stories of men who boasted of their sexual exploits with pride rather than remorse and of women who were degraded by their experiences with such men crept into their conversations with painful regularity. A man who fathered children out of wedlock was regarded as a *macho* hero by his peers while the unfortunate mother was labelled a slut. Millie's depression was noticeable enough for Albert to suggest that she spend some time with her mother in Talparo.

Millie gladly accepted the offer and the three of them travelled to Talparo for a change of air. Millie and Andrew would stay for the week but Albert returned to Sangre Grande the following day. He did not trust Celia to take enough care of their livestock.

Andrew was allowed to ride on a donkey which he thought was great fun. He also improvised a sled from the branch of a Royal palm and used it to slide down the grassy hill at the side of the house. He climbed the King Orange trees and picked the ripe fruit which he enjoyed. There were no little children to play with, however, and he became bored and asked when they would return home.

Millie took him to Mahaica to visit her Maclean relatives where Great Uncle Ian made a fuss of him, calling him *a wee bonnie laddie*. He played with his cousin Irene who was only a few years older than he and acted like what his grandmother called a *tomboy*. She climbed the cashew and guava trees and raced him up and down the little hills on their estate. Andrew was attracted to her and asked Great Aunt Marie if she would let Irene visit them in Sangre Grande.

"Her father doesn't like to let this one out of his sight;" was the reply. "He misses the other children who left home and unless he's going there too, he doesn't let her go anywhere. He doesn't like Sangre Grande and wouldn't go there." Andrew was sad and surprised that anyone would dislike Sangre Grande, his special home.

Millie was able to tell Aunt Marie all about Aunt Cecile and her family and regale her with the tales she had heard of their life in Grenada. Aunt Marie promised to try and visit them one day. Millie sensed that Uncle Ian would be the stumbling block in this venture.

Meg was not surprised when Millie related their experience at Mahaica. She knew of Ian's possessiveness of Irene as Irene had been told by her father to eat her lunch at school rather than visit her auntie at lunchtime. Ian was very disappointed with the way his other children had deserted the homestead. He would do his best to keep at least one child at home.

Chapter 94
Millie's Suspicions Are Strengthened

Millie returned to Sangre Grande the following week feeling refreshed by the visit. Her first meeting with Celia, however, brought back the anxieties that had nagged her before.

"Albert couldn't stay the whole week without you then?" Celia asked.

"You mean with me. That's why he came back," Millie corrected.

"No, I mean without. He didn't sleep home for three nights," Celia affirmed.

Millie felt a tightening in her stomach. She took two deep breaths then said, "Excuse me. I have to go and lie down."

Celia wondered if she had *put her foot in it*. She had honestly assumed that Albert had gone to be with his wife in Talparo. It now seemed that she was telling tales. She hated tittle-tattlers and now she was one. She hoped that Albert would have a good excuse.

When Albert came home that evening Millie accosted him. "Where did you go last week?"

"I came here to Sangre Grande," he protested. "You know that."

"Yes," Millie countered, "but you didn't sleep here."

"I see, someone has been spreading rumours. Well, the fact is that the boys had organized a chess competition and were staying at a beach-house in Balandra, and I joined them for a while," Albert explained. Millie wanted with all her heart to believe him but had serious nagging reservations as she said: "That's why the milkman said no one was here to buy milk." She did not want to implicate Celia in the matter.

Changing the subject, Millie remarked, "Andrew wanted me to bring home his cousin Irene. He developed a great attraction to her."

"Really!" Albert replied, "I thought she was about four years older than Andrew."

"Yes, but he has always been attracted to older girls. Look at him and Phyllis; they've been getting on together since he started school."

"True," Albert agreed. They let the matter drop as Millie placed their dinner on the table and Albert washed his hands before they ate. They consumed the meal in unaccustomed silence. This marked the beginning of a cooling in the relationship between man and wife.

Chapter 95
Andrew Gets a Brother

Baby Joseph, who, before he made his appearance, was referred to as Josephine, was born to an anxious Millie. She hid her disappointment at having another boy as the nurse said to her: "You have another lovely baby boy. You wanted a girl I know. Better luck next time."

"Thank God he's all right," Millie answered. Belle, who had been summoned by Albert as Millie began having labour pains, handed the baby to her and she cradled him to her breast.

"Andrew will be very pleased when he wakes up to find he has a baby brother," Millie declared. "He wanted a brother to play "bat and ball" with."

"He'll have to wait a few years for that," Belle answered. "But perhaps he'll enjoy helping to push the new wickerwork pram Albert bought." Albert had bought a "*baby carriage*" as it was called in the shop, made of rattan canes and having a movable hood to shade the baby from the sun. He had also made a wooden slatted cradle with one side that lifted up or down to allow easy access. He was currently working on a wooden rocking horse for Andrew. This pleased Millie greatly as she saw it as a sign that he loved having a family.

Albert appeared to be delighted that he had another boy and set off to celebrate with his friends, saying, "We've got to "wet the baby's head," a fitting reason to drink rum and Coca-Cola." Belle had to admit that this baby was fit and healthy looking although Millie was twice as physically active than when she carried Andrew. Millie also felt fitter and stronger than she did after her first pregnancy. She was out of bed the following day and assured Belle that she could manage on her own, promising that she would send for her immediately if she felt ill. Ma Henry, the midwife, lived nearby and looked in every day. A reluctant Belle returned to her own home. Millie breathed a sigh of relief. At last, she thought, *we'll have the house to ourselves again.* But this wasn't going to be for long.

Chapter 96
Aunt Gertrude Appears

A buggy pulled up in front of the house the following week. A large young woman of about thirty years of age descended from it. A small boy of about eight or nine followed her. They were both very white in skin colouring but the tight curls in their hair spoke of African ancestry.

"Is this the Kong residence?" She enquired of Millie who had come to the door.

"I am Mrs Millicent Akong," Millie stated, putting an emphasis on the A. "Can I help you?"

"I am Mrs Gertrude Kong, the wife of Rodrick A. Kong," the woman announced, "and I was told that his mother lived here." Mr Mongolas, the buggy owner, had retrieved two large suitcases from the buggy and was wondering where to deposit them.

"She doesn't anymore, but you're welcome to come in," Millie replied. The two strangers and their luggage were taken into the drawing room and Mr Mongolas left. "You do know that Rodrick is supposed to be lost at sea?" Millie enquired.

"Yes," the woman answered. "But no one knows for sure. That's why I'm here, to find out if his family knows anything and to ask for help. This is his son, Rudolph, I need help to take care of him."

"Well!" Millie exclaimed, "I don't think his family even knew he was married, but his mother, Ma Belle, would be thrilled to know that he left a son. I'll send word to her that you are here. You must be tired after traveling. May I ask, where did you come from?"

"I thought my Guianese accent would be a dead giveaway," Gertrude Kong replied.

"I guessed as much," Millie responded. "But I meant today; you might have been living in Port of Spain or San Fernando."

"It's a long story, but I'll tell you all," Gertrude related:

"My two sisters and I were on a trip to New York when I met Rod. He was very attentive to us when we got seasick and I fell in love with him; much to my sisters' displeasure, I might add. Weeks later, on our return journey to Georgetown, we met Rod again. But this time my sickness wasn't due to the sea, I found I was pregnant! My sisters threatened to tell the captain about Rod. He would lose his job and never be allowed to work on a ship again as crew were not supposed to fraternize with passengers in that way. He said he would tell the captain the incident happened at a hotel in New York when he was off duty, and he would marry me.

The captain, in his official capacity, married us on board in a ship's ceremony. That's when I saw Rodrick's birth certificate and noticed that he was born in Arima, Trinidad. I had to return to my parent's home in B.G. but he supported me by sending money from time to time and visited when his ship docked. Because of the war, this stopped. Things in Guiana became desperate. We heard that because of the Americans in Trinidad, everything was better, so I decided to come over.

I had an old school friend who joined the nunnery and was teaching at the convent school in Arima. I came to her a week ago and she put us up while we tried to find Rod's family and look for work. Fortunately, I met a Cezair girl who said she might have known Rod's brother. That's what brought me here."

"That's quite a tale!" Millie exclaimed. "What I mean is, you've had a remarkable experience. The children are just coming home from school and I'll get word to Albert and Ma Belle."

As Aunt Gertrude introduced herself and Rudolph to the children, Millie instructed Kenric to get permission from his mother to go and tell his grandmother of her arrival. No sooner had Kenric left, than Albert appeared. He had been told by Mongolas of his sister-in-law's visit. Gertrude embraced him in a warm hug, exclaiming: "You look so much like Rod, for a moment I thought it was. You are both such handsome men!" Albert actually blushed at this flattery.

"I think," he returned, "that this child of yours is more like him. He wouldn't be able to deny that he is the father."

"You have a lovely son too," Gertrude replied. "He is the spitting image of you. Your new baby though, looks more like his mother, he is so pretty."

Andrew was quite bemused by this effusive auntie and her silent son who had an aura of mystique about him. He asked Rudolph, "Did you come to Trinidad by boat?"

"We came on a big ship," Rudolph replied. "And when I'm older I'll be a sailor like my Dad." (This prophecy was to come true and will be reported in a subsequent volume).

Upon the arrival of Isabelle and Emma, brought there in a truck driven by Eric, the house suddenly became crowded as Celia and Edith also came to meet their new sister-in-law. Rudolph became the center of attraction as they all exclaimed how much he resembled Rodrick. Isabelle said to Gertrude, "When we heard of Rodrick's ship sinking, I gave a Mass for him and prayed that somehow, something of Rodrick's would be saved and be given to me. God answered my prayers. This is it."

"The Lord works in mysterious ways," Gertrude agreed. "I've been looking for someone to look after Rudolph as I've found a job as housekeeper for a lawyer, a Mr Hansell-Smith, but he doesn't want children in the house."

The Akong siblings went quiet at this, seemingly waiting for someone else to volunteer to take on responsibility for Rudolph. Millie looked at Albert and nodded. He spoke up. "If Rudolph wants to stay with me, I'll take him as long as he's prepared to be treated same as my own children."

"I would have him with me and Emma but we haven't got enough room," Isabelle admitted.

"Rudolph, will you stay with your Uncle Albert?" Gertrude asked.

"Yes Ma," Rudolph answered. So it was that Rudolph, baptized Rudolph Kong, came to stay with the Akong family in Sangre Grande.

That night, as they lay in bed, Albert asked Millie: "Are you happy with Rudolph staying with us in Emma's old room? I know you wanted to have it as a sewing and handicraft work room."

Millie replied: "Yes, he has lost his father, his mother's family can't take care of him, he has just found his father's family and we can't desert him now." She then wondered: "Would my father's family have welcomed me?" Sighing quietly, she drifted off to sleep.

Chapter 97
The End of War Gives Birth
to the Steel Band

In 1941, the British government in Trinidad had not only incarcerated anyone who had come from Germany (including some innocent Jews), but also probable insurgents, like T.U.B. Butler, and had prohibited the celebration of carnival. With the defeat of the Germans, mainly due to the help that Churchill was able get because of to his maternal affiliation (he had an English father and an American mother), VE day was celebrated on May 6, 1945.

People took to the streets in large and small bands to celebrate. Defying the prohibition on drums, anything that made a sound was beaten, biscuit tins, metal pails, even dustbin lids were beaten, and so began the evolution of *the Steelband.*

The Japanese, however, who had overrun China and had taken over many British protectorates in the Pacific area, were still at war. The annihilation of Hiroshima with an atomic bomb dropped by the Americans on August 6th was not enough to make them surrender. A second atomic bomb on Nagasaki, on August 8th, with the threat of making the Japanese nation extinct, plus the invasion of Manchukuo by the Soviet Union on August 9th, brought about a surrender to the Allies on August 15th by Emperor Hirohito.

Although President Truman declared September 2, 1945, VJ Day, many factions of the vast Japanese war machine were still at war. It wasn't until the 9th of September 1945 that the Japanese commanders in China signed an act of surrender to Generalissimo Chang Kai-shek. Labuan, a British Crown Colony in Borneo (which was expected by the British to become a second Singapore), was not surrendered until September 10th (Also, many pockets of Japanese guerrilla resistance held out even into the 1970s).

In Trinidad, for some obscure reason I'm unable to fathom, I think it had something to do with Taiwan, the 10th of October was celebrated as VJ Day, and a calypsonian sang:

You must try and remember,
De tenth of October.
China never had a VJ Day,
Lay yo, low san e yea.

Chinese people in Trinidad were heartened by the news and Attao, who owned the barracks opposite Albert's house, decided to sell up and return to China. He, like many other shrewd Chinese businessmen, had acquired a small fortune, and with the sale of his property, was able to book passage for himself and a partner to return to China with enough money to enjoy his retirement. (Sadly, it was later reported that he died at sea and was tossed overboard).

The Waterfields, Bertie and May, who bought the barracks, continued to rent out rooms and operated a parlour to sell bread, cakes, candies and sweet drinks (sodas) instead of running a grocery shop. The Le Blanc family were allowed to stay there until they were time qualified to obtain places in the Brooklyn Land Settlement scheme. Cuthbert and Rudolph, being nearly the same age, became great friends and went fishing or hunting birds together. Andrew was deemed too young and did not get the chance to tag along.

As Cuthie and Rudy (the names they used for each other) came past old Mr Nelson's house with their fresh-caught fish one day he called out: "Want to sell me some fish? I'll gi' yuh tuppence fo' dem two Catfish!" They readily agreed, for they had several large Wabeen and Coscorob to take home to cook. "I see you two youngfellas go by regular like," he added. "Yuh mus' live nearby. I need somebody to go to the shop fo' me. Me rheumatics too bad deese days. Yuh'll get another penny fo' doin' me shoppin'." Cuthbert and Rudolph were only too glad to do that service for him.

When they got home they told Millie of their encounter with Mr Nelson and she promised herself to visit the old man and render whatever help she could. Andrew was also interested in their story, perhaps from a more mercenary standpoint. The fact that they had three shiny copper pennies to show for their enterprise influenced him. Shortly after, when his mother did pay Mr Nelson a visit, he went with her and was introduced to him. Thereafter, when Cuthie and Rudy were going fishing, he would be permitted to go with them to Mr Nelson's house and to volunteer to do his shopping, but, at his mother's insistence, without charge.

Chapter 98
Infidelity Confirmed

Eric Le Blanc, who had lost his job with the sale of Attao's property, found work as an odd-job man wherever he could. His specialty was joinery, as he enjoyed working with wood. He was also very good at fitting windows. Mr Romaine, a popular carpenter, often employed him for this particular task. While fitting a window at a house on Henderson Street one day, he observed Albert, his cousin Millie's husband, enter the house next door. Thinking little of it, he carried on with his work. He was surprised, however, to see Albert emerge from the back door of the house with a little baby dressed in pink in his arms. Albert was followed by an Indian woman who admonished him saying: "Yuh ent put yuh chile hat on an' de sun hot on she head."

"Is all right," Albert answered, "We go sit in de hammock under de mango tree."

Eric was shocked as he observed the woman take a seat next to Albert in the hammock and embrace him. It was certainly Albert, no mistake. Yet, he spoke differently, using the local vernacular which he didn't use when talking with Millie. Eric decided he would find out more before relating the incident to Millie.

As he finished the work, he enquired of Romaine who lived in the house next door. Romaine told him that it was a *coolie* woman called Poolsie. Apparently, Albert was a regular visitor and the baby's name was Maria. Eric was disturbed at hearing this news which he felt compelled to tell his cousin Millie. He would discuss it with his mother first.

On getting home, he told his mother what he had discovered. She said that Millie should be told and they went over to see her before Albert got home from work. Millie was saddened by the news but said it was confirmation of what she suspected for a while. Keeping a brave face on the affair, she made them cups of tea and offered them coconut drops which she had just baked.

After they had gone, she went to her bedroom and broke down in tears. Andrew, who had been spinning tops in the neighbour's yard with Ooshman, came in and heard his mother weeping. Running into the room, gravely concerned, he asked: "Mommy! What's the matter?"

"Nothing for you to worry about," she answered, responding to his hug, as his little arms were put protectively around her. "Sometimes mommies get upset and sad, just like you do." Wiping her face with a hand towel, she added, "A warm hug is what I needed, and you are making me better already."

Andrew, still perplexed, scanned her out of the corner of his eyes, looking for cuts or bruises which might explain her behaviour, and finding none.

Chapter 99
Say the Rosary

Millie desperately needed advice. As a Roman Catholic, she couldn't seek for a divorce. She didn't want to talk to Albert's family about him. If they brought it up, all well and good, but she wasn't going to be the first one to bring up the failings of their kin. There was little point in asking Albert about the affair he was having. *Ask no questions and be told no lies.* She decided to talk to the parish priest about it.

Fr. McKenna received her in the drawing room of his presbytery where Mrs Francis, the widow who did his housekeeping, brought them a pot of tea. Mrs Francis then took Andrew outside to see the turkeys, while his mother, holding baby Joseph in her arms, discussed her problems with her confessor.

Millie managed to control her emotions as she dispassionately described her situation to the priest. He listened attentively without interrupting, then asked, "Have you been too ill these last few months, because of your pregnancy, to keep your husband happy?" Millie translated this to mean "have you allowed him his marital dues?" She replied, "I've been quite normal; I was healthier with this baby than I was with the first. I've been there for him and cooked him his favourite meals."

"My child, all we can do is pray for him. The devil sends temptations to everyone. As you know, even Christ himself was sorely tempted by the devil. In the meantime, you could divert yourself with charitable work. There is the St. Francis Society which helps the poorest of the poor and of course the Legion of Mary."

Millie fumed inwardly as she considered his advice. She thought, *If a man had come to him and told him of his wife's infidelity, would he have advised him just to pray and to join the Knights of St. John?* Not likely. There would probably be a plan to threaten to expose her publicly to shame and ignominy.

Depending on the status of the husband, marriages have even been dissolved. Everywhere women are treated unfairly. She composed herself, however, and asked the priest: "Father, would you have a word with him about his behaviour? He told me he trims your hair."

Fr. McKenna thought for a moment, then answered, "I cannot tell him I heard a rumour. We priests are not supposed to listen to rumours. You said you came to me without his knowledge. I can congratulate him on having been married for eight years and having two sons, but I doubt whether his conscience would be affected enough to effect a change his ways. You can say the rosary every night and I will offer masses for him. We'll try our best."

Millie left the presbytery feeling little better mentally or spiritually than when she came to it. At least, she had unburdened herself to one person and perhaps the repetitive mantra of the rosary may have a sufficiently numbing effect on her brain to lull her to sleep at nights.

Chapter 100
A Heroic Rescue Is Punished

Andrew went one day with his cousins to Mr Nelson's house and found that the old man did not need any shopping done. He decided, against his mother's wishes, to go and watch the fishing. Cuthie and Rudy were fishing with their bamboo rods at their favourite basin about twenty feet apart. Andrew took up his position between them so that he could watch their floats as fish nibbled at the bait and caused them to dance in the water. After half an hour of this, with only two Coscorob caught, Andrew wanted to peer into the coffee coloured water to try to see if there were any fish, and as feared, fell into the river.

Struggling and gasping for air, he stuttered: "He-elp!" Rudolph immediately dived in, grabbed Andrew's arm and pulled him to the side where Cuthie reached down and dragged him out of the water.

Wet and muddy, the two boys returned home, leaving Cuthie to sort out the fishing. Millie was alarmed at their condition. "Why did you go to the river when I expressly forbade you?" She admonished Andrew. "And why did you let him?" She screamed at Rudolph.

"We were already fishing when he suddenly appeared," Rudolph explained. "He sat well back on the bank, and I thought he was safe there. When I wasn't looking at him he went down to the bank and fell in. I went in and pulled him out immediately."

The boys were showered and in clean, dry clothes when Albert appeared. "I hear these boys were in the river!" (News travelled fast on the village grapevine.) When he had been given an account of what happened, he took Andrew and slippered his buttocks with his alpargata three times, saying: "This one is for disobedience. This one is for foolishness; and this one is for being clumsy enough to fall in." Then, taking Rudolph, he administered three of the same, saying: "I promised I would treat you same as my own children. You being older, should have sent him home rather than let him stay by the river. He could have drowned."

Rudolph felt this treatment grossly unfair. After all, it was his quick action that saved Andrew's life. He should have been rewarded! He had received a letter from his mother who now lived at the lawyer's home in Tunapuna. If he took the train to Tunapuna, which she described as being about the same size as Sangre Grande/Cunapo, he was sure he could find the address. He had been saving his pennies from the sale of catfish and had picked up coins from the American soldiers. Getting some additional help from Cuthie and Kenric, with whom he confided, he sneaked away early one morning and got on the first train.

On discovering his absence, Millie enquired of Cuthbert as to Rudolph's whereabouts and was told of his intention to go to his mother. Millie had been appalled that Albert had spanked him also but did not say anything. She considered herself an Akong only by marriage and therefore not entitled to interfere with Akong methods of discipline. When she had entered Rudolph's room that morning, there was a piece of cardboard on his bed with the words: KILROY WAS HERE written on it. Those words were popping up everywhere since the Americans had come to Trinidad. No one knew what they meant. On informing, Albert of Rudolph's departure his reply was: "Don't worry, his mother will send him back with his tail between his legs." That did not come to pass.

Chapter 101
Rudolph Goes to the Abbey School

On getting off the train at Tunapuna, Rudolph was given directions to St. John's Road where Mr Hansell-Smith, the lawyer, lived. He found it easily enough but had to trudge quite some distance uphill carrying his suitcase before he came to the house. This large house commanded a view not just of Tunapuna, but all of central Trinidad. Rudolph stopped in front of it to gaze at the panoramic scenery before him. Two large mastiffs bounded to the gate to bark at him. He stood still while his mother, wearing a white apron and headscarf, came out to quieten them. She then noticed who he was and opening the gate, embraced him in a motherly hug.

"What are you doing here?" She asked.

"I've run away," he answered simply.

"Come inside out of the heat and tell me what happened," Gertrude replied, drawing him into the house. After drinking a glass and a half of cold water, Rudolph related what had happened to his very sympathetic mother who claimed to be "absolutely appalled" at the treatment meted out to her dear son. She fussed over him, giving him treats from the pantry and promising that she would never send him back to that horrid uncle.

That evening, when Hamilton Hansell-Smith returned from work, she related Rudolph's plight to him and pleaded for Rudolph to be allowed to stay. She even asked if some action could be taken against Albert. "Hammy, can't we get Albert to pay damages or some sort of compensation for mistreating the boy?"

"No," he replied. "You told me that Albert agreed to accept him and treat him as one of his own. He was therefore acting *in loco parentis* and entitled to do what he did."

"But we can't force Rudolph to go back there, can we, Hammy?" She entreated.

"I'll think of something, but he can't live here," Hamilton replied.

The next week, the lawyer had made arrangements for Rudolph to become a boarder at the recently opened Abbey School at Mt. St. Benedict. He had been able to "pull strings" with the management of the school, which at that time only allowed boarders from other countries (mainly Venezuela). The fact that Rudolph's mother was from British Guiana and his Trinidadian father was declared a war victim, probably helped his cause. (At The Abbey School, Rudolph's talent for music was discovered and nurtured, but that topic will be related in another book dealing with the diaspora of Akong descendants to Britain, Canada and the United States of America.)

Chapter 102
Distractions Are Found Outside the Home

Millie had joined the Legion of Mary and also immersed herself in the work of the St. Francis Society. She taught her handicraft skills to many who wanted to learn and became one of the most prominent parishioners in the district. She was even approached by the wife of the magistrate to become a founding member of the Ladies Auxiliary to the Knights of St. John and hold the office of Secretary. Albert was encouraged to join the Knights of St. John (which he did with some reluctance), but continued to live his double life, that of a respectable married man and the gay Lothario many of his friends admired.

One of Millie's new friends in the St. Francis Society, Elmina Clarke, a young teacher at the Sangre Grande R.C. School, invited her to go to a political meeting held by a Mr Victor Bryan. Although Millie claimed to have little interest in politics, as the meeting was being held in the Mutual Help Society Lodge almost opposite her home, she agreed for the sake of friendship.

Mr Bryan spoke of the need to have government assistance in agriculture and the awakening of people's attitude towards self-sufficiency instead of reliance on the crumbs handed out by an imperial government. He praised the farmers who produced the best cocoa in the world, but lamented the fact that this was then exported to be refined by Cadbury's in England. We then had to import the finished products at great cost.

"Should we not have our own factories providing work for our own people and exporting our own goods?" he argued. "Then, not only would we have created new employment opportunities, but our farmers would get a fair price for their produce and be able to pay agricultural workers more."

His arguments must have struck the right chord with Millie for she agreed to be introduced to him by her friend, Elmina. Victor Bryan was trying to win one of the eighteen seats in the newly established Legislative Council which would give Trinidadians and Tobagonians greater say in the running of their affairs. He, a man of mixed race, was running against Wharton, a white man regarded to be from one of the upper classes in Trinidad. She found Bryan to be most affable. He enquired about her Talparo background and on learning of her being brought up on a cocoa and citrus estate, talked her and her friend, Elmina, into attending his next meeting and canvassing on his behalf.

Thus it came about that Millie used politics, as well as religious and cultural work, to distract her from the problems of her marriage which were daily becoming unendurable. Her cousin Eric had reported to her that the Indian woman, obviously pregnant, was seen going into the barber shop and demanding shopping money from Albert. He had made a show of giving her ten dollars. Millie usually received ten shillings from him for market shopping. ($2.40).

Chapter 103
Meg and James Spend a Week in Sangre Grande

As time went by, Millie could observe a deterioration in her mother's handwriting. Her stepfather, James Browne, was becoming crippled with arthritis and she thought her mother to be only marginally better. With Albert's consent, she invited them both to come and spend a week with her. Belinda would be happy to look after their farm in the meanwhile. Albert had occasionally taken her and Andrew to spend a week or two in Talparo during school vacations, so having her parents visit was a natural exchange of hospitality.

Meg was pleased to spend time with her sister-in-law Cecile and had long chats with her about Grenada. The old ladies would prattle on in French Patois for half the night! Meg's connection with her brothers had been cut short when Papa Leon took her with him to Trinidad as a small child. She barely remembered Jerome and Gerald who were then in their late teens. Cecile was able to regale her with stories of their exploits. Both brothers had married and had families. Jerome had come to Trinidad while Gerald remained in Grenada until his recent demise.

Cecile's children were delighted to meet their Aunt Meg, who had brought them gifts of woven baskets, patchwork bedspreads, and an assortment of fruit and vegetables. They were also surprised that the two old ladies looked more like sisters than sisters-in-law. Millie decided that her Uncle Gerald had loved his sister so much that he married someone who looked just like her.

There was a certain "Le Blanc look" in all of Cecile's children. People who met them at Millie's home could see that they were related to Meg and therefore to Millie. Their comments testified to their observations. One said: "If you had a daughter Millie, I'm sure she would look like Joan." The Lamont children, Kenric and Cedric, who also resembled Millie, however, did not have the "Le Blanc look."

As the Lamont boys popped in one day, Millie introduced them to her parents. She added, "Their father was a Lamont who works for the Ministry of Agriculture. Perhaps you have met him, as he travels a lot in his job."

"No," replied her mother, "I don't recall that name."

James, however, replied: "Yes, I knew a Lamont who was a witch broom inspector. He came to the De Verteuil estate from time to time to keep a watch on the cocoa trees." While her mother's reply seemed ingenuous, Millie harboured doubts about it. Could it be that her mother did not know the name of the man who violated her? If so, she would surely have described him and had him exposed.

Millie persisted: "I think you might have known Kenneth Lamont, the children's grandfather. The son. Louis, followed In his father's footsteps and took over his job."

"Yes, you're right," James admitted. "The Lamont I knew would have been too old to be the father of these children." The name Kenneth Lamont did not seem to arouse any reaction from her mother so Millie was no nearer to discovering who her real father was. She busied herself cutting slices of cake for the children who then ran off to play marbles in the back garden with Andrew.

Chapter 104
Difficulties of the Post-Bellum Recession

After her parents had returned to Talparo, Millie decided to paint the larger spare bedroom which had become shabby since Belle left it. She had not noticed the deterioration until her parents came and used it. This encouraged Albert to get the outside of the house and the roof painted. In addition, the front gallery was beginning to show signs of wet-rot where rain blew in. Albert decided to get rid of the bannisters and put in wooden jalousies. It was brought home to them both how much property needed constant maintenance.

Millie had realized that both her parents were becoming frail and would soon be unable to upkeep their small farm. Their only son, Pedro, had forsaken agriculture to earn oil money and Maria, who loved agriculture, was now living in St. James, Port of Spain, with her husband and having a child every year. It would be up to her, Millie, and Olivia, to help their parents in their declining years. James had written a will, giving each of the four children an equal piece of his twenty-acre estate, but they were unlikely to use their share. A subtle migration of the children of subsistence farmers from the countryside to urban habitation was taking place.

The "War Effort" had made townspeople more self-reliant. The rationing of flour and rice had helped considerably. Many reared their own chickens and milked their own goats. Others cultivated their own vegetables and relied less on market produce. Country farmers began finding it harder to sell their goods unless they could be part of the American supply chain. But as the war ended, even that lifeline was extirpated. The economy was in recession and the eventual closure of American military bases exacerbated the situation.

Workers refused to return to the low wages of the cocoa and coffee estates and these fell into decline. Without proper pruning and maintenance cocoa trees became diseased and yields fell. The Browne estate was no exception and

James Browne, attempting to undertake the work normally done by three men, took ill and had to be brought to Millie's care in Sangre Grande. As Millie reminded Albert, James was the one who looked after her from babyhood and was the only real father she knew. It was now her turn to take care of him. Her mother came as well but her arthritis was getting worse and Millie therefore had the brunt of the nursing to undertake. Olivia, at the time was expecting another child and unable to help.

James was suffering from a severe case of pneumonia and the doctor who examined him in Sangre Grande said that it was so advanced that there was little hope for him. Meg claimed that it was his own fault. He would go out to work on the estate all day and neglect his meals. He would fall asleep at the table in wet clothes after coming in from the fields and then stumble off to bed without eating. He refused to go to the doctor's when he developed a chest cold. He was more stubborn than the mules he worked with. Her litany of his faults seemed endless.

In spite of the best care Millie could give him, her step-father was found unresponsive one morning and the doctor said he had passed away in his sleep, which was the best way for him to go.

Chapter 105
Meg Comes to Live in Sangre Grande

After the funeral, which was held in the San Raphael church, Meg returned to Talparo, where she spent a month sorting out her husband's affairs. The house and parcel of land it occupied was hers for her lifetime, after which it was willed to Pedro. She had agreed, however, to go and live in Sangre Grande where Millie could "keep an eye on her." They had decided that it was never a good idea for mothers-in-law to live in the same house and Millie had procured the corner apartment in the barracks opposite the Marshall's parlour for her. Rebecca was left in charge of the estate.

In that part of Sangre Grande, barrack rooms were the order of the day. They were homes for many who worked in the rubber estates owned by the Robinsons in Caigual. Workers from the cocoa and coffee estates owned by the Marlays in Cunapo were also housed in them. Sundry folk, seeking temporary lodging, sought accommodation in them too. There was no such thing as a hotel in Sangre Grande and there wouldn't be for a number of years.

The Waterfields had found it more convenient to rent out rooms rather than continue to run a parlour. The parlour was therefore shut down and those rooms rented out to the Benn family who had come over from Barbados, like many other *small-islanders* at the time, seeking a better life. The rooms vacated by the Le Blancs who had moved to the Brooklyn Land Settlement, were let to the Guerra family and other rooms, to Cyrus, a shoemaker, Sonny, a barber, and "Shorty" a taxi-driver. These young people, however, were music lovers who were taken up with the emerging cult of the Steelband. They were involved in making the instruments as well as practising to play them. Millie's mother, Meg, was therefore happier to live a little further away from her daughter than have to endure the noise.

Chapter 106
Steelbands Come of Age

Young children like Andrew were fascinated, not just by the sound of the music, but by the atmosphere created by the pan beaters. They would gather round an open fire on which the oil drums, cut to various sizes, were heated. The circular face of the drum was then hammered into a concave bowl shape, on which concentric note areas of diminishing sizes were drawn. Indentations were then made along the borders of each note with hammer and chisel. There was usually a *chuner,* an individual with acute hearing and tone-sensitive ear, who would hammer away at each note in the steel drum until the right sound was produced. The *ping-pong*, or tenor-pan, the drum for playing the main melody, had the most notes. The other drums, used for accompaniment, had fewer notes and were usually taller, as taller drums produced lower bass notes.

The Steelband was mainly pioneered by men from the lower working (or non-working) classes and the first popular bands, such as Hell Yard, John John, Tombstone, Invaders, Renegades, Desperadoes etc. fostered a gang mentality in their players. A typical calypso of the period featured the line: *Red Army coming down, Tombstone drop dey pan an' dey run.* Children from "respectable" families were therefore admonished for showing an interest in Steelbands. It took very hard work from important patrons, such as Beryl MacBurnie, Lennox Pierre, and Canon Farquhar to affect a degree of change in people's perception of the Steelband. By 1950, when a truce between Invaders and Casablanca was brokered, attitudes began to change, so that the following year, a Steelband took part in the Festival of Britain.

This was a momentous occasion. Young men from the slums of Laventile who grew up bare-footed and in rags, were able to perform and be applauded by the cream of British society! No lesser a person than Dr Eric Williams, the acclaimed Father of the Nation, was heard to advise: "*If you let this movement die, then you will drive a nail in the coffin of our aspirations.*" Young Andrew, however, was never permitted by Millie to join a Steelband.

Chapter 107
Moving House Is Made Desirable

Before moving into the barrack rooms, Meg, with Millie's help, removed the Gazette paper which was used by the former occupant to line the walls and replaced it with a flower-patterned wall paper. All the crevices were painted with a solution of boric powder which Meg believed kept insects away. The barracks were noted for cockroach infestation. The floors were carefully scrubbed with vervain in the water. This gave the rooms a pleasant lemony scent and furniture was moved in. Her bed and mattress were brought from Talparo, as were the table and a few chairs. Although Millie had arranged to do all the meals, her mother insisted in having her own coal pot and cooking utensils. These were installed in a partitioned area at the back of the building.

There was a communal latrine used by the other two tenants of the barracks but Meg paid her nephews Eric and Cuthbert to dig and construct a new outhouse for her own use. This she kept locked as she considered the standard of hygiene of her new neighbours to be, in her words, *execrable et absolutement effroyable.*

Meg saw more of her Le Blanc family than she had seen of the Macleans when she lived in Talparo and was very pleased with the new state of affairs. Her nephews brought her Seegin vines and other material for making baskets and trays and she kept herself as busy as her rheumatism allowed. She hung out her baskets under the awning in front of the barracks and sold enough of them to pay her rent.

Millie was concerned that her mother was working too hard but was reproved and told that her doctor's advice was to keep working or deteriorate and die. Once joints were not swollen and painful, they needed to be exercised. Millie was happy to act as masseuse when her mother needed a massage.

Millie's sisters, Olivia and Maria, claimed to be appalled that their mother was reduced to living in barrack room accommodation, but when they actually paid a visit, they were impressed by how comfortable and suitable for her it was. They also visited their Le Blanc relatives in Brooklyn (as the Land Settlement Scheme came to be called). Maria especially, noted how every plot of land allotted had a river or stream running through it. This made it ideal for agriculture even in the dry season. She wished that a similar scheme could have operated in St. James but realized that the densely populated environs of Port of Spain did not allow for it.

Barrack room dwellers were looked down upon by other members of society, and the Akong families were relieved when Celia moved to the Charlerie's old house in Upper Sangre Grande. Aldon's family was growing and he built a larger house for them on the neighbouring plot of land. He therefore was able to offer his cousin Celia the use of their former home. This house, though small, would provide twice as much room for Celia's family which had now grown by the addition of Louis and the latest baby, Cindy.

The move proved fortuitous for the older children's schooling. They were about to change schools from Sangre Grande Government to Sangre Grande R.C. so that they could receive their First Communion and Confirmation sacraments. Fr. McKenna had stipulated that they must be at a Roman Catholic school in order to attend catechism classes before receiving the sacraments. Their new home was now the nearest building to the school. This meant that their usual visits to Millie were discontinued and Millie considered that her most probable link to her biological father was now broken. It was like having a treasured photograph of a loved one removed from the wall. Paradoxically, it was unclear in her mind what her feelings were towards her unknown father.

Chapter 108
Filial Visits

From time to time, her siblings would visit. Her sisters had marital problems of their own and they would commiserate with each other. Millie considered that this, rather than alleviate their pain, served to spread the irritation further. She therefore tried her best to divert their conversations to other directions. Their visits were primarily in the form of filial obligation, so their mother's ailments were a natural source of distraction.

"Mother said her knees are causing her a lot of pain these days. On top of that, she gets breathless whenever she has to walk up a hill or even climb steps," Millie informed her sisters.

"But she used to go up and down the back stairs from the kitchen in Talparo about ten times every day without any trouble," Maria replied.

"I suppose that's because for months now she's been living in a flat place and didn't get the regular exercise she was accustomed to," Olivia offered.

"You're probably right, Ollie, she says her doctor told her she must exercise her joints regularly, once they are not swollen."

"Then you should take her for regular walks," Olivia suggested.

"I try to get her to go to church with me but she says Bravo Hill is now too steep and long for her," Millie replied.

"The church in St. James is just around the corner from my house with no hills to climb. If she was staying by me, I would take her to church regularly," Maria boasted.

"You'll get that chance one day," Millie replied, making a mental note to keep her to her word.

After her sisters left, Millie broached the topic of a visit to St. James to her mother. "How would you like to spend a week or two with Maria in town?" She asked.

"Did Maria ask for that?" Meg inquired.

"Not in so many words," Millie explained. "She did say that her church was just around the corner from her house and she could take you without any trouble. It's all flat land."

"Ah, so you know that I miss going to church. It's me knees, they can't manage the hill."

"All right; one day, we'll visit Maria."

Chapter 109
Meg Goes to Stay with Maria

The Ladies Auxiliary to the Knights of St. John was having a conference in the United States of America and Millie was invited to be one of the delegates from Trinidad and Tobago. When she told Albert about it he was impressed. To her surprise, he suggested that she should attend. It was during the August holidays and the children could stay at relatives for the holidays as they sometimes did. Andrew had been invited to spend some time at his godmother's in Belmont and Olivia in Arima would be happy to have Joseph stay with her. Millie thought she would solve the problem of her mother's care easily enough.

She wrote to Maria thanking her for her "suggestion" to have her mother visit and go to church in St. James and explained that she, Millie, was chosen as a delegate to represent Trinidad and Tobago at the Ladies Auxiliary Convention in the U.S.A. It would be a fine time for her mother to see a little of Port of Spain and get to know Maria's children.

Before Maria could reply to her letter, Millie arrived at her doorstep with Meg and Andrew. She couldn't stay long as she had to take Andrew to his Godmother's in Belmont.

Maria was flummoxed. She vaguely remembered saying something about how easy it was to go to church from her home but couldn't recall an invitation to visit. She was barely managing to feed her children at the moment, but at least Millie gave her some money which would considerably boost her house-keeping allowance. Her husband had gone to Tobago "on business" and she didn't know when, or even if, he would return.

Chapter 110
Andrew Stays at Godmother's as Millie Shops for Her Trip

Millie and Andrew took a trolley bus back to the train station where they collected their grips from the left-luggage counter and took a tram-car to Belmont. The tram took them to Norfolk Street and they alighted in front of the Hodgkinson's residence. Andrew's godmother greeted them effusively and Millie asked if she could impose on her hospitality and stay for the night. "As I explained in my letter, I'm going to the convention in America and I need to buy some suitable clothes. The shops in Cunapo are very limited."

"I'm sure you'll get what you want from Salvatori Scott and Co. or Stephens," Juanita informed her. "I'd be delighted to have you spend the night. Since my children left I'm very lonely and I'm afraid I'll talk your ears off. I don't get many people to talk to."

Cold drinks were served and they were shown to their rooms which Andrew thought were very spacious and had glass windows through which he could see soursop trees and birds feeding on the ripe fruit. Returning to the living room, Juanita put on the rediffusion speakers and they listened to the news which was about the partition of India into two countries and something called "The Marshall Plan" in Europe. The US Secretary of State was saying that if Europe wasn't given aid it would *face economic, social, and political deterioration of a very grave character*. This was followed by a music programme which featured the songs: *Cruising down the River* and *My Guy's Come Back*.

After they had had their supper and Andrew put to bed, the ladies talked well into the night. Juanita told her that the house they were in was up for sale and she would be moving to a smaller apartment on Jerningham Avenue. Millie learned that Isabelle and Juanita had been inseparable childhood friends and that on the day of Isabelle's marriage to Peter Akong, the two friends were bathing in the river when another friend, May Homer, came to tell them that Peter was waiting at the church! Juanita subsequently made sure that she didn't put her own husband through such an ordeal.

The following day, Millie bade goodbye and departed to do her shopping. She was amazed at the choice offered and also the prices. Fortunately, she had been doing embroidery work and had earned herself enough money to buy what she wanted. She was able to procure material to make uniforms for herself and two of her Ladies Auxiliary "sisters." Millie then did something for the first time in her life; there was a readymade dress in a fetching turquoise colour that she fancied. It was just her size; she bought it! She then boarded the train to return home.

Chapter 111
"First" Discoveries for Millie

Millie's trip to the United States of America was more exciting than she imagined it would be. There were many "firsts" for her. She had acquired a passport and visa for the first time. It was her first visit to Piarco and she went as a traveller, not a mere onlooker who went to the "waving gallery" to wave the travellers goodbye. It was her first trip in an aeroplane. She stayed in hotels for the first time in her life. White men carried her suitcase for her, served her and treated her like a lady. There were white road-sweepers and garbage collectors. What impressed her most, however, were the parks and gardens. She had bought a Box Brownie camera and took pictures of nearly everything she saw. She admired tulips, daffodils, narcissi and other flowers she had only read about. The meetings, lectures and parades seemed secondary to the whole great adventure.

On her return, her excitement was still so great she had difficulty sleeping. In Millie's absence, her uncle in Mahaica had passed away, but Albert had gone to the funeral on her behalf. Olivia was there with her children and Joseph, but Maria had sent her apologies. A nagging worry about her mother's health possessed Millie's mind. No news about her mother had come to Albert during her absence and Albert told her not to worry, no news is good news. Nevertheless, she had a presentiment and decided to go down to town the next day.

"You come back at last!" Maria greeted her as she entered the door in St. James.

"Of course. What happened?" Millie asked.

"Well, Mother only gone and get pneumonia, same as Papa. She went to church last week and came back in the rain. Now she gasping for breath and the doctor only prescribe inhaling hot Vicks vapour !"

Millie hurried into the bedroom to see her mother who was sitting up in bed with pillows at her back, a towel over her head and a steaming bowl, held by Merle, Maria's eldest, under her chin.

"Oh Mama!" Millie cried. "I shouldn't have left you!"

"You h-had to g-go," her mother gasped. "My time h-has c-come."

"Don't talk now Mama, just try to relax and breathe," Millie told her. Her mother took a few deep breaths and seemed to relax.

"I brought presents for everybody," Millie said, opening up her suitcase.

"The only p-present I want is your p-presence," her mother wheezed.

"I brought you a mantilla, Mama; I know how you admired the lacy ones those Spanish ladies wore in church," Millie remonstrated.

Meg wasn't impressed. "Well, you'd better give it to Maria, I don't want it buried with my coffin."

"I brought Maria one for herself too and something called T-shirts for the children. It's what they're all wearing in America now."

Having handed out the presents, Millie took over the task of getting her mother to inhale the hot vapour. Her mother was breathing easier and Millie removed the pillows from her back and lay her down. She was alarmed that in three weeks Meg seemed to have become much thinner. Talking soothingly to her, Millie wiped her forehead and said, "Ma, you can't leave us yet. We are not ready to be orphans although we left home. You've got to be there to advise us and pray for us."

"My time has come," Meg whispered, "and at last I can tell you the secret you wanted to know and you'll realize why I couldn't tell you before." She took a couple of deep breaths and added, "Your Uncle Ian was your father."

Millie nearly dropped the bowl she was holding. She gasped: "And he never even gave me an extra sausage as lagniappe!" From a house nearby, a radio was playing one of the latest calypsos and they heard the words: *Woe is me! Shame and scandal in me famalee.*

Finish

Glossary

Accra: Small savoury patties made by frying chopped pieces of saltfish (Cod), or chip-chip in a batter with chopped onions, peppers and tomatoes.

Baigan: (Solanum Melongena), Eggplant, Antrober, Aubergine. A member of the nightshade family, related to potato and tomato.

Bul jol: A type of Choka (relish), with saltfish, onion, garlic, red pepper, tomatoes, lime juice, and olive or coconut oil.

Bobolee: A stuffed effigy of Judas Iscariot which is tied to a tree or post on Good Friday and beaten to destruction.

Chip-chip: (Donax denticulata) A shiny wedge shaped clam, about one inch long.

Chadon bene: A green leafy shrub with a flavour like coriander, particularly suited for flavouring game.

Coconut bake: A type of flatbread made from flour and grated coconut.

Craf': (Craft) A dialect way of referring to young women, likening them to sea-going vessels.

Cush cush: A root vegetable commonly added to stews and soups.

Dasheen: Another root vegetable, bluish in colour, giving rise to the name "blue food" attributed to most West Indian ground provision.

Dhalpuri: A Trinidadian split-pea stuffed flatbread.

Dhoti: A type of sarong tied in a manner that outwardly resembles loose trousers.

Douen: A mythological entity in West Indian folklore pictured as a small child with backward facing feet.

Flambeau: A flaming torch which, in Trinidad, is made with a thick cloth wick immersed in a bottle of paraffin.

Gyul: The local vernacular pronunciation of girl.

J'ouvert: (Jour Ouvert) Literally, daybreak. The first carnival bands to parade the streets on the Monday before Ash Wednesday in Trinidad.

La-diablesse: (Sometimes pronounced "lajabless") A siren-like character in Caribbean folklore. She was born as a woman but made deals with the devil to acquire eternal youth and became a demon. She has hooves instead of feet.

Laglee: The gum obtained from the bark of a breadfruit or chataigne tree.

Lagniappe: An extra piece given to secure good will.

Loup garou: (Werewolf) A man who turns into a wolf-like creature, especially at full moon.

Manicou: A tropical arboreal rodent that carries its young on its back.

Ma Terre: (Mother Earth) An entity who resides in the forest and protects it.

Mauby: A refreshing drink made from an infusion of the bark of the Mauby tree (colubrina arborescens) usually flavoured with aniseed, bay leaf and cinnamon.

Moko jumbie: A colourfully dressed stilt-walker.

Paime: A sweet desert pie made with maize flour (cornmeal) and raisins, wrapped in a banana leaf and steamed.

Papa Bois: A mythical father of the forest.

Parang: Derived from the Spanish word "parranda," meaning a spree or a fete, the parang bands (parranderos) of Trinidad embody this tradition with lively and colourful performances that reflect the Christmas festival.

Pastelle: A savoury pie containing minced meat folded into cornmeal, rolled in a banana leaf and steamed.

Peong: (Peon) Derived from the Spanish meaning a common day-laborer.

Phulourie: (Polourie) A fritter made with fresh dhal (split-peas).

Pierrot Grenade: A colourfully dressed comic figure or clown.

Sada Roti: A leavened flatbread similar to Nan bread.

Sari: A draped garment worn by Indian women.

Seegin: A tropical aerial root used in weaving baskets.

Sorrel: A wine-hued drink made from sorrel (Rumex) or hibiscus calyces and infused with spices.

Soucouyant: A shapeshifting Caribbean folklore character who appears as an old hag by day but at night sheds her wrinkled skin which she puts in a mortar. In her true form as a fireball, she then flies in search of victims from whom she sucks blood while they sleep, leaving blue-black marks on their skin.

Sweetbread: A dense rustic bread made with freshly grated coconut mixed with dry fruit and spices.

Tannia: A root vegetable similar to dasheen, used in stews and soups.

Tamboo Bamboo: A carnival tradition involving the hammering of carved sticks (usually bamboo) on the ground or against each other to create complex musical rhythms.

Tantie: (Tante) Aunt. Often used to address any older female, as a form of respect.

Toolum: A black chewy candy treat made with sugar, ground coconut and molasses, usually flavoured with lemon-peel and ginger.

Topi Tambu: (Calathea Allouia) A tuber that is eaten boiled; popular around carnival time—tastes like water chestnuts.

Travesau: A person of (more than two) mixed races.

Washeekong: Rubber soled canvas shoes.

Wild-Indians: Native South American tribes (Canchi, Colla, Lupaca, Ubina, etc.) called "wild" to distinguish them from Indians from India, called East-Indians, or other Caribbean peoples, called West Indians.

Some of Millie's pictures taken in USA: